INTO
THE
ABYSS

ALSO BY STEFANIE GAITHER

Falls the Shadow

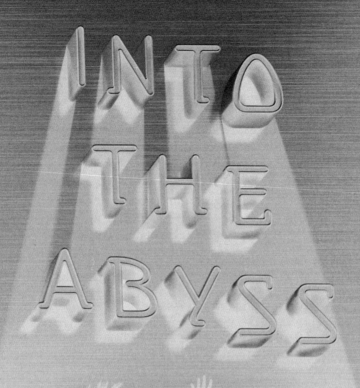

INTO THE ABYSS

STEFANIE GAITHER

SIMON & SCHUSTER BFYR

New York   London   Toronto   Sydney   New Delhi

SIMON & SCHUSTER BFYR

An imprint of Simon & Schuster Children's Publishing Division
1230 Avenue of the Americas, New York, New York 10020

Text copyright © 2016 by Stefanie Gaither
Jacket illustration © 2016 by Justin Metz

For information about special discounts for bulk purchases, please contact Simon & Schuster Special Sales at 1-866-506-1949 or business@simonandschuster.com.
The Simon & Schuster Speakers Bureau can bring authors to your live event. For more information or to book an event, contact the Simon & Schuster Speakers Bureau at 1-866-248-3049 or visit our website at www.simonspeakers.com.
Also available in a SIMON & SCHUSTER BFYR hardcover edition
Cover design by Laurent Linn
Interior design by Laurent Linn and Hilary Zarycky
The text for this book was set in Arrus Std.
Manufactured in the United States of America
First SIMON & SCHUSTER BFYR paperback edition November 2017
2 4 6 8 10 9 7 5 3 1
The Library of Congress has cataloged the hardcover edition as follows:
Names: Gaither, Stefanie, author.
Title: Into the abyss / Stefanie Gaither.
Description: First edition. | New York : Simon & Schuster Books for Young Readers, [2016] | Summary: Her memory and personality erased, and accused of betraying the CCA, Violet Benson runs away with her foster brother Seth and discovers new information about her city's history—and the truth about cloning.
Identifiers: LCCN 2015037167| ISBN 9781481449953 (hardcover)
ISBN 9781481449977 (ebook) ISBN 978-1-4814-9660-0 (pbk)
Subjects: | CYAC: Identity—Fiction. | Cloning—Fiction. | Brothers and sisters—Fiction. | Science fiction.
Classification: LCC PZ7.G1293 Int 2016 | DDC [Fic]—dc23
LC record available at https://lccn.loc.gov/2015037167

To Karla, because volcanoes.

And to Erin, because finally, right?

INTO
THE
ABYSS

"He who fights monsters should see to it that he himself does not become a monster. For if you gaze for long into the abyss, the abyss gazes also into you."

—Friedrich Nietzsche

PROLOGUE

At first there is only the feeling of fire.

Burning. Twisting. Scorching the spaces just beneath my skin, in the emptiness between my fingers. My toes. My lips. It blazes its way up into my brain, destroys every conscious thought. So I'm not sure how long I lie there, body stiff against the cold surface beneath me, before I open my eyes for the first time, and I see.

Sight. It is a glorious thing.

But too much of a glorious thing, too fast.

Far too fast. I don't dare move at first, while my new eyes adjust and try to make sense of the surface high above me. Eventually I grow braver though, and I look down, see pale hands (five fingers each, no burning around them now) and wrists wrapped with wires that twist out and into a tall . . . something beside me. Something rectangular (a rectangle is a basic geometric shape). It flashes and it beeps, and for some reason I don't like looking at it.

I turn to the other side and see gray silhouettes surrounding me. Other eyes peering at me, squinting in the dimness. I stare back, and the smoldering haze over my mind clears further. More thoughts and words and definitions begin to flash in my head. They seem pointless at first—annoying, really—but soon they begin to take form, wrapping around the gray shapes and giving them deeper meaning.

Suddenly the darkness in this room doesn't seem so absolute.

My eyes continue to watch those silhouettes. My thoughts continue to rush rush rush until they reach kingdom: Animalia. Class: Mammalia. Genus: *Homo.* Species: *sapiens.* Bipedal. Social. Well-developed neocortex and frontal lobe.

Finally, a conclusion: humans.

These are humans.

I sit up. The group before me takes a collective step back, save for two in the very center—a tall human whose body type suggests female, and another female who appears much younger. The second female's face doesn't have the fine lines, the subtle creases that my brain is able to rapidly identify as age markers. I study this one for a moment, taking the pieces of her appearance apart and putting them back together in a way I can understand. Eyes that equal a number first: 006600—the color evoked by an energy wavelength of approximately 520 nanometers. Connotations: nature, grass, hope, youth, envy.

Green. Hair that equals 330000, dark brown superimposed over red.

She takes a step toward me. The rest of the humans stay where they are, their gazes downcast, feet shifting, mouths moving with hushed words. And their actions mean something—I know—but what that something is, I don't understand right away. It's more difficult than the appearances, than the simplicity of colors I can see and make sense of so easily. It's a feeling. An emotion. Intangible, untouchable, even as the air slowly chokes with it.

Fear.

The realization slides in and snakes its way around my thoughts, squeezing tight.

It's fear.

Yes. I'm fairly certain they are afraid of me.

All of them except for the girl with the red-brown hair and the bright green eyes.

She takes a few more determined steps toward me. I sit up fully, my gaze zeroed in on her. The rest of the room fades into the background, into a blur of shadows and sounds without significance or meaning. There is only me, and her, and then her voice loud against the wall of whispers behind her—

"Do you remember me?" she asks, coming to a stop a short distance away.

Memories. Preservations of knowledge. Retained impressions of events. Of places and people. People like her? Am I supposed to have impressions of this female? I close my eyes, trying to focus on a thought—brightness and warmth and a high-pitched sound I don't under-stand—that is suddenly flitting around me, up and over my head and just out of reach. But I reopen them almost immediately. I don't like the deeper darkness that shut-ting them brings. I stare harder at the girl in front of me instead. Her eyes are shining, because there is a thin sheen of moisture over their green, and it's catching the little bit of light in the room and throwing it back out. And my mind is racing too fast now to make complete sense of it, but somehow I know my silence is causing that moisture.

Tears.

The knowledge is a weight in my stomach, and I hate it, and I want to sink back into the ignorance of sleep.

But the fear of closing my eyes again is still there. So instead of sleeping, I try harder to grab at that flit-ting thought, at that strange brightness and warmth that staring at this girl brings. At that noise I keep hearing whenever I look at her. The pitch has changed now; not so high, but it's the same melody as before.

But the more tightly I try to hold these things, the fur-ther away they all seem to slip.

"You don't, do you? . . ." Her tone is odd. Like she meant to ask a question, only it came out sounding more like an answer. And her expression is equally confusing; her eyes are even more wet now—a profusion of liquid that my thoughts have managed to identify as generally an expression of strong, often painful emotion such as sad-ness—but the corners of her lips are upturned. A smile. A determined and shivering smile that doesn't fit with the rest of her face. Our gazes meet again. She inhales sharply. That smile falls open, as if to let more words out, but the older female speaks first.

"I told you not to expect much, Catelyn." There is no trembling in this other female's expression, or in her words; the latter seem weighted only by their definitions, and part of me immediately likes her for this. There is nothing extra to understand when she speaks.

The younger one's—Catelyn's—attention snaps away from me, though, as if those definitions are not enough for her. "You've hardly given her a chance," she says.

The whispers in the distant crowd grow louder, but the older female doesn't seem to notice them any more than she notices the girl's staring. She just keeps watching me in her easy, unconcerned way. "I allowed you to be here when she woke up, didn't I? Even though it's clearly confusing her, as I told you it would." The tone is still mostly flat. Simple. But something about the way she said "her" feels wrong. The word and its wrongness linger in the silence, growing claws that dig into my mind and make me sit up straighter, which for some reason causes one of the woman's eyebrows to arch. It's almost as if she is surprised that I have noticed the word at all.

Surprised that I have figured out that I am the "her" she is speaking about as if I am not here, even though she is looking right at me.

I decide I dislike her as quickly as I thought I liked her. And I wonder if it could ever be as simple as that first thought I had of her, if any of these humans truly mean only the words they say, and if those words could be worth anything at all on their own.

"We could get my—our—parents." More words. Catelyn's this time, coming more quickly and quietly than before as she looks back at me. "Seeing them might help you remember more."

"Or it might make her even more confused and over-stimulated than you have already made her."

My hands begin to tremble. I splay my fingers out—try to brace them into stillness—but they keep shaking against the metal below me. The air fills with a hollow echo, a *tat tat tatatattat*, and my thoughts are rushing again, faster and faster, and I can't make them stop.

I am not just a "her."

I am not as confused as you think I am.

I am awake and—

"I have a name." If not for the way they both jumped slightly at the words, I might not have realized they were my own this time. But I am, it seems, a fast learner.

I am a fast learner and I have a voice and I can make them listen to me—

"I have a name," I repeat, trying out that voice again. A bit more deliberately this time, and this time the words are strong and satisfyingly clear. "I have a name. And it is not 'her.'" Catelyn's eyes mist over again, which, for all my quickness, is still a difficult reaction to understand. Her attention darts from me to the woman and back again. I sift through the tumbling currents in my mind and come back with a word: "nervous." She looks nervous.

"Yes," says the woman to me. "You do have a name. But do you remember it?"

A hush has fallen back over the rest of the crowd. They're just watching me now. Waiting. Everyone is waiting on me. The shaking in my hands gets worse. It sinks into me, makes my insides tremble and my head feel like it is spinning.

Because I don't remember.

I understand names. I know there is one that belonged to me, though I don't know why or when or how I got it. I dig and I reach through my thoughts, but I find nothing to grab except ash and dust where my name should be.

The woman tilts her head a bit to the side. My silence doesn't seem to surprise her as much as interest her. I seem fiercely, terribly interesting to her, and that causes a new emotion to hit me: anger. So easy to feel, and suddenly it is the only thing I want to feel. The only thing worth feeling. The only thing worth thinking.

Because what is the point of anything else if I can't remember my name, if I couldn't remember the name of the girl with the green eyes, or the reason I feel brightness and warmth when I look into them?

My head is full and rushing with facts, but they are facts that I want nothing to do with. Facts that seem to be taking up space and pushing out the things that matter.

And I am already so, so tired of them.

My fists clench. The shaking in my hands stops, and my insides feel solid again. Every inch of me feels solid. Strong. Like I could leap across this room and over the entire crowd, and I could run fast enough that I could escape their eyes and their whispers and everything about them—everything about all of this—that doesn't make sense.

But I don't do that. I leap only far enough to clear the metal bed beneath me, to jerk my wrist free of the wires that trap it, and I land directly in front of the older female. She doesn't move. The anger in me burns stronger still, because I wanted her to move. I wanted her to fall back and away, to throw up her hands, to jump aside, to do anything except keep studying me the way she is.

I can't stand to meet her eyes, so my gaze drops instead to the embroidered letters on the jacket she is wearing.

D-R-J-A-C-Q-U-E-L-I-N-E-C-R-O-S-S

Letters that make words—a name—that I can't force my mind to put together, either because I don't want her to have a name when I don't, or because this anger is doing exactly what I am so glad to let it do: It is scorching away so many useless things. Who cares what this woman's name is? Who cares what she is saying now, in her unconcerned voice, and with that thin-lipped smile?

Behind me, the rectangular machine that my wrist wires dangle from has started beeping more frantically. It seems to be begging a reaction from me. Each silence-splitting beep tries more urgently to cut through the warm anger that is blanketing me, protecting me.

I want it to stop.

It's not a thought so much as a primitive need, and that need makes my muscles flex and my arm swing. My fist connects with the machine, sinks in deep, and crunches the metal face and cracks and shatters several of its blinking screens, and the whole thing topples backward, stray wires whipping through the air behind it. It crashes loudly to the floor. A heavy silence sinks over the room. No more beeping, no more nervous shuffling from the crowd—no more nothing, until the woman clears her throat from behind me. I twist back around. My fist is still clenched, and an image flashes briefly in my mind: her face crumpling, shattering the way the metal and its screens did. It was so easy to destroy that machine.

It is the easiest thing in the world, maybe. To destroy.

And destruction made the noise stop, at least for a little while.

Would destruction make this woman stop smiling like that? Is she the same as that machine?

I take a step back toward her.

And I believed my thoughts belonged to me and me alone; that this was the way things worked, the reason I had a voice that I could use only when I chose to share those thoughts. But apparently things don't work this way at all, because though I have not said a word, this woman already seems to know exactly what I am seeing in my mind.

"I wouldn't try it," she says.

Footsteps punctuate her threat. From the crowd around us, several people walk forward. They all move with the same tense, practiced stride. They all carry shining black and silver objects in their hands.

Weapons.

Guns.

Destruction. They're tools of destruction.

But the silent and broken machine behind me is proof that so am I, and so they don't scare me.

I take another step.

Sounds of movement come then—the clicking and whining of those guns, the shuffling of feet, the tapping and scraping of uncertain fingers against the weapon metal. And then a shuffling much closer, and with it I feel a sudden pressure on my arm. I glance down and see a hand wrapped around it, just above my wrist. The hand is gripping so tightly that every vein of it is visible, every knuckle white and distinct.

"Don't. Please." The green-eyed girl again. Catelyn. That's her name. It's grown flimsy somehow, a flickering light that keeps trying to disappear back into the shadowy parts of my mind.

"Please," she repeats. "Please listen to me, Violet."

Everything stops with her last word. My breathing. That flickering in my mind. The awareness of everything, of anything happening around me. I see her fingers still resting on my skin, but I don't feel them. And I just keep hearing that same word over and over:

Violet. Violet. Violet.

Again and again until even it feels strangely unreal. Incorrect. But it still refuses to flicker away. *Violet. Violet. VIOLET.*

A bluish-purple color seen at the end of the spectrum opposite red.

A herbaceous plant of temperate regions.

A given name.

My name?

I jerk my wrist from Catelyn's touch. The room swirls violently as awareness crashes back into me. My awareness. Violet's awareness. And with it comes a feeling of nothing and of everything all at once, of an ending and a beginning and a desperation to go back, back to my nameless self. I clawed so frantically for this name only minutes ago, but now that I'm holding it, the weight seems unbearable. Confusing. Loaded down with things that belonged to this Violet that Catelyn knew—things that she wants to give to me but that I can't possibly take.

Can I?

How could anyone take something like that?

"So you have a name again," says the woman. "An old name, but this is a new life." Her voice lowers as she adds, "One I've worked very hard to give you. And don't you ever forget that."

My balance sways. I lean back against the cold metal bed and breathe in deep, so slow and so deep that I swear I can feel my very lungs inflating with it. Bit by bit. Breathing. A sign of life. A new life.

A life like hers? Like Catelyn's? Like the lives of all the ones standing and staring at me?

Human. These are humans.

And they have hands like me. Feet like me. Legs and eyes and lungs and names just. Like. Me.

So why do I feel so alone here?

CHAPTER ONE

Six months later

I dive and roll across the cracked concrete floor, missing the fist swinging at me by mere centimeters.

But I take too long springing back to a formidable position. The second fist flies even faster than the first, and it cuts roughly into the curve between my neck and jaw. I feel warmth oozing, trailing down my skin.

Blood.

Why am I bleeding?

A flash of silver catches my eye. The boy who hit me doesn't even try to keep me from looking more closely at it; his hand hangs lazily at his side, and around each of his knuckles, there is a band of metal. The edges of each band look like they've been filed to a rough surface. A blood-drawing surface. My eyes dart up.

He smiles at me.

All of this takes only seconds, but the distraction lasts long enough to prevent me from dodging the knee that slams into the small of my back a moment later. I fall forward, breath seizing in my throat. The palms of my hands absorb most of my weight. It stings and it stuns, but I grit my teeth and manage to find enough strength to launch myself back into the air; I flip backward and land lightly on the balls of my feet, facing my attackers.

Six of them now.

They started with two—and that was supposed to be the limit. It's what we agreed on. But judging by the four more who have joined the fun since that agreement, and by the blood drying sticky against my neck, they seem to be rewriting the rules as we go.

So why shouldn't I?

The one closest to me is a girl I've fought several times before—Emily, I think her name is. She wears a smile identical to that of Metal-Knuckles. And I know she's quick. Much stronger than her tiny frame suggests too. Her right leg is weak, though, still recovering from a year-ago accident that shattered her kneecap; she was hobbling around on crutches the first time I met her. She seems determined to act as though that accident never happened, but my eyesight is much too sharp, my brain much too predatory, to miss the weak way her muscles quiver when she tries to brace that leg. She sees me watching those muscles. That determination in her eyes becomes almost feral.

She darts at me.

I wait until the timing is perfect, bank hard to the left and drag one leg behind me so it catches her right foot and knocks her off balance. As she tumbles, I catch her roughly by the arm and sling her forward—straight into the chest of Metal-Knuckles. The force is hard enough to knock him to the ground.

Hard enough that neither of them moves much once they're down.

Hard enough that I've made my point.

I should stop.

The four still standing are hesitating a bit now. Worried, maybe, that they've pushed me further than they should have. But their mouths are still moving perfectly quick. Jeering, talking threats, and swearing words much braver than their body language suggests.

I should stop, I think again.

But then, it isn't me who started it.

One of the four has a spark of bravery and lunges toward me. It's the last clear image I have for several moments, because my vision goes mostly black after that. I glimpse flashes of light and edges of moving things, and I still hear very clearly—shouts and thumps and a scream of "Cut it out!" that I think belongs to Emily. But it's not until something slams into my head and sends me stumbling—until I hit the ground flat on my back and I have to make a conscious effort to remember how to breathe—that my eyes manage to blink some sort of clarity back into the world around me.

Only one of the original six remains standing. He looms over me, a gun in his hand. It isn't aimed at me though; instead, the blunt butt of it is tilted up toward my head, which makes me guess that this is what slammed into me and knocked me out of my rage.

"Are you insane?" he asks through panting breaths.

I remember the way they were all smiling at me just

moments ago. And now, instead of answering his question, I simply return the gesture. He stumbles, as if I've physically assaulted him with my grin, and he flips the gun around and shakily points it at me. I ignore it. Likely it's nothing more than a weak Taser gun; he's too young to have clearance to carry much more than that around here. And if it is something stronger than that, he knows as well as I do that shooting me with it would be a mistake. It likely wouldn't stop me, for starters, and he would end up just like his friends. And beyond that? Metal knuckles are one thing, but explaining a gunshot—and the potential damage it could do to me, to the president's most precious tool—is something he likely wants to avoid.

So I go on smiling and ignoring Gun-Boy—his name is Josh, I recall after a split second of processing—as I climb back to my feet. In the process, I nearly step on Emily, who has managed to make it back up to a crouching position. "This was supposed to be controlled combat," she hisses at me, swiping at the strands of hair that have escaped her disheveled ponytail.

I touch a finger to my throat, tracing the place where the metal knuckles cut in. "It seems we could all stand to work a bit on control, doesn't it?" I say drily.

But I know she won't be the last to hiss those words—"controlled combat"—at me today. It's very likely I have a lecture in my future, perhaps from President Cross herself. Precious tool or not, I have parameters that I am supposed to work within here; namely, I am supposed to keep my inhuman strength in check—to give these young trainees an idea of what it's like to fight the others like me, but to not actually put them in any sort of mortal danger.

Whether they deserve to be put in that danger or not.

Whether they outnumber me, cut me, taunt me, spit on me—it doesn't matter what. Because to most of the people of this organization, I am not a tool they want to use. My risks, they say, outweigh my benefits: I'm unpredictable; I'm a traitor-in-waiting. . . . Pick any argument against my existence, and it's likely I have already heard it. I was born a monstrous thing, a thing that should have been left for dead. A life that the president shouldn't have brought back.

And maybe there is truth to some of that. Maybe not. All I know is that one step too far—one deadly "accident" with any of my opponents—would be more fuel on the fire those people would like to use to burn out my existence.

I should have stopped.

It isn't the first time I've blacked out like that.

But it needs to be the last.

I glance at the screen high above us, fastened to the center of the far wall in this enclosed room. A timer counts down on it, angry red numbers telling us there are still nine minutes to go in this training session. Underneath the timer is the shaded window of the control room, which is exactly what it sounds like; everything from that timer, to the lights, the temperature, and even to the gravitational force in some of the better-equipped rooms, can be controlled from that tiny room. It also serves as an unobtrusive observation spot for instructors overseeing the scheduled sessions that take place here.

This one wasn't scheduled, though. It was an open challenge. One I would have been better off ignoring, where Josh and Metal-Knuckles set most of the rules—which I should have known they wouldn't bother following. They never do. I should have seen the other four, unfair additions coming long before they sauntered out of the shadowed corners and into the arena. Should have known prohibited weapons would be used.

But the alternative to stepping into this unfair fight would have been to hide, to avoid them until they forgot about their challenge—which I wasn't going to do. These pickup sessions are the norm around here, especially among the younger, more ambitious members. Nobody says "no" to them, and I am different enough without being the one girl who does. Besides, being called things like monstrous is bad enough.

I won't be called a coward, too.

Out of the corner of my eye, I see that two of the ones I sent to the ground have pulled themselves back to their feet. They've moved back to the corner bench they were sitting on at the beginning of the session, before they so eagerly entered the fray. They don't seem to care about the still-ticking timer; they look more than finished with this little exercise, regardless of how many of the agreed-upon minutes are technically left. They aren't the only ones either.

I head for the door.

But there are still those other four to deal with. All of them are standing now, shaking off their stupor, and they all seem to notice me at the exact same time and with the exact same, hungry-for-more-blood gleam in their eyes. Without a word they catch up, two flanking to either side of me. I keep walking, staring with all my concentration at the metal door ahead.

"Session isn't over," Metal-Knuckles says. His voice is viciously prideful. It's the sort of mindless pride that I've found drives so many of these trainees to keep going—particularly when they really should just stop. Worse than his words, though, is how he is so close to me now that his arm brushes mine with each step we take. My entire body cringes. I hate being touched like this; his skin so intimately glancing against mine. I hate how close he is. How close they all are.

Twenty steps to go, I estimate, eyes still on the door. I breathe in deeply through my nose and exhale several times, wiggling each of my fingers through the air, one by one to the count of ten. It's a trick Catelyn taught me to help stave off the violent blackouts.

"There are still eight minutes left," says Metal-Knuckles, curling his way around me and attempting to block my path.

"Which is eight times as long as I need to put you permanently back on the ground." My words don't sound like they're coming from me, a detachment that I've learned is a warning that my control is slipping. Again. Already. Maybe it's how stiflingly thick and hot we've made the air in this particular training room, or how close his arm is to touching me again, but I seem to be having a harder time clearing my head than I usually do.

"Do it then." I shouldn't glance his way, shouldn't pay his words any attention at all. But I do. And his smile is back.

"You know she won't," says Emily from somewhere on my left. She sounds like she's getting bored with this. I try to siphon some of that boredom from her and make it my own. "She knows better, don't you?" The question is mocking, inviting no answer from me. "Even a monster has its limits, doesn't it?"

My hand is around her wrist, twisting it, before I realize what I'm doing.

"Let go of her!"

The other three are all in front of me in a flash, eyes wild and hands lifted slightly in gestures of almost-surrender.

Almost. The word splinters through my thoughts. *Almost isn't good enough though, is it?* It's the same voice that urged me on before my blackout, that told me I wasn't the one who started this, but I can end it. That other voice, the one telling me to stop, that we're finished with this, seems to have retreated so deeply back into my mind that I wonder if it was truly there to begin with.

Why should I stop?

My fingers tighten on Emily's wrist, thumb tracing the thin bones beneath her skin. I can almost hear those bones popping already, so helpless against my strength. She utters something—a plea, a threat, something in between maybe—but it comes out more amusing little squeak than actual words. Her arm tenses.

She tries to jerk away.

Black dots flash across my sight.

But the darkness doesn't last this time. It's driven away by the beep of the timer resetting, reverberating through the room. I blink, and my vision clears completely as the lights go from their dimmer, hazier setting to bright and almost blinding. There's a whir of mechanics as cool air breezes down from the massive ducts above.

Someone was watching from the control room after all, it seems. Someone who has decided this session is over.

I still can't seem to unclench my fingers from Emily's wrist.

"Let go of her," repeat the others around me. I'm not listening to them, though; a new sound, a more important sound, has reached my ears: the door opening and shutting. The same person from the control room most likely, slipping in to interfere completely. I brace myself for the inevitable lecture as footsteps approach, my eyes focused on the soft indentations I'm leaving in Emily's wrist. The voices in my head—all of them—are gone now. There is only silence beneath an odd prickling along my scalp . . . a silence that's interrupted by a familiar voice a moment later.

"Six against one, Josh? Really? And even with those odds, I still have to intervene so you all don't get your asses kicked. Pathetic."

Josh holsters the gun and turns to the newcomer with a smug frown. "No one asked you to intervene, Seth."

Instead of answering, Seth reaches for the grip I still have around Emily's wrist. I drop my hand and jerk away from both of them the second Seth's fingertips sweep over mine. I actually find him one of the more tolerable people in this place, largely because Catelyn seems to think I should—but I still don't want him touching me.

That same touch, on the other hand, seems to have erased the hateful look Emily was shooting me. Her freshly grown smile is full of innocence. She's still absently rubbing her wrist, but that smile and the rest of her focus is completely on Seth now, her eyes sweeping down over his tall frame and dark skin, and then back up to his earth-toned eyes and the half-cocked grin he's giving the group. "Thanks," she tells him. Then with a hasty glance at me, she holds up her wrist and adds, "I thought she was going to break it with her freakish strength."

I consider pointing out that I still could if I wanted to, but decide it's not worth the effort. Instead, I shove past them and continue my interrupted path for the door. I hear Seth telling them that it's over, to not follow me. Part of me is annoyed that he stepped in. But the other part is simply glad that this time, no one tries to follow me.

The headquarters of the CCA—which stands for Clone Control Advocacy—seem much quieter than usual for this time of evening. I pass only a handful of people as I walk the twisting corridors back to my assigned room. Most of them hug closer to their side of the hall when they go by me, lowering their eyes and lifting their phones or communicators or whatever else they have to distract themselves with.

Exactly one person meets my gaze, though—Zach, a

boy I only know because he usually hangs out around the same people as Catelyn. And I don't know if he actually meant to look me in the eyes, but once he has, he manages to keep looking at me long enough to offer me a hello in the form of a quick head bob. Not an overly friendly gesture, but at least he's acknowledging my existence in a halfway normal manner and not tripping over himself to get away from me.

Not that I care about the ones who are doing that.

It's probably for the best that most aren't like Zach, actually; there is still blood on my neck, and that strange tingling across my scalp is still there too, only it seems to be penetrating through my skull and down into my mind now. In a way, it's even worse than those violent, warring voices in my head.

And until all of these things go away, the fewer people I have to interact with, the better.

If I believed I could get away with it, I would lock myself away from all of them indefinitely. Away from their hateful stares and words, away from these stupid training sessions—the scheduled ones or otherwise. But I have run through possible escape scenario after possible escape scenario in my brain, and they all come back with the same conclusion: The truth is, I have nowhere else to go.

Because after all, it is those stupid training sessions that have been earning me my place among these halls these past months since my "awakening"; I am a weapon, that precious tool—though not for destruction, like I first thought, but for teaching, as the president so eloquently explained to me within hours of waking me up. It gave me an objective at least. Something to cling to. A way to somewhat belong within this organization, which is the only home I've ever known.

Though "home" is not exactly the best way to describe it; I understand enough after all these months to realize that it is not a normal home. There are few warmly colored walls here, and none of them holds safe memories, or familiar stories, or embarrassing old family photos. People live here, but they do so in neat, orderly rows, on neat, orderly schedules that keep the CCA running. And the CCA must keep running. President Cross—the woman who woke me up, who granted me refuge within these cold walls in exchange for my cooperation—never misses an opportunity to remind us of that.

Because outside these walls, the world is a dark place.

A world growing darker every day, thanks to the ones those training simulations are meant to prepare CCA members to face: clones. An untold number of clones created by the CCA's nemesis: a corporation known as Huxley, which, years ago, began slipping those clones quietly and certainly into the population at large. In time Huxley had created a sleeping army, brainwashed, programmed, and prepped to fight for the future this corporation envisioned. Simply waiting for the command go.

And I was one of the sleeping. I was born—created—in Huxley's laboratories. Another monster for its ranks.

I was apparently different, though; I managed to rebel against that programming. I couldn't tell you how, because when I woke in this place, I remembered none of what came before. I have since pieced together some things—from stolen glances at reports of the fighting between Huxley and the CCA, and from what I could squeeze out of Catelyn, who it turns out was my sister in this before-life. But the one who I most want answers from—President Cross—refuses to say much about my monstrous past. Only that I am different, and that it doesn't matter so much where you're born. Only where you end up. This is why I was given a second chance at life.

And why would I question being allowed to live?

For all the confusion and chaos in my head and the uncertainty in my existence, there is still a beauty to my artificially beating heart that makes me reluctant to give it up.

I manage to make it close—so close—to my room when I hear an awful word I was hoping to avoid for the rest of the evening: my name. And worse still, it's come off the lips of Seth. I'm not especially surprised that he managed to catch up with me; he's the adopted son of President Cross and has spent years living among these halls, so he knows them better than anybody. Including any and all shortcuts. Which partly explains how, no matter what happens around here, somehow it seems he is always in the middle of it. Even if it doesn't concern him. Actually, *especially* if it doesn't concern him, as most things—such as what happened in that training session—don't.

"Hey," he says as he reaches my side. At least he has the sense not to try touching me again—though when I glance at him, he's in the middle of drawing his hand back, as if he'd at least thought about doing just that.

"Hello," I say stiffly, only because I've learned that ignoring greetings rarely gets people to leave you alone anyway. I've also learned that when people run up to you and greet you like this, they generally have a reason for it. But the next time I glance at Seth, he's only watching me with the same sideways grin he wore back in the training room. Which is irritating, because it forces me to keep speaking. "What do you want?"

"To say you're welcome."

I stop walking. "For what?"

"For getting those creeps to leave you alone. You're welcome for that."

I wonder if he might be joking. Even after six months, humor is still something I haven't quite managed to grasp. And it's especially difficult to tell with this one, because it seems like he is always wearing that bright, arrogant smile, like he's in on some grand joke the universe has not bothered to tell anyone else.

"*They* should be the ones thanking you," I say, not returning his smile. "Things would have ended badly for them if that timer had kept going."

"Mm-hm." He leans against the wall in front of me, partially blocking the short distance left between my room and where we stand. "And then what do you think would have happened to you?"

His question makes that tingling across my scalp worse, turns it into more of a buzzing that drowns out everything

I'd been thinking of saying to try to get rid of him. So instead of speaking, I only glare for a moment before going around him, making sure to hug the right side of the wall so there's no chance of us accidentally touching. I've made it perhaps ten steps before he calls to me again.

"Hey."

"What?"

"Can I ask you something?"

I sigh, because short of ripping out his vocal cords, I doubt there is much I can do to stop him from talking. I never can stop him. It didn't take me long to realize this— or that, unlike most of the people in here, he is indifferent to my glaring and oblivious to the fact that I could break him in half without breaking a sweat. Nothing I do, and no rumor that has started about me yet, seems to have made him afraid to follow me around and annoy me like this.

Which makes him a bit of an idiot, maybe, but it also may be the real reason I find him a bit more tolerable than most.

I don't intend to answer whatever his question may be, but I stop all the same, and without turning around, I wait for him to finish. It takes him a moment. And then finally, in a voice not as obnoxiously loud as normal, he asks, "Do you ever wonder why she brought you back? Just so everyone here could hate you?"

The only part of me that I can manage to move right away is my head, and just barely; I tilt my face back so I can see his in the corner of my vision. He is still smiling, but it's less arrogant than usual, and more . . . haunted. A ghost of his normal grin. This is far worse than the arrogance I have come to expect from him. I don't like the way it makes me feel, and I don't want to look at it anymore.

So I lie.

"No," I say. "I never have."

And then I turn and I walk straight to my room and shut the door, locking it behind me—something I never bothered to do before. I've always thought that trying to lock things out was a sign of fear. I have no use for fear. I have absorbed everything from the moment I woke up. All the dark and monstrous things in the world outside these headquarters, all the hateful words and unfair expectations inside of them—all of it. And I am afraid of none of it.

Do you ever wonder why . . . ?

I back up against the door and slide down it, onto the cold faux-marble floor. How could such a simple question turn me into a liar and door locker?

Just so everyone here could hate you?

The room in front of me is dark. Simple. Everything is clean lines and function. Bed, desk, chair, closet. It has all been designed with a purpose, just as I have been designed with a purpose.

And as confusing and chaotic as it may feel right now, I am still reluctant to give that purpose up.

CHAPTER TWO

There is only one person who knows the code to my locked room—aside from perhaps President Cross, who knows everything that happens around here. Only one other person. And I should have known that she would show up before the night was over, and that no matter how many times I told her to leave, she would still insist on staying. On battering me with an endless barrage of pointless questions.

"I'm not leaving until you tell me what happened," Catelyn says again. She sits cross-legged on my bed, staring at me. Her eyes are far too full of spark and defiance for this time of night. We ate breakfast together at eight o'clock this morning—more than fifteen hours ago. How is she still so wide awake? I can stay awake for days on end, but she isn't like me. In many ways, really, but the most noticeable of which is that she is completely human. All normal flesh and blood, and a brain and body that function best with regular, plentiful amounts of sleep.

But from moments like these, you would never know it.

"Violet," she presses. "Seriously. Tell me."

I finish wiping away the last of the blood from my neck, using one of the more ragged shirts from my closet, which I've dipped in the medical alcohol Catelyn brought. The disinfecting alcohol wasn't really necessary; once I've cleaned away the blood, there is nothing to see except pale, smooth skin that looks as though it was never damaged in the first place. There is no scar to even face the possibility of infection. My skin cells are much more advanced than a normal human's, and controlled by a brain that drives them to reproduce at lightning speeds in the case of minor injuries like this. Which is why I am not worried about it—and even less willing to talk about it. With the blood washed away, all signs of that training session are already gone. There is no point in carrying on about it.

But out of all the people here, Catelyn seems to have the most trouble remembering that I am not human.

Which is why she is still looking at me worriedly. Expectantly. "That looked like a lot of blood," she says.

"And now it's all gone, just like that," I muse. "I'm truly a marvel of modern science."

"I heard Emily talking in the hall a few minutes ago," she continues as if I haven't spoken. "She was talking about you, about your training session earlier and how you'd . . . I don't know, gone crazy or something. That you tried to break her arm off after everyone else had already stopped fighting."

My fingers clench around the bloodstained cloth I'm holding. "If you already heard what happened, then why on earth do you need to hear it from me, too?"

I've gotten better at reading tones since that first day she spoke to me, and I can almost hear the frown in her voice when she replies: "Because I thought your version of the story might be different."

Of course it's different. It's less trouble, though, to simply let her take Emily's word for things. So I shrug. "No. That's essentially how it happened." I reach for a clean sleeping gown and change into it before I turn back to her. "I am crazy. Completely outside my strange little mind. You should probably escape now, while you still have both your arms."

"Shut up, idiot."

"Don't call me names. Name-calling is one of my triggers."

"I'm serious, Violet. Stop being dumb."

"I feel another violent rage com—" She flings the bed pillow in my direction, forcing me to cut off midsentence and block it. I throw it back. Harder than I meant to, maybe. She manages to catch it, but the force almost sends her toppling backward off the bed. There is a long, uncomfortable silence as she rights herself and places the pillow back at the headboard, taking the time to smooth out every wrinkle on its case before turning and doing the same thing with the sheets along the edge of the bed.

"Didn't you stay at headquarters last night too?" I ask. "Isn't your father going to wonder if you don't come home tonight?"

"Our father," she corrects, that wide-awake defiance from before flickering back into her eyes. It's weaker than earlier, though; or perhaps now it's just dimmed with grief. She tends to get emotional when the subject of her parents comes up.

I still can't think of them as anything other than her parents either; though once upon a time, they really were both of our parents. And apparently we lived in our house on a beautiful tree-lined street, and we did all the things that real and perfect families do: birthday parties and dinners and picnics and after-school plays—things I have seen pictures of, things that Catelyn has told me about. She took me to that house once too, a week or so after I first woke up here with no memories of it all. It's nice enough, I suppose. All white and grand and tall. It looks like the sort of house the now-resigned mayor of Haven would live in.

But it is not my home.

And the now-resigned mayor of Haven is not my father.

I have to credit him for attempting to be though. In the beginning of my short life, he was there soon after my awakening, and he insisted that I come home, back to stay in that grand white house that still has a room filled with all the things I used to call mine. All those things, though, are just dust-collecting reminders of how I am a stranger in my own skin. I don't remember them. They don't belong to me. I don't know what does belong to me, but it is not that house, or that man Catelyn calls Father, or the woman she calls Mother, either.

That woman was there in the very beginning too. But she was quiet and fading into the background as I stepped forward, and now that single memory I have of Natalie Benson is the same way—so washed out I can hardly picture it. And there has been no chance of building bolder memories of her; she left months ago, off to live with distant family in Germany. To escape the violence, she claimed, between the CCA and Huxley, both of whose operations are focused mainly along the Atlantic Seaboard, here in this city and beyond. After everything I've been told "our" family went through because of these two companies, I guess it makes sense that she would want to get away from this place. To try to find peace somewhere else. Germany is a long way from Haven, North Carolina, though, and sometimes I wonder why she went so far.

I wonder what else—or who else—she may have been trying to escape from.

Do you ever wonder why . . . ? Why you were brought back? Just so all the people here could hate you?

I give my head a little shake, trying to spill Seth's words from my brain. I can feel Catelyn staring at me, and I imagine she is thinking about the same thing I am now: what a strange pair the two of us are. And maybe wondering why she didn't get on that same plane and escape with her mother to Germany, away from all of this. Away from the whispers and hateful words that follow me through the halls of this place. Away from me and the blood on my strange skin.

I can't escape my own skin, though.

Yet another difference between us. Because Catelyn could escape me. I don't know if I will ever understand why she hasn't, particularly when I start thinking about her mother and all the ways I'm certain I am the one who drove her away, and about all the cracks my existence has cut into the foundation of that grand white house we all used to live in. But whatever the reason, Catelyn is still here. Still trying to rebuild what we were, as though that foundation could never be broken beyond repair.

The more I think about it, the more desperate I am to at least redirect the conversation away from me, if I can't get rid of her altogether.

"I know why you're staying." I focus on trying to buff out a scratch in the metal closet door as I speak, though it's obvious the scratch is going nowhere. I'm trying to appear nonchalant with my words.

"What are you talking about?"

"He doesn't want you to go home, does he?" I know she knows who I mean by "he": Jaxon Cross, the president's biological son, the adoptive brother of Seth—and the best chance I have at distracting her. Because when she isn't bugging me, she is usually with him. And maybe at her insistence, he has always been much nicer to me than most of the other CCA members our age. Even if it is a wary sort of niceness, full of almost-but-not-quite-eye-contact and the timid sort of smiles one might give a dog he was afraid could be rabid. But he seems to be trying, at least.

And I would much rather it be Jaxon she stayed here for. Not me.

"He suggested I stay, maybe. Yes." She pulls up a corner of the sheet she so painstakingly smoothed only moments ago, starts twisting it around and through her fingers.

I watch her hands, thinking maybe these are the things we would talk about if we were normal sisters: these simple things, like this boy who makes her fidget and makes her voice go shy. These are the things I would tease her about, maybe.

But there is little that I would call normal or simple about our lives, which is why I'm not surprised when she stops fidgeting and follows up her statement with: "It's mostly because it's gotten so late, though, and because there have been several more . . . incidents in the city today. Father doesn't want me going anywhere either—not without a few dozen bodyguards, at least. Not worth the trouble. So here I am." She shrugs. "But for the record? As soon as I heard you were fighting again, I planned on staying until I could see you. You know, you don't have to prove anything to those jerks. I've told you before that Josh is bad news. You're better off just walking away from him."

I ignore this last part, determined not to get back on that subject. "What sort of incidents?" I ask. She looks reluctant to go into details, so I have to guess. "More deaths?"

Her lips remain pursed, unwilling, but eventually she shakes her head and explains: "Two houses in the Magnolia District burned to the ground earlier today. The families got out, but now a member of each of them is missing. A child from each family—Catherine Robinson and Rachel Davis. They're best friends, and your age, and they used to hang out with—" She catches herself. "Well, I know you don't remember them now, but you would if . . . you know. They went to high school with us."

"They're clones?"

"Not registered, but yeah. The CCA members who've

investigated think so. This makes too many incidents like this in the past couple of weeks for it to be coincidental; they think it's Huxley again, just adding two more to their army and continuing their string of activations."

"Activated" is the word the CCA uses when a clone goes from the normal replacement it was supposed to be—the one that families were promised when they agreed to clone the original loved one—to the brainwashed, potentially deadly machine that Huxley intended it to be all along. Those activations slowed, at least in the city of Haven, about seven months ago—part of the aftermath of a battle that left both of the organizations' headquarters heavily damaged. Huxley's damage was far worse, though. I've never been, not during any of my rare trips outside the CCA, but I've been told that the once massive laboratory compound suffered the same fate as those houses in the Magnolia District—burned by fire, choked by smoke. The hollowed shell is still standing, but most of what remained inside has been stripped out and carried to other operating facilities.

It's strange to think that I was there while it was burning. Like everything else that happened before I woke up, though, I have no memory of any of it. It was actually during that same battle that the brain Huxley had given me was damaged beyond repair, taking every uploaded piece of the old Violet Benson with it.

But at least that blank-slated mind means that Huxley can't touch me anymore. Can't control me. I won't be burning down any houses to make any statements for them. Because that's what this most likely is: activations increasing again, coupled with acts of violence to remind the CCA that Huxley is still around, that it still has a presence in Haven and clones who are ready to fight for it. Clones that I don't want to believe are anything like me.

But I can't help feeling that this girl sitting on my bed isn't anything like me either.

So what am I, exactly?

"Are you okay?" Catelyn asks.

"Tired," I lie, and she frowns, I assume because she knows I'm lying. But all the same, she finally stands and walks toward the door.

"Fine, I get it. Leaving now." She's halfway outside before she pauses, glances up and down the hallway a few times before looking back over her shoulder at me. "Just promise me something, all right?"

"What?"

"Just . . . lie low for a while."

"I have scheduled training sessions I have to participate in."

"I know that. But the other ones, the unmonitored ones, like with Emily and Josh and all of them—seriously. Ignore them. Everyone's acting crazy because of all these activations and stuff going on in the city, and they're just eager and out for blood." She doesn't say it, but I know what she really means: They're out for blood like mine. Clone blood.

"I'm not like the activated clones that burned down those houses."

"I know you're not," she tells me. But she doesn't meet my eyes when she says it.

CHAPTER THREE

I fall asleep still picturing Catelyn in my doorway, almost hoping she might come back just to look me in the eyes one more time.

Hours later I wake to an empty doorway and the sound of gunfire and shouting outside it.

Lie low for a while, Catelyn's voice hisses in my ear as I jump to my feet, grab a pair of sweatpants, and jerk them on. I wish I could listen to that voice. But by the time I reach the door and fling it open, her plea is already nothing but static in the back of my mind.

Once outside, it's easier to tell where most of the noise is coming from: near the south wing, where the main computer systems—the nerve center of these headquarters—are located. It's also where the president's living quarters are—including the spare bedroom that Catelyn usually sleeps in when she stays here.

I run.

My mind may have been free of memories six months ago, but nearly everything that's happened since then is a permanent file, fixed and clear and easy to open the instant I want it. So I have no trouble finding my way through these halls even at blurring speed. Even with the distraction of those shouts getting louder as I get closer, and with the pungent scent of metal seared by gunfire growing stronger by the step. Left, right, right, left, right, and then I've reached a small room that serves as a security entry point, protecting that central nerve center on the other side. There are two computers in here, each with its screen smashed, one on either side of a far door that looks like it's been peeled back and pinned open as easily as if it were made of paper.

The same strange tingling I felt in my scalp earlier comes rushing back. I don't want my eyes to keep searching this room, but they do it anyway. And they fall on the two bodies—one operator for each of those destroyed computers—crumpled together in the dark corner. Neither of them looks like he's breathing. I step closer. There's bruising around the necks, but no burns or bullet holes that I can see. Just like the broken door, this was clearly done with bare hands. Which further confirms my worst fear: This looks like it was done by a clone. Because we don't need weapons.

They, not we.

You are not the same as them.

"Not the same, not the same . . ." I keep chanting that under my breath as I stumble back and turn toward the makeshift opening in the door, bracing myself for whatever's on the other side of it. *I'm not the same. And I have to help Catelyn—*

I burst through the opening.

And I collide with a solid body. A pair of strong hands grab me, shove me back into the security room, and my instincts react before I manage to get a good look at the person trying to stop me. Instincts that say *fight* and *we need to free ourselves*, and that yank my right arm free, swing my fist and connect it with a jaw. That solid body staggers into the wall, and the room fills with curse words a second later. So many colorful and elaborate curse words, and some that I'm almost certain are made up, and for the second time today I recognize Seth's voice over the chaos around me and in my head.

"Oh my god," he says in between spits of blood. "What is with you Bensons and this need to punch me whenever I'm just trying to help?"

"Help?" I sidestep to avoid the blood he is showering over the floor. I would apologize for causing it, but I am too busy glaring suspiciously at him and edging toward the peeled-back door. "I don't need help. I need to—"

"Yes, you do," he says, positioning his body in front of me and grabbing my arms again. He's surprisingly brave for someone still bleeding profusely from the mouth as he speaks. Surprisingly strong, too. But he isn't stronger than I am, and if he doesn't let go in the next few seconds, I will give him a painful reminder of that.

"Get out of my way. Now."

"You can't go in there."

"Watch me." I try to jerk my knee up into his stomach, but somehow he's quick enough to let go of me and jump backward, avoiding the blow. "I'm going in there," I say, voice nearly cracking with frustration. "I need to find Catelyn."

"Catelyn is fine."

"You're lying."

"No, I'm not—she's with Jaxon, and I just talked to him and they're both fine. And why the hell would I lie about that, anyway?"

Instead of answering, I squint in the darkness, sizing up the narrow bit of space between Seth and the door. Just enough of an opening to slip past, so long as I am fast enough.

And I am more than fast enough.

I take a few backward strides to give myself enough room to gain momentum.

"Don't," he says.

"Move."

"Don't." He steps forward to stop me, and I see my chance. I sprint, and in a flash, I'm past him, through the opening and into the fluorescent-lit room on the other side. I dart to the left. But I make it only maybe five steps before Seth slams into my side and sends me to the floor. He falls with me, and in the next motion, his hand is on my shoulder, pinning me in place. I struggle, but even the smallest movement is much more difficult than it should be. And I should be angry, frustrated by the way he's managed to stop me—but all I can think is, *How?*

He shouldn't have been able to catch me.

He shouldn't be able to hold me down like this.

It's one thing when I'm in a training session and I am purposely holding back my strength and speed to even things out. But right now? I am holding nothing back, and it's all I can do to fight my way out from underneath him and get back to my feet.

What is going on?

What is wrong with me?

And why is he looking at me like he's the one who's been caught?

My head is swimming with questions, but before I can ask any of them, we hear voices heading in our direction. Seth grabs my arm. And maybe because I'm still so stunned at the strength in his grip, he manages to pull me back into the destroyed security room. He presses me against the wall and out of sight just as two CCA members round the corner outside. He places a finger against his lips and makes a soft shushing noise. I stare at him silently. There is too much going through my brain for it to form words right now, anyway, between my confusion and that creeping, violent humming that always fills it when someone gets this close to me. Because he is entirely too close. Our shoulders are touching, and he's turned in toward me, near enough that I can feel the heat from our struggle radiating off him. His right hand is close enough to my arm that with every deep attempt at a silent breath he takes, his fingertips brush my wrist.

I find a focal point—a drop of blood that's stained the collar of his shirt—and force myself to focus on it until the people outside pass by us.

"I recognized their voices," I say, still staring at that drop of blood. "Those were CCA members. Why were we hiding from them?"

"There were clones wreaking havoc through there, a dozen of them at least. Mostly contained now, but they made an ugly mess of things before they were stopped."

I realize he hasn't answered my question, but what he's said makes me think of another one: "How did they get in?"

"They didn't." His voice is barely a whisper. "They were let in. This broken door here? It's the only damage anyone's reported—every entrance from the outside is fine. No destroyed alarms, no wounded guards—nothing. They didn't have to force anything until they got all the way in here."

My confusion officially overwhelms that vicious hatred of his closeness, and I abandon my focal point and jerk my eyes up to meet his instead. "Who would have let them in?"

He laughs: a small, savage sound without humor. "Does it matter? Who do you think they'll blame first?"

I want to look away, because I don't want him to see the slow realization dawning across my face. Because it seems so obvious now. I should have seen this coming.

Who would let a bunch of clones in, if not another clone? One who the rumors were already saying had gone crazy or something. Who tried to rip off Emily's arm after everyone else had already stopped fighting.

"Come on," Seth says. "You need to get out of here—at least until the dust settles."

I don't move. "I'm not like those other clones." I am whispering. I don't know why.

Who am I afraid will overhear?

And since when am I afraid of anything?

"The president knows that," I mutter. "Everyone here knows that, whether they want to admit it or not; they can't—"

"Everyone here does not know that, or think that, or whatever," Seth interrupts, "which is exactly why we were hiding from those CCA members you heard. They weren't members you want to be anywhere near right now."

"I don't care what they think," I say, as much to remind himself as me. "Or what they want to accuse me of. I don't care about any of them."

"But you might care if they put a few bullets in the back of your head, right?"

I have always been an expert at keeping my face impassive, unreadable—but this time I almost don't manage it. My silence must give away my shock, though, because it makes Seth sigh, and then try to convince me with one last, hurried explanation.

"Listen," he says, throwing a cautious glance through the broken door, "things are changing in this place. And I don't think the president's orders are going to keep you safe much longer—especially not after what's happened tonight."

I think of my conversation with Catelyn. About the city above, and the activated clones, and all the things they've burned and ravaged. That city knows I'm a clone. They know my face, and my former politician "father," and all the well-publicized exploits of my former self. So if I left here, I would be walking into that entire city full of fear and uncertainty about me, into those hordes of people who really know nothing about what has happened to me since the events of seven months ago. They don't know that I am any different, or that I have been freed from Huxley's grasp.

"Do you actually think leaving here is going to be any safer for me?" I ask.

I don't really want an answer, but he gives me one anyway. "At least the air is clearer up there," he says. "Which is why I'm leaving myself."

And then he turns and he disappears into the hallway before I even have a chance to ask why.

CHAPTER FOUR

I don't follow Seth.

I've made a point of following as few people as possible these past months. I follow President Cross's orders. I listen to Catelyn—when I'm in the mood. But Seth? I don't trust Seth. Not enough to follow him through the dark. Not enough to leave the familiarity of this place—of everything I know—and run with him into a world above that doesn't promise to be any better than this one.

Even so, every moment that happened in the security room keeps playing over in my mind as I sneak toward Catelyn's room. Those still bodies. The way Seth moved, too quick and too strong for me to make sense of.

His concern about the CCA members we overheard.

Seth has a tendency to exaggerate, but is that the case this time?

And even if it isn't, maybe he is still right about the city above being clearer, safer, for now. Because there will be some sort of backlash from what is happening here tonight, I'm sure; all that extra fear and anger that tonight has caused will have to go somewhere. Once Huxley's clones are gone and their dust has settled, I will be the only place left for it to go—and there isn't much room in here to hide, even if I decide I want to.

So why am I still here?

I don't like the next answer I come up with, but it surfaces before I can stop it anyway: Catelyn. I set out to make sure she was okay, and I am not taking Seth's word for that, either. I don't trust words. I trust what I can see, and right now I want to see her.

That need to see her is making me feel stupid and human, but I can't seem to get rid of it, even though I am usually remarkably good at that sort of thing. At minimizing things I don't want to think about, or "compartmentalizing" things, Catelyn calls it. Usually with a hint of distress, or perhaps jealousy, in her voice.

Most people can't just shut off the things they don't want to think about, she tells me. I imagine it is because most people are not like me. Most of them can't so easily picture each of their thoughts and memories existing as tidy little files, ready to be closed and stored in a brain made of wire and circuit. And they can't do what I do now, and pull up one of those files—the one that shows me the way to Catelyn's room, in this case—and bring it to the front center screen of their vision, maximizing it so that all other distractions fall behind it.

Even with my mind focused on that path, my heightened senses are still picking up a frenzy of sounds that don't seem safe to simply ignore: sounds like frantic voices and steps that still number far too many for this late at night. I haven't heard gunfire for a while now. I refuse to let myself guess at what that last bit might mean, good or bad. It doesn't matter right now. All that matters is one foot and then the next. Down this hallway and then that one. Melting into the shadows here to avoid people, darting into a storage room there to avoid more. And all the while I am quiet, so quiet, footsteps falling soft, silent, sure. It's an odd thrill, being able to move through these halls unnoticed while the remnants of pandemonium echo around me. To know that I am aware of any of the CCA members long before they could possibly notice me.

But it is something of a curse, too. Because hearing everything within such a large radius makes it hard not to at least notice even the sounds I would rather miss—sounds like the muffled crying that makes me pause as I round the next corner. I'm on one of the railed walkways now, a bridgelike path that stretches above the first floor of the main control room below, and from this angle I can easily see where that crying is coming from: There is a desk surrounded by high privacy walls, and underneath it, a person, curled up and whimpering softly in the dark. A girl, I think. Her face is buried in her huddled knees, long dark curls cascading over them. She must feel my eyes center on her, though, because after a moment she glances up with wide eyes—eyes that take me a moment to recognize, because I have never seen them look frightened.

Emily.

I shrink back against the railing behind me, away from the overhead lighting and any chance of her scared and searching eyes finding me.

Compartmentalize, I think. *Don't worry about what she's doing down there. About why she looks so afraid.* And I succeed, again, in pushing Catelyn's room back to the forefront of my mind. I start back on my interrupted path without a second thought—just as the bridge shakes with the lightest of vibrations. The tremble of footsteps, coming from behind me.

I turn and find two people facing me, standing shoulder to shoulder. Silently. Still as stone. A male and a female, both a little older than me, maybe, and wearing identical smiles that look as though they've been painted on.

I didn't hear them coming. I don't recognize them either, and they wear none of the symbols the CCA members often have: no bright red emblems stitched onto their jackets, no torches of truth hanging from their necks. The silence stretches on as they look me over, and I have the same uncomfortable feeling I get when I am walking through one of the dozens of security scanners that grant access to the rooms around this place—like I am being taken apart, all my inner workings put on display for everyone to see.

They stop scanning, as suddenly as they appeared out of nowhere, and they exchange a glance.

The female dives.

My body evades her without thought, legs rocketing me to the top of the tall bridge railing and out of reach. But the railing is wickedly narrow, and my balance teeters dangerously for several seconds. I crouch, press the tips of my fingers into the cold metal, and find my center. When

I glance down, both of the bridge invaders are staring up at me. Neither of them looks especially surprised that I just leaped six feet straight up to land on this railing. They look almost . . . amused by it. As though I've just signaled the start of some sort of game.

And they make the next move: Just as quickly, just as effortlessly as me, they both jump and land on the railing opposite. They stand facing me, balanced on tiptoe and still without speaking. But they don't need to say anything. I realize now why they were scanning me so closely. Why that girl dived at me.

Because she wanted to see how I would react.

She wanted to make sure I was like them.

They're clones. And I couldn't see it immediately, even though they obviously noticed I was different from the start. To me, they were only strange—but normal—humans that I didn't recognize. This is the first time I've encountered others like me, and it makes me feel odd and uncomfortable to have not seen them for what they are. Like I've betrayed them, somehow.

Maybe you didn't recognize them because they aren't like you at all, that voice from earlier reminds me. And that's right, isn't it? I didn't want to be like them.

The boy has dark splotches of what looks like blood on his sleeve.

I don't want to be like them.

How strange it is to actually see them, though. To see how human clones really do look to the unexpecting eye. So strange that I am mesmerized, my normally reliable computer of a brain refusing to pull up my original objective for crossing this bridge.

The universe feels as if it has shrunk to nothing except the three of us.

They don't stay as mesmerized by me, though. Maybe because they don't know what to do about me now that they've realized what I am. And because, a moment later, something in the room below catches their attention anyway, and both their heads turn toward it, instead. Without their gazes locked on me, the universe again expands outward a bit. I become aware of more of the sounds and sights around me—including the one that must have caught their attention below. Emily. She's asking for help now, talking into the com-bracelet on her wrist, her voice hoarse and interrupted by the occasional whimper that she tries desperately to stifle. Still trying to be proud, even as she crouches under a desk.

Stupid girl, I think, watching the two clones watch her. Doesn't she realize they hear her? But then I remember that even I didn't notice them until they were dangerously close to me.

Suddenly I am shivering, and I don't think it has anything to do with the air vents that just kicked on above me. I feel my balance slipping. I grip tighter, just as the other two clones tumble backward—deliberately and gracefully—off the railing.

It has to be at least a fifteen-foot drop to the ground floor below, but I don't hear them landing. All I hear is Emily's loud gasp.

Stupid, stupid girl.

I fall back to the bridge, maybe not as gracefully as the other two but just as quietly. And from it, I watch those other two close in on Emily, and I scan the rest of the room below and see that it's empty. No one she was so desperately calling has come to help her yet. By the time they reach her, it will likely be too late. Not that I know what those clones are planning to do to her, exactly. Because I am not like them. I don't think like them.

Am I CCA, though? Should I be answering Emily's cries? She wasn't calling to me, but I heard her all the same. And I could swear she is looking directly up into my eyes now, even though I am still hidden in shadows and I don't think she could possibly, truly be seeing any part of me. Why would she look to me, anyway? To her, I am the same as the ones that have cornered her. No, she hasn't seen me. She is only looking up in desperation—to the heavens, maybe. Saying a prayer to the god Catelyn has tried explaining to me so many times. Looking for one of his angels, perhaps.

But I am not an angel. I am only thinking it, but I feel my mouth moving in sync with the words, as if she was close enough to read my lips. As if I want to make certain she hears my thoughts, even if something is keeping me from saying them aloud.

I close my eyes, and I am back in that training room suddenly. I feel the cut in my neck. The blood trickling down it. I hear her mocking voice. I feel her and all the others pressing close to me. Too close.

I am not your savior. My mouth forms the words slowly, relishing the release of each one in a terrible sort of way.

I am a monster, remember?

I am not coming to save you.

But I have moved. Pressed closer to the railing again. Because from my higher vantage point, I can see something the ones below can't: a bit of fluorescent light spilling into the far corner of that room below. A door opening. I watch as person after person slips quietly through it, all of them armed, their guns casting giant shadows on the wall beside them. The CCA, answering Emily's call. More than a dozen of them.

I press my hand to my left temple as my head begins to throb and the room pulses in and out of focus with it.

The clones are so centered on Emily at this point—each of their steps focused and deliberate, their gazes locked on her cowering figure—that I wonder how soon they will notice the firing squad sneaking toward them.

The door is shut, the CCA members and their guns are lost in the darkness of the room, and suddenly I have forgotten, again, how I ended up on this bridge.

And so with nowhere else to go, I jump down.

I don't bother to land quietly. Both clones snap their heads toward me as I circle around, positioning myself between the two of them and Emily, so that the clones have no choice but to take their attention from her. They fall silent again. Emily does too. And it's quiet enough now that the soft echoing of footsteps from the approaching CCA can be heard.

The female glances back over her shoulder. Her partner's eyes slide to Emily's for a moment before darting back to mine, and then he takes a step toward me. Challenging, almost. But I don't budge. The faint hum of charged weapons joins the oncoming footsteps, and I can almost see the calculations both of the clones are making, their stares cold and unblinking as they compute their next move.

And then, with one last curious look in my direction, they leap past both Emily and me, and they run. They head straight toward a door that I know leads to an exit hallway. I don't know if they know this—if they plan to escape, or whether or not they actually stand a chance of making it out.

"Why did you do that?"

Emily shrinks back as I turn to look at her. Before I can answer her question, though, the other CCA members emerge from the shadows with their guns lifted, their appraising glares training on me. Emily looks at them. For a moment I think she might step back and let them draw whatever conclusions they want about what's happened, and let them deal with it however they want to.

But then she surprises me by stepping closer instead.

"Why did you protect me from them?" Her voice is oddly strangled sounding. Angry, almost. "Why would you do that for me?"

I keep my eyes on hers, but I can hear and sense movement around me; a few of those guns being lowered, uncertain glances being exchanged. I should be relieved by this, I know.

The only thing I can think, though, is: *Wrong.*

Emily is wrong.

I understand how it might have looked from her angle. Looks can be deceiving, though. And I could pretend that she was right, because it would make things easier for me—or at the very least, lower a few more guns. But I am growing tired of pretending. So, instead, I shake my head, and I tell her: "I didn't do it for you."

I am not entirely sure who I did it for, or why, but it doesn't matter.

It's done now, and I am leaving, and they are all too slow and too stunned to stop me.

CHAPTER FIVE

No more detours, is the mantra I keep repeating to myself as I walk the rest of the way to Catelyn's room. Over and over. Because I can still hear the sound of clones and CCA members violently crashing together in the distance, and my mind keeps threatening to crash with them. My thoughts flicker in and out, the same way they did while I watched the CCA members from the bridge. And I still feel the same as I did while standing between Emily and those clones. Still caught in between them, even as I move alone through these hallways.

I pause midstep, my eyes clenching shut and my hands moving to my aching head again.

No more, no more, no more. . . .

When I finally look up again, I am no longer alone.

Catelyn is in front of me, and the first thing my little sister does is grab my hands, pull them from my head, and hold them still.

"Where have you been? And why the heck didn't you answer the messages I sent you?"

"I didn't see them," I say, sliding my hands from hers and taking a step back. "I was . . . distracted."

"Distracted by what, exactly?" Jaxon asks as he catches up with Catelyn.

"By a terrible headache," I answer without looking at him.

After a few more unsuccessful interrogation attempts from Jaxon, Catelyn insists I need someplace safer and quieter if my head is hurting. And that is how I end up standing in the doorway of Jaxon's room, wishing I had simply stayed in my own bed and slept through all of this.

This is only the second time I have been in his room, and I feel every bit as out of place as I did the last time I was in here. Maybe it's because the room itself feels out of place—a soft spot in the middle of the hard, practical world all around it. Where outside there are gleaming metal walls and sensible fluorescent lights, this room is one of the few exceptions to the mood that permeates most of the base: This room feels like a home. Not my home, of course, but Jaxon has had plenty of time to make it feel like his. He and his mother have a house in the city that serves as their official address, but from what I have seen and understand, they're almost never there. It's easier just to stay here, I suppose. More comfortable. You spend enough time in a place, and pieces of your life start to rub off on it, and suddenly leaving means abandoning all of those pieces along with the place.

Maybe that's part of why I am still here too.

Besides that, looking around I can understand why Jaxon stays. Why Catelyn spends so much time in here. Even I find something warmly alluring about the soft-piled rug and butterscotch-colored walls. And I appreciate the posters and pictures he has covering those walls too—prints of cars, mostly, and a few framed photos of him with his mother and Seth—because they give me something to focus on instead of having to talk to him or Catelyn.

I sit at Jaxon's desk because it's in the corner farthest from his bed, where the two of them are huddled together with a laptop between them. They have been talking in hushed voices ever since we came back here. Not to try to keep me out of the conversation, I don't think—because they both know I could easily hear every word if I cared enough to pay attention. I don't, though. I'm much more interested in the wall decor, and in pushing the slider on the base of this desk lamp up and down, up and down, repeatedly dimming and brightening its light. I'm considering taking it apart, to see how it works, when Catelyn walks over to me and puts a hand on my arm.

"We've messaged the president and told her you're with us," she says. "But she, um . . . When things have settled down outside, she wants to talk to you in private."

I stop messing with the dimmer, leaving it halfway between the lightest and darkest settings, and wait for Catelyn to elaborate. I can tell, just by glancing at her face, that there is more she could say. That she knows exactly what the president wants to talk to me about. But she doesn't go on.

I wonder if I am as easy to read as she is.

I hope not.

"She wants to know where you were when all of this started," Jaxon says from his place on the bed.

"I was in my room," I say evenly.

"By yourself?"

I don't answer. President's son or not, he has no business interrogating me. Catelyn frowns in his direction, but it doesn't stop him from adding: "And she wants to know exactly what happened in that training session earlier today too."

Catelyn's hand is still on my arm, and she must feel it tense. "She just wants your side of things," she says in her best peacekeeping voice.

My eyes, eager for more distraction, slide to the picture nearest to me. It's a family portrait, with both Jaxon and his mother looking stiff and posed, and Seth looking like they only woke him up and informed him they were taking the picture maybe thirty seconds before it happened. They all look much younger. Seth's hair is longer, dreadlocked and very different from the short-cropped style he wears it in now. His eyes seem lighter too. I study them, trying to determine whether or not this is just a trick of the camera, and his name slips out of my mouth before I can stop it.

"Tell her to ask Seth, then," I say to Catelyn.

"Seth?"

She gives me a strange look, and I remember instantly why I didn't bring up Seth's name in my room earlier: because I still can't make any sense of his odd behavior today. And I don't like talking about things I can't make sense of.

Jaxon is on his feet now, though, and wearing the same look as Catelyn. "Have you talked to Seth recently?" His question catches me off guard. Or maybe it's the demanding way he asks it. He seems much more on edge than usual.

My eyes drift back to the portrait. "Maybe I have. So what?"

"We haven't seen Seth for hours," Catelyn says. "And he isn't answering Jaxon's calls or messages—or anybody else's, as far as we know."

So he was lying, earlier, when he said he'd just talked to them. Did he really know if they were both fine? Or was he just trying to convince me to leave with him? And if so, why? Why does he care about getting me out of here, enough that he would lie to do it?

Whatever the reason, this is precisely why I don't trust words.

"If you've seen him, or talked to him . . . ," Jaxon begins. He seems to be making an effort to soften the edge from his voice. And between that and the hopeful look Catelyn is giving me, I decide it's easier just to tell them the truth.

If it makes Jaxon pissed at Seth, all the better. That's what he gets for lying to me.

"He was in the training room earlier," I say, "and we walked part of the way back to my room together, and I saw him again on the way here. He was on his way out, though. Probably running away from everything going on." I shrug. "He asked me to leave with him, but I told him no."

"Why would he ask you to go anywhere?"

"I don't know, nor do I care." The last part is a half lie, of course, but I manage to hold my trademark blank stare this time, keeping my curiosity to myself.

"I don't understand why the idiot won't answer me," Jaxon says. "He always has his phone on him." He moves to the door, apparently already giving up on the possibility of forcing anything else out of me. "I'm going to go look for him."

But Catelyn steps in front of him. "Your mother already has people out looking for him. And she told us both to stay in here until everything calms down, remember?"

They keep arguing. I tune them out by spinning back and forth in the desk chair and focusing on the creaks and whirs of its wheeled base instead of on their voices. *Creak. Whir. Click. Whir.* The mechanical sounds are predictable, soothing. Empty sounds, empty motion. And my mind circles wonderfully, emptily, with them.

But my eyes keep drifting back to the family portrait on the wall, and every time they do, my mind threatens to stop. To focus, and to reopen all the thoughts from tonight that I have so carefully filed away.

Those bodies in the security room.

How quickly, how anxiously Seth confronted me.

Those clones staring at me.

Emily staring at me.

Why hadn't I simply stayed on that bridge and let whatever was going to happen below happen?

I only left my room to find Catelyn. I never wanted to

be in the middle of all these other things, or to care, or even think, about anything or anyone else. And I am so used to not having to care about things I don't want to that for a moment I actually feel my awareness slipping, my computer-brain apparently freezing in its attempt to process all these unwanted things.

I close my eyes.

Reboot, reboot, reboot. . . .

Open my eyes and look away from the portrait.

No. I won't think about any of this. Only emptiness. Empty *creaks. Whirs. Click click clicks—*

"Let me see your phone."

Jaxon and Catelyn both turn to me, and I realize then that I've said this aloud, and that my hand is outstretched and waiting. And waiting. And waiting.

"Why?" Jaxon finally asks.

A good question. And one I don't have an answer to, despite all my brain's eagerness to fill my mouth with other words without my say-so. Fortunately for me, though, Jaxon seems distracted enough by his argument with my sister that he doesn't bother pressing his question. I just stare expectantly at him until he silently tosses me the phone.

I don't know why I am doing it, but as soon as it hits my hands, I pull up his recent calls and I dial Seth. After four rings, I am greeted by a recorded message of his voice, telling me to "leave it."

All I leave for him is a number—mine. A number I have given to almost nobody else, and that I forget I have most of the time, even though the communication device that it goes to is always around my wrist. It's another condition of my living here: The president wants to be sure I am always reachable.

I'm sure Catelyn recognizes the number too, though she only watches me curiously as I hang up the phone. I can tell she is dying to press me for more answers and explanations. But she knows it's useless too. Maybe once I understand Seth better—if I ever do—I will try to explain today to her, if I can.

Or maybe not. In a way I am starting to feel possessive of my strange conversations with Seth, feeling that need to guard them the same way I protect everything Catelyn tells me, whether she wants me to or not. I am a hoarder of words and secrets. I suppose because most girls with bodies as old as mine have plenty of secret things of their own by this time: moments that only they know about, things given to them in confidence to keep for themselves. But I have precious little that feels like it is only mine. Six months is not much time to collect a life of your own.

So I turn around and I keep to myself, pulling the scraps of my life that I do have around me like a thin and ragged cloak, and I leave Jaxon and Cate to their own hushed conversations and secrets.

An hour and a half later, the communicator around my wrist beeps.

Catelyn lifts her head from the pillow in Jaxon's lap and blinks sleepily at me. "Who . . . ?"

I glance down at the number that has never flashed on this tiny screen before, and I almost want to laugh, though I am not sure why. Catelyn has told me several times now that my sense of humor needs work. And she is clearly right, because both she and Jaxon are wide awake now, and watching me with decidedly grim, less-than-amused expressions.

Beep, beep, beep.

I pop the earpiece from the screen's edge and slip it into my ear, then tap the answer button—which responds only to my individual fingerprint—on the device's other side. But I don't lift it to my mouth to say anything. Not even hello.

I don't have to, though, because Seth is quick to speak first: "Are you alone now?"

Why does it matter? I want to ask. But then I glance up and meet Jaxon's eyes, and think of his earlier frustration when Seth wouldn't answer him. Clearly, for whatever reason, Seth doesn't want his brother to be able to contact him. If he knows I am still this close to Jaxon, he is likely to hang up on me.

"Yes," I lie. "I'm in my room."

"Good." Silence, then the sound of his breathing, quickening as if he's suddenly started walking fast. "Stay away from Jaxon. And Cate, too."

"Why?"

"You need to get out of the CCA headquarters."

I spin around in the chair, hoping once more for the empty motion to lift emptiness into my thoughts—this time so I can be sure to sound as detached as I want to when I answer him. "You know, I was hoping you would have something more interesting to say this time."

I don't hear his reply to this, because at that moment I sense movement. I jerk around just as Jaxon reaches for the earpiece. I twist so fiercely up and away from his touch that the chair skids out from under me and hurtles into him.

"That's Seth," he says, knocking the chair away and ignoring it as it totters on half its wheels for a few seconds before crashing to the floor. "Let me talk to him." His voice is even, but loud. Loud enough that Seth hears him.

"Liar," he breathes into my ear, sounding almost amused.

"Given that you haven't been exactly forthcoming with me," I say, backing away from Jaxon, "I assumed lying was just part of the game."

He laughs darkly on the other side. A tiny black hole of sound, one that feels like it is swallowing up everything between us until he says, "We're not playing a game here—we could call it that if you like, but I'm not sure it's possible for either of us to win. Just so you know."

I don't know if he is trying to intimidate me with this last part, but if he is, he is wasting his time. "Impossible games are my favorite kind," I say. And then I mean to hang up, because I am finished with his evasiveness and with trying to carry on a conversation while both Jaxon and Cate are trying to wrestle me away from it. My hand is slow to find the end button, though, slow enough that Seth manages to leave me with a few last words:

"Perfect. Then you should meet me downtown, at the statue in the center of Market Square, around dawn."

Click.

Found the end button, finally.

I pull the earpiece out and snap it back into its place. "I seem to have lost the connection," I say in response to Jaxon's incredulous look.

"Call him back," he says. "Give me that earpiece, and call him back."

Catelyn sighs in a way that clearly tells me she is too tired for this argument. I can't do what Jaxon asks, though. I won't. Not even for a second do I want Seth thinking I am calling him back, or that he has any of that sort of control over me. I have to maintain some sort of command over whatever is happening tonight.

"You know he's alive at least," I say, picking up the chair and pushing it back under the desk.

"Why is he answering you and ignoring me?" Jaxon's face seems perfectly impassive when he says it. But Catelyn must see something in his eyes that I don't; her body language and expressions are more familiar and easy to read, and I've memorized that look she is giving him now—the way she bites her lip and tilts her head to the side like that, the way her body sinks deeper into her seat, bit by tiny bit, as if absorbing whatever perceived hurt she senses rolling off someone.

Empathy. I know the word for it. And Catelyn has tried, several times, to explain when I need to put myself in someone else's shoes, so to speak. It's difficult, though.

Maybe the shortness of a six-month life is to blame again; it seems as if it would be easier to sense someone else's hurt if you had spent a lifetime collecting and recognizing pain for yourself.

I don't think it would be worth it, anyway, however much or little time it took. I have no plans to become more like Catelyn—to be any more in touch with hurt, whether mine or anyone else's. Whatever pain I notice, all I want to do is file it neatly away where I don't have to feel it. Where I can control it, and not the other way around.

Because the second I start worrying about other people hurting, I end up in places like this, with my mind racing with all these things I don't understand. I end up forgetting about myself, and the danger I might have put myself in by staying because of Catelyn.

"It's been calm outside for a while now," I say quietly. "The president is probably wondering why I haven't come to see her yet."

Anger is one of the simplest, easiest emotions to read. And now it's unmistakably written all over Jaxon's face. "Yeah. You should go," he says, and I can feel him glaring after me, all the way out the door.

CHAPTER SIX

The hallway outside the president's room is dimly lit, aglow only with the pale-white security lights that line the bottom half of the wall. The headquarters are almost completely quiet, wrapped in an uneasy hush and forced calmness as members follow protocol to finish restoring order. Our walk here didn't contribute any extra noise either. Yes, *our* walk, and not simply mine, because Catelyn supposedly wanted a change of scenery. And Jaxon didn't want her to go alone, so he came too.

I am not sure why they had to walk with me, though.

They remain quiet company, at least. Quiet enough that all three of us hear a voice long before the person it belongs to—a middle-aged man with graying hair and a sharp chin—rounds the corner ahead. Catelyn averts her gaze, but I keep staring at the man walking toward us as she whispers, "That's Silas Iverson. Josh's dad."

I already know this, but I don't bother to point it out. I've seen him before, and all it takes is once; I remember him the same way I remember everything I see and hear. And he and Josh look so much alike that I don't think he could deny his son even if he wanted to.

His attention remains fixed on the conversation he is

having over his communicator, his pale-blue eyes staring straight ahead until he has almost walked right past us. Only then do those eyes dart toward Jaxon. He gives a curt nod. Indifferent, still—at least until he truly catches sight of me. Then his step slows. His voice starts to trail off, almost to complete silence before he realizes it, and he has to apologize to whoever is on the other end of his communicator.

He doesn't say a word to us, though. He just averts his gaze and picks up his pace again.

"I wonder where he's heading off to," Catelyn says, once he is well out of earshot.

Something in her tone strikes me as odd; she sounds too concerned about what looked like nothing more than a man going for a walk to me—especially since half the CCA is awake right now.

I think it might be simply because she is still worrying about my run-in with Josh earlier, until Jaxon turns to her and says, "Probably off to another of his committee meetings. I'm sure they'll have lots to discuss after tonight."

"That's what I'm afraid of." She turns the direction Iverson disappeared toward, and takes a step as if she is thinking about following him.

"What meetings?"

Catelyn hesitates before glancing back at me. "He and a few others formed this . . . group thing, a few months back. They said their goal was to help bring the CCA back to its roots, to the philosophy they started with, which . . ." She doesn't seem like she wants to finish her sentence, but all I have to do is think about his son, and the way Silas himself hurried away from me just now, and I can guess the rest on my own.

"Which probably didn't include harboring a clone within the very walls of the CCA, for whatever reason?"

Catelyn picks at her fingernail instead of looking at me. "Something like that."

"It was only a few of them at first," Jaxon says. "Mom figured it was just a knee-jerk reaction to her bringing you back here, a protest that would die out before it gained much momentum. But more and more people seem to be listening to him lately, and they're getting more secretive about things. We're pretty sure they're holding meetings somewhere outside of headquarters, but we haven't been able to figure out where—or what they're planning, exactly."

I suppose this means Seth wasn't lying when he mentioned the changes taking place around here, then.

Should I have trusted some of the other things he said, after all?

Almost as if she can read my thoughts, Catelyn forces her eyes to mine again and says, "Maybe you should talk to the president about leaving for a while? If you won't go back to our house, I'm sure she can figure something else out. She has plenty of connections."

Is there really no other option for me, other than running away?

Catelyn is watching me closely, waiting, but I just silently walk over and press the buzzer outside the president's room.

We messaged ahead, so she knew I was coming. Still, it is several long moments before someone comes to the door: a man with a bruise on his left cheek, who I could swear actually jumps at the sight of me. I hold in a scowl. I haven't done anything to startle him.

Though I will admit, the longer I stand here under his wary gaze, the more tempting it is to offer him something frightening to jump about. To simply become what they all seem to expect of me.

But I restrain myself. This time. What I can't stop, though, are those stupid words Seth said earlier from running through my head: *Do you ever wonder why she brought you back? Just so everyone here could hate you?*

Maybe it is time I stopped wondering and started asking.

I like this reason for my still being here better, at least: the idea that I was pursuing knowledge, instead of being dragged along by some connection to Catelyn that I couldn't manage to control.

I leave Catelyn and Jaxon and follow the man inside. There is another door once we step through the first, one with a security code panel beside it. I watch his fingers move over the panel, slowly, as if he hasn't been entrusted with the correct numbers for long enough to have them fully memorized.

The next space we enter is set up as a formal kind of sitting room, not as cold and clean lined as the office the president usually operates from, which is just down the hall. But it is still clearly a place meant for business. She and a handful of others are gathered around a large table in the corner of it, their heads bent over a flat display screen in its center.

The man who escorted me in walks over to the president, and only once he is directly beside her does she seem to notice his presence. From him, her eyes travel to me, and they linger there as she stands up straight and dismisses most of the table, informing them that they will finish their discussion in the morning. While the others file out, my escort stays by the president, as does one other woman, who I recognize, though I don't know her name. Her eyes are cold, her hair pulled back in a tight, severe-looking bun. Both she and my escort stand like sentinels on either side of the president.

I am not surprised they're staying. Now that I think about it, I don't know that I have ever had a conversation with the president alone.

I feel that scowl from before threatening again. Not even she—a woman who I have never seen show anything like trepidation—can brave the sight of me on her own.

Can that be true?

I want those other two to leave, suddenly. I want to be alone with the president, and I want her to tell me, and only me, all the things that I deserve to know. Why am I here? Why am I the only one? And is there a way to bring back the Violet I was before—all eighteen combined years of her?

There is so much I should know that I don't.

"You look like you have a lot on your mind," President Cross says.

"A lot has happened tonight."

She nods, and takes a seat in one of the tall leather chairs around the table. "Come sit," she says, gesturing to the chair beside her. I would rather stand, and normally I would, but I decide to simply go along with whatever she asks for now. It might make her go along more easily with me when I start asking my own questions.

"A lot has happened tonight," she repeats, leaning back in her chair as I slide stiffly into mine. "I'm glad to see you escaped all the violence unscathed."

"I slept through most of it."

"Though you weren't in your room the whole time."

"I went to find Catelyn."

"I know where you were," she says thinly. "I have security cameras. Plenty of them, in strategic places—one above the right wing bridge over sector C, for example."

Having a conversation with the president is often like playing a game of chess. And this time is no different. I consider every angle of everything I could say next, all the ways it could leave any pieces of me vulnerable to capture and defeat, before I finally say, "I had to pass by there to get to Catelyn's room."

"Did you see anything interesting while you were there, by chance?" she asks. And then she just leans back and watches me. Waiting, I assume, for me to move a pawn into the wrong square.

I am already tired of playing this particular game, though, so I look directly into her challenging gaze, and I say, "You have cameras. You know what I saw."

"Perhaps. But I am still trying to decide exactly what *I* saw. The personnel who responded to Emily's distress call found only you when they reached her. They're convinced you warned the other clones and allowed them to escape. And they did escape, if you wondered."

"I didn't," I lie.

"All the same, the security footage was interesting, if inconclusive."

"And what did Emily conclude about what happened?"

"Nothing. She claims to have been too shocked to remember the exact details of it all."

I try to hold back a derisive snort. "Well, I think I may be suffering the same problem, unfortunately."

The president's guards shift uncertainly at the mocking tone of my voice, but she only smiles at me, and her voice is equal parts steel and ice when she says, "We both know your memory is flawless, Violet. And so you remember, too, who brought you back? It wasn't Huxley. Just keep that in mind the next time you encounter their clones and you have to decide which side you're on."

"I was not on their side," I say.

But I know I wasn't on Emily's, either.

Watch your footage again, I want to tell the president. *And you'd see me standing in the middle.*

In the middle, and alone. As alone as I was on that day she brought me back. I wonder if she can understand that, somehow—that I don't feel like I could ever completely belong to either side. Did she think about that while she watched the shell of the old Violet sleep, all those months ago? Did she consider it at all before she decided to wake me up?

That should be the first thing I ask her, I decide, out of all the questions spilling their way into my thoughts.

But before I can settle on exactly how to phrase this question, President Cross stands and pushes her chair in.

"Wait a minute," I say, getting to my feet as well. "I need to ask you some things."

"And I need sleep, unfortunately. You know the way out—and do me a favor, will you, and have the decency to look like you've received a proper scolding in here. It probably won't be enough to pacify the members you've upset, but we might as well make the effort. Right?"

I haven't made any movement toward the exit. "I have questions," I say, more firmly this time. She gives me the same cold, placeholder smile she used earlier, and then turns and disappears through a door on the far back wall, one that I'm fairly certain leads to her own private quarters.

No one follows her.

My escort clears his throat. "Curiosity killed the clone anyway, right?" he says, giving me a pointed shove toward the door I first entered through. I recoil from his touch and throw a wild glare his way, no longer caring whether I frighten him or not.

He lets me walk myself out.

The security door clicks behind me. I stand for a moment in the low-lit vestibule on the other side of it, thinking. I already have two messages in my communicator—both from Catelyn; one wants to know how the meeting is going, the other suggests that just the two of us get together in her room afterward and talk. But there isn't much to talk about, is there? None of my questions have been answered—they weren't even asked.

Nothing about tonight, nothing about me, makes any more sense than it did before.

What should I have done? If I had tried to stop the president from walking away, things might have turned violent, and it wouldn't have been a fight that ended well for me. It will never end well for me, as long as she is surrounded by bodyguards and personal aides—most of whom are eager for an excuse to take a swing at me anyway. And then I will only have proven all of the president's detractors right and made the division among the members here that much greater.

Do I care, though?

Should I care?

I lean against the wall, clenching my fists. My eyes lift upward, searching. Just as Emily's did earlier.

The only difference is that mine actually find a possible solution.

Or a hiding place, to be exact.

On each of the walls left and right of the door to outside, there are knockouts that look like they're intended for storage. They are high—the bottom at least seven feet above me—and reach to the ceiling. I can't tell from where I am how far back they go. But if it's deep enough for me to fit inside, then the chances of anyone walking by and actually noticing I'm up there will be slim. And as far as I know, there are only two people I have to count on not noticing me.

Even as the plan is unfolding in my mind, I realize how crazy it is. All of the painfully bad ways that it could end. I can already see that disappointed look Catelyn does so well, her frown falling deeper as I try to explain what I was thinking, attempting this.

I press my ear against the security door behind me, listening. And suddenly I am out of time to think my plan through, because I hear two sets of footsteps approaching from the other side. I look to my left, determine the angle quickly, and hit the wall with as much speed as I can gather in the small space. My reflexes do the rest, legs bending and then pushing off with enough force to propel me across to the storage space on the other side. With no time to calculate a more graceful landing, I hit hard, my upper body flopping into the open storage space and my knees slamming hard against the wall beneath. I scramble the rest of the way inside and curl back as far as I can—which unfortunately isn't very far. At least this space is dark.

The security door opens.

I hold my breath and stop trying to curl myself smaller. The president's bodyguards are talking quietly among themselves as they step inside. It's hard to make out exact words, though, between the way my arms are cramped awkwardly up by my ears and the beeping sounds of the security panel below as one of them tests to be sure it's armed.

What feels like an eternity later, they leave. I still don't move right away, waiting and listening for any new voices or footsteps of bodyguards who might be coming to take their place. The president is known to enjoy her privacy, so I don't think she regularly sleeps with any more security than the alarmed doors and whatever other computerized defenses lie between here and her.

But after tonight that may have to change.

Luckily for me, though, after five minutes I am still the only one here. Keeping an eye on the outside door, I slowly untangle myself and slide out of my hiding place, dropping soundlessly to the floor. I turn my attention to the glowing white screen of the security panel next. With a bit of concentration, I access the memory I stored of my escort's hand moving so slowly across it earlier, and I copy his movements with my own hand. My first attempt fails, but on the second try the screen glows green as I pull my hand away, and the door's latches release with a click.

Motion lights flash on as I step back into the room on the other side. I almost freeze up, but there is no point in stopping now. I rush forward and open the door the president disappeared through . . . only to find another entry hallway. And at the end of that, yet another door. There is no security panel beside this one, but I am not foolish enough to think it will be that easy. If it isn't locked, then other security measures must be in this hall. I just can't see them.

I slip the communicator from my wrist and press a few buttons until it opens the device's digital camera. Then I point it toward the seemingly empty hallway, and with the

aid of the camera's lens, I can see them on the communicator's screen: infrared beams. Invisible to the naked eye.
Waiting for me to cross them and set off an alarm. There
are several sets of them, crisscrossing my path and reaching from the floor up to two, perhaps two and a half, feet
from the ceiling. An abysmally small space to try to jump
cleanly through, even with inhuman strength and grace on
my side.

I could simply trip the alarm; it would get her attention
I'm sure, send her running out here within moments.

But how many others would it attract?

Even one or two would be too many. So instead, I creep
back to the room behind me, quietly grab a chair from
around the table and carry it back to the hallway, taking
care not to drag or bump any of its feet against the floor. I
don't trust even the smallest sounds; there may be things
monitoring for those, too. It's going to be impossible to do
this completely silently, though, so I need to be quick. The
less time she has to react to any noise I make, the better.

I climb onto the chair, size up the space one last time,
and dive through it.

I hit the ground in a tumbling roll on the other side,
and spring back to my feet—only to find myself facing an
open door.

CHAPTER SEVEN

President Cross stands in the center of the open doorway, gun drawn.

"I thought I heard something," she says.

And since I have already broken every rule of my existence at this point, I decide there is no point in stopping now. I dart forward and wrap my hand around the gun, jerking it out of her grip before she has a chance to protest. I fling it away, and it skitters across the floor and underneath a couch on the other side of the room.

True to her seemingly unshakable nature, the president doesn't as much as flinch at this. She only watches the gun disappear out of the corner of her eye, and then turns her full attention back to me.

"Tell me," she says, arching an eyebrow, "in all of your programming and all of the knowledge uploaded into your brain at your rebirth, was there perhaps, within all that, an understanding of the phrase 'biting the hand that feeds'?"

"Yes." I know exactly what that phrase means. But like so many of the things filling my head, that meaning is cold. Sterile. A fact I can regurgitate but do little else with. What I really want to know is why that hand bothered to feed me in the first place.

But how to get that out of her?

"Emily hates me." It sounds childish, the way I blurt it out. And it's not what I meant to say at all, but it's the first sentence that comes to my mind—and refuses to leave—when I start thinking about everything that has happened today. "They all hate me. Why did you bring me back just so everyone here could hate me?" I force myself to keep staring at her, to not think about Seth and how I couldn't answer when he asked me this same thing.

"'Why' can be a dangerous question," the president says. "Lots of people go mad trying to answer it."

"I'm already mad."

She glances toward the couch I threw her gun beneath. "So it would seem."

"You made me this way."

Her eyes flutter shut for a moment, and the bemused grin she's been wearing slips a little. She reaches up and absently rubs her shoulder. It's hard to tell if she's grown thoughtful all of a sudden, or if she is simply fighting a losing battle with sleep. "No, I remade you. Into a blank slate that could go this way or that."

"Right. And then gave me an ultimatum."

"You still have the free will to ignore it."

My face grows hot. "But at what cost?"

She stares blankly at something behind me as she answers in a quiet, careful voice. "One of your new life's little paradoxes, isn't it? You're free to choose, but you aren't free from the consequences of your choices. Welcome to the human existence."

The room feels like it is growing smaller, frustration and irritation pinching my field of vision and blurring it together. These are not the answers I came in here for. They aren't answers at all—just the sort of philosophical musing that I hate. And this is the reason I never bothered to ask her why before tonight.

Because questions like "Why?" only lead to conversations that circle, and I prefer straight lines.

I search for a question that's easier—something to keep the conversation going, to keep her from turning and locking me out again. "Is that really all you had to say to me earlier? You dismissed the entire room just so you could give me a halfhearted lecture?"

"No. I dismissed the entire room because I was tired of talking to them," she says, still rubbing her shoulder. It doesn't sound like the sort of thing a president should admit to, but she doesn't seem to care that I've heard it.

But then, what CCA members would I repeat it to, anyhow?

None of them would be interested in anything I had to say about her.

"And the only reason I called you in at all was to hopefully prevent a riot starting over you." The word "hopefully" seems to choke out of her, as though she isn't ready to admit that she is relying on that hope. "If you haven't noticed," she adds, "my bringing you back and having you stay here has not been the most . . . popular decision I've ever made as president. And you certainly didn't do much to help my cause tonight."

"Why did you do it?" There it is again. That question I can't help asking, even knowing it will lead to nowhere.

"Why, indeed?" She seems to be searching for an actual answer at first, but then the president's eyes refocus on me, and both they and her tone grow laser sharp once more. "It's late," she says. "See if you can manage to leave more quietly than you came in, why don't you?" Her hand finally drops from her shoulder as she turns away from me.

And I don't move, and I don't answer, because I am too busy staring at the skin her falling hand revealed. I've never seen it so exposed as this; she wears only a tank top with her navy, uniform-style leggings. And where her back and shoulders are normally completely covered, by stiff-collared blazers or CCA-emblem-embroidered jackets, right now they are completely bare—except for the strange purplish marks on her skin. Like bruises, only raised and stretched and twisted. There are dozens of them.

"What happened to your back?" I don't know why I ask. I don't know why I care.

She stops walking, tilts her head toward the ceiling, and lets out a quiet sigh. "What does it matter?"

I stare at her until a realization surfaces in my mind. "Those markings. They're from the virus, aren't they?" The same virus that made Catelyn's parents decide to clone their two original daughters. Catelyn has told me about it, about how sick it made her mother and so many others, and the way it left these permanent, ugly reminders of itself on their skin. I have never seen them in person, though. Because so many of the sick sided with Huxley, not the CCA. It was Huxley, after all, that promised cloning as part of a way back to a healthy population, a way to "fix" that sickness they were passing on to their children.

"Everyone knows that I am a former Huxley employee," the president tells me. "But not many know why I worked for them. They don't know that I was once sick—quite desperately sick. And I would prefer they didn't find out."

Even as she talks, I don't take my eyes off the scars she has revealed. I suppose she hid them to avoid reminding people of her sickness and her connection to Huxley, but it still seems strange to me, going to such lengths to cover up such a large part of her past. Although, maybe that's only because I find myself so desperately wishing I could uncover at least part of mine. Especially after today.

"So let's keep this our little secret, shall we?" For the first time since I broke in, the president's tone carries a low threat with it. And I know it isn't hollow.

There is something else in her voice too, though, something that moves me farther back than any threat ever could have. I understand threats. I've heard enough of them that they don't faze me much anymore.

What I don't understand, though, is the quiet sadness tangled in with her threatening words—and that is why I back away from it, leaving her alone in the darkness of her room.

CHAPTER EIGHT

I can't stand the thought of going back to my bed, so instead I slip out and into the city above—though I go only as far as the ruins of the parking garage that sits above the CCA's underground headquarters. I'll admit that Seth's cryptic invitation to meet him downtown does surface in my mind, but I crush it away just as quickly. I don't want to see anybody else right now. Especially not him. I have too many questions for him, and if my attempt to get answers from him were to go as well as my attempt to get them from President Cross, there is a good chance I might actually go insane.

So for the moment, at least, I head straight for the stairwell in one of the garage's corners instead. Its concrete steps are crumbling and crawling with weeds, and broken and burned-out light fixtures make most of my upward climb a blind one. But I don't need to see. I have made this climb several times before.

Aside from the few excursions I have made with Catelyn—to her house, once to the library, and to a handful of other places—I haven't seen much of the city that stretches below me. It's mostly silhouettes and shadows now. The nearly full moon is still gleaming overhead, even though far in the distance I can see the eastern sky beginning to lighten. Bright streaks of blue reflect on some of the shinier steel buildings. The damp, heavy dew scent of coming morning saturates the air, and the city is already beginning to wake up, with the occasional quiet roar of the electronic shuttles over their tracks, and the rumble of jet-bike engines echoing between houses and businesses.

The safety walls along this top floor are in worse shape than the stairs, but I find a relatively sturdy looking stretch and hoist myself up. I creep forward bit by bit, until the toe of my left boot presses against the outer edge. Just far enough that it fires a warning through my brain. Then the other foot, just a little farther. . . .

I stop moving forward and straighten up. The wind seems to whip harder with every inch taller I stretch. I have excellent balance, but looking down—down, down, and farther down to the near-dead streets below—is dizzying. And I love it. All my thoughts from the past twenty-four hours weigh heavy on my mind, refusing to be filed away as neatly as I normally manage, but something about all the open air beneath me makes me feel lighter. Free.

What would it be like, I wonder, if I actually was free and able to go out into that city below? If people knew what I was, but it didn't matter? If I could be in that world below, instead of standing up here outside of it?

No more whispers, no more stares, no more questions.

On either side of my sturdy patch of wall, bright-yellow caution tape droops over some rougher-looking breaks in the concrete; but other than that, most everything else around me looks as if it was given up on decades ago. I know there are city officials who are also CCA members, which is how I assume they keep this garage from being torn down even when its decrepit appearance probably makes most outsiders see it as a hazard at worst and wasted space at best. And there are others besides those officials, too, tasked with keeping unsuspecting civilians from wandering up and down these parking levels.

So I can usually count on being safe and undisturbed when I come here.

Which is why I almost lose my balance when something suddenly stings me in the back of the neck.

I spin around. Drop to a sturdier, crouched position and wrap my hands over the wall. At the top of the stairwell are half a dozen CCA members, led by two of the training-room group: Josh and Metal-Knuckles. On the ground below me is a tiny piece of chipped concrete that one of them must have thrown. Part of me is surprised they didn't try harder to sneak up on me and just shove me over the edge.

Part of me still wants them to try that and see what happens.

A taunt rises in my throat, but new warnings fire through my brain before I can get it out. I'm well past outnumbered. We're alone up here. They're likely armed.

There is something else stopping me too, as much as I don't want to admit it: my earlier conversation with President Cross. So much of her own organization is turning against her, at least partly thanks to her decision to have me stay here, and yet she continues to provide me with food, with shelter. And tonight she led them all to believe that I would be punished, that she would treat me as the scapegoat they want me to be—only for her to then dismiss me with barely a harsh word. She called for no one when I cornered her in her room.

My stomach does an odd little flip, because here it is, happening again: a connection I don't need, to someone I don't want to be thinking about right now.

I glance behind me and over the edge, sizing up the distance between me and the next parking level, wondering if I could angle my drop well enough that I could roll safely into it. Probably. And perhaps I owe it to the president to not get in any more trouble than I can help.

Except I don't want to run. What she said about me having free will may be true, but running endlessly from this group still seems against something programmed deep in my brain.

"There's a rumor going around about you, you know," Josh says, stepping forward.

I step down from the wall but don't answer him. My communicator buzzes at almost the exact same moment my feet hit the ground—Catelyn again, most likely. I ignore it, refusing to take my eyes from Josh's.

"People are saying you helped those clones earlier tonight," he says. "That they saw you talking to them."

I still don't believe "help" is the right word. But it isn't worth arguing.

"So they all expected you to run away, same as those others did," he says. "Is that what you're doing up here? Or are you thinking of doing the world a favor and jumping?"

He saunters toward the wall. I can't help noticing—with a grim, almost-satisfaction—that he makes certain to keep a wide berth between us. "Would it kill you then?" he asks, casually glancing over the edge. "A fall from this height, I mean."

"Maybe. Maybe not." I return the smirk he gives me. "But I have a feeling it would kill you. Would you like to jump together and see how we're both faring when we get to the bottom?"

Someone in the group lingering by the stairwell coughs something that sounds like "crazy bitch." My attention snaps toward her before I can help it. I fully expect to see another of the training-room group—Emily—since it sounds like something she would say.

But it isn't her.

Because for once, she isn't here in her place among my regular tormentors.

And whether it is because she has simply dealt with enough clones for one day, or because she still mistakenly believes that I was thinking about helping her when I intervened earlier, I may never know. But it doesn't matter right now. The girl who did call me that has fixed a shaky but determined glare on me, and she is fumbling with something in her hands—a gun.

"Crazy," I snap, taking a step toward her, "and yet I am not the one who thought following me up here and attempting to corner me was a good idea."

"There are six of us," Metal-Knuckles gruffly points out,

"one of you, and this time there's no one here to interrupt. No one here to witness anything, so there's no reason for us to hold back."

No one else here, warns that voice in my head again. *Alone, with no one to stop them.*

But then a more vicious voice from someplace deeper answers it—corrects it.

We are alone, with no one to stop me.

"What do you plan to do then?" I ask. "Push me off the edge?"

"We could make it look like an accident so easily," Josh assures me. "Alone up here, just a bunch of stupid kids messing around, sometimes things get out of hand."

And suddenly I realize: "Someone sent you to cause this accident, didn't they?" This is not a coincidence, or another one of their casual, violent attempts to remind me of my place among them. They're serious about creating this accident. I can see it in Josh's eyes, hungry as they are in a way I don't quite understand, and in the still-not-quite-committed shuffling of some of his group by the stairs. Maybe the older, more experienced CCA members aren't quite ready to make a demonstration out of me like this, however much they might want to. But it doesn't mean some of them wouldn't sink so low as to bribe the younger, more reckless among them to do their dirty work.

"What did they offer you?"

"Offer?" Josh says, moving closer. "They didn't have to pay me for this. I've been planning this ever since you woke up. I only had to wait until we had enough on our side that we wouldn't have to worry about whatever retaliation this might cause from the president and her mindlessly loyal drones."

"And you think you have that now?"

"Let's just say that it's a shame you won't be around long enough to see the way things are changing around here," he says. "We're on our way toward quite the revival."

"I don't want to fight you," I say quietly. But it isn't true. I don't know why I say it. I do want to fight them. I want to tear them all to pieces and then parade those pieces across headquarters as a warning, as a promise that if they want to paint me a killer, then I can live up to their expectations. I can make them regret every word they have ever said against me.

I don't, though. Not yet. Because some part of me is still desperate not to be like them, any more than I wanted to be like those clones.

But my choices are narrowing, along with the distance between myself and the stairwell group. That group moves almost in unison across the deck, their eyes burning with the reflection of the sun creeping up behind me.

"You don't have to fight," Josh says, drawing my gaze back to him. "There's still time to jump." There is something about the way he says it. Still so casual. Without a hint of the chill a mention of death should carry with it. My fists clench. My pulse quickens. My control slips—for only a moment.

But I am lethally fast.

So a moment is all it takes.

I lunge, slam hard into his side and knock him into the crumbling stone wall. Hard enough that a few bits of it chip free and scatter down around him. He's slow to get up, but the others have reached me now; I spring sideways to avoid one of their punches, only to be met with a knee to my side that sends me stumbling and almost tripping over myself to regain my balance. When I look up, I find myself staring into the eyes of a dark-skinned girl with hair the color of coal and lips stained a startlingly bright red. She smiles. I catch a glimpse of a lipstick stain against her teeth, and it is the last thing I see before a sudden sharpness lightnings through my neck. I reach up, and my fingers close around a thin metal dart.

Tranquilizer.

As I yank it out, another hits near the hollow of my throat.

I don't think these are normal tranquilizers either. I have heard other CCA members talking about them; they're doctored by some of the scientists and weapons specialists here, strengthened past the point of anything you could legally obtain outside these walls. They're strong enough to kill a normal human with just a small dose.

And more importantly, strong enough to stop most clones with relative ease, even in spite of their genetically enhanced bodies and organs.

My neck tingles where the poison's seeped in, itches just out of reach beneath my skin. It takes only a few seconds for my vision to start to fade. For the roof to start spinning. The space around me seems to collapse, the entire group around me falling into one blurry shape of hatred.

I fight to stay on my feet as that shape breaks apart and allows a single piece to step forward. Josh, I realize—but only once he is mere inches from my face. There is blood dotting his skinned cheek. Not much, though, and being slammed into that wall doesn't seem to have shaken his confidence much either. His smug grin is still there as he leans in close, whispers words that I am just barely still lucid enough to understand: "I'll tell Catelyn good-bye for you, don't worry."

My wrist feels oddly heavy as my attention shifts to it, dimly recognizing the device resting there. Communicator. Full of messages from Catelyn that I never answered. My eyes close, and I can somehow still picture her much more clearly than I can see anything that is happening now. And I can picture Josh talking to her, wearing that same awful smile as he tells her what he's done.

That burning, that itching along my neck grows more intense, spreads down through my whole body.

I know what should come next. I am waiting for it: that flash of black, the violent shock of my mind unhinging, releasing its grip on the strength it usually makes me hold back. I am hoping for that darkness, almost. Because it likely would end this, and I wouldn't have to think about what I was doing, or even remember it.

But that darkness doesn't come.

The tranquilizer is to blame, maybe. The way it seems to be dulling my world, softening the sharp edges of my furious thoughts along with everything else.

Josh's hands grab my arms and shove me against the

wall. The edge of it digs into my lower back, and my feet fly up, and suddenly I'm flat against the top of it, my head and shoulders hanging out over emptiness. My eyes dart open to wide sky above, interrupted a second later by Josh peering down at me as his right hand moves to my throat.

I'm not sure where the strength to do it comes from, but I grab that hand and I twist, pulling him off his feet and crushing him down against my body. I'm not strong enough to hold him, though, and the two of us roll over and over along the perilously uneven wall, breaking and shifting even more of the cracked bits of concrete as we go. I can't shove him off me—I don't have enough control left in my muscles to manage it. And I am losing what little bit of strength I managed to muster; bit by bit he keeps shoving me farther out over the edge, and I can't fight my way back.

I am tired of fighting.

Now I am just hoping to scramble enough power and momentum together to bring him over the edge with me.

The group behind us has gotten louder. Or maybe my hearing is getting stronger, to make up for my vision and everything else that continues to fade. What I originally thought was that group jeering and cheering Josh on sounds more frenzied and frustrated now—more like the sound of scuffling. As if they can't be still, can't help fighting among themselves since Josh is taking care of me alone.

My attention is ripped brutally from whatever they're doing, though, as my now mostly numb body is spun over and thrown against a particularly run-down bit of the wall. There isn't enough concrete left to support me here, and the entire upper half of my body slides down along the crumbling slope. My legs make a feeble attempt to close over something—anything.

But all it takes is one last shove from Josh, and then I am falling.

CHAPTER NINE

There is no sensation of being crushed toward the ground like I expected. There is only a careening, out-of-control weightlessness. And I should be terrified of it, I suppose, but the only thought in my mind is: *Josh is still up above.*

I wanted to drag him down into this weightless abyss with me, but I've failed.

My hands stretch out, as if I still had some hope of snatching him. They hit something else instead. Even in my numb, drugged state, I feel the pain of impact strike up through my arms—such an unbelievable amount of pain that it's all I am aware of for several moments. Then my eyes flutter open much like my hands reached out—on their own, with me only distantly aware that I once had the full power to control them.

It takes what feels like hours to make sense of what I'm seeing.

A dark level of the parking garage unfolds to my left. Both my arms are lying out in front of me, and underneath me, from my stomach upward, I feel solidness. Only my legs are dangling in open air now; the rest of me is safe on that solidness underneath—on the narrow top of one of the giant, faded signs affixed to the side of the garage. That is the only thing I can think of that it might be, and I can't seem to get my body to cooperate, to move so I can see if I'm right.

All I remember are my hands hitting, and that pain. . . . I don't remember pulling myself up. Yet here I am. Alive. And once again, I don't understand how or why I am breathing. But maybe now isn't the time to question it.

What I do wonder, though, is how much worse that impact against this sign was. How much of it I didn't feel. If I don't remember moving and pulling myself up here, what else is my brain blacking out? Why can't I make myself move? Is it still the tranquilizer at work, or something worse?

How broken and bruised am I, really?

The thought is fuzzy at first, but it repeats itself enough that soon it becomes clear—the only clarity I have. Everything else feels scrambled, rimmed in darkness along with my vision.

And very soon I grow tired of caring even about my injuries. About not being able to move. Why do I need to move? I am fading into that darkness, the edges of it expanding and engulfing. It feels warm. Comfortable. I don't need to make sense of the noises above or below me.

I don't need to do anything about that figure crossing the parking garage, moving toward me. They can't want anything to do with me—nothing in this world has anything to do with me anymore.

So I close my eyes again, and I keep falling.

• • •

Strange voices.

"She's lucky. Bit deeper and this cut probably would've caused some serious hardware issues."

"But it hasn't, right?"

"Chip's a bit banged up now; probably why she seemed so scrambled. But everything on it should still be intact—just needs cleaning, and then we can let the healing program work its magic and cover things back up, safe and sound like."

Strange smells.

Industrial smells, mostly—metal and rust and oil—but with an overlay of something that doesn't seem to belong. Vanilla? Or honey, maybe? I've only had honey once, but when I swallow to try to clear the dryness in my mouth, I can taste its sticky bitter-tinged sweetness all over again.

"It looks like she might be waking up."

I don't remember falling asleep.

"Violet? Can you hear me?"

Why does this strange voice know my name?

"Can you move anything?"

Maybe I can, but I don't rush to prove it. This voice, these people looming over me, waiting and watching my every move . . . I feel vulnerable—like they already know too much more than I do. I don't like it. I don't know what I will see when I open my eyes, how surrounded I might be, and I just want to be still for a few more moments until my mind and my senses have gathered as much as they can with my eyes still closed.

But then I hear a more familiar voice.

"I know there's no way you'd let those assholes kill you."

Seth.

"Language," the other voice scolds with a light *tsk* of her teeth.

Seth ignores her. "You're fine, Violet," he says. "It's been almost two days. Stop milking this and open your eyes already."

I stubbornly keep them closed. There is a rustling sound to my left, and then the woman speaks again: "Don't rush things, Seth," she says. "Just keep a watch on her for a moment. I'll be right back." I listen to her footsteps fade as she leaves the room.

"You look like a corpse just lying there, you know. It's sort of freaking me out."

Maybe the familiarity of his voice should be a comfort to me. But it only makes my muscles tense more, because it sends a deeper flood of uncertainty washing over me. I refused to follow him earlier. I didn't meet him like he asked me to on the phone, and I had more or less made up my mind that the best way to win this so-called impossible game we're playing would be for me to keep avoiding him.

So how did I end up here alone with him?

And more important is that ever-persistent, ever-annoying question: Why? Again, I'm not sure I want to know; whatever his motives, good or bad, my life so far has only proven more complicated with every person I have tried to get close enough to understand.

But I can't keep my eyes shut forever. So I open them, and I find Seth more than a little too close, crouched down beside me with his gaze leveled into mine.

I fight the cornered-animal instinct to strike that ridiculous smile off his face.

"You're alive," he declares. "Awesome." He's either unaware or indifferent to the way my body is bristled, possibly prepared to attack, because his grin doesn't so much as twitch.

"I'm a miracle of life," I deadpan, and then quickly roll over so I can stare at the ceiling instead of him. It soars high above me, exposed beams and ductwork crisscrossing through the wide-open space. Three small windows near the top let in a minuscule amount of daylight through grimy glass, but most of the space is lit by the warm glow of mismatched lamps strewn throughout the room, perched haphazardly on tables here and chairs there, and most of them connected by extension cords and power strips that look far from fire safe. And there are plenty of tables and chairs to perch them on too, more tables and chairs than I think any one room could ever possibly need, and all of them overflowing with more than just those lamps and electrical cords. There are books on some of them—dangerously teetering towers of books—computer parts on others, along with random tools, colorful piles of scarves, and even half-empty bottles of paint beside stiff, unwashed brushes. None of it seems to follow any sort of organizational pattern. It is simply a trove, a hoard of anything and everything in a space that doesn't make any more sense than its contents; because while the exposed ceiling and ancient windows clearly make this feel like a dusty old factory or warehouse of some sort, the lamps warm walls that—even though they're braced with metal poles and piping—are splashed with soft shades of brown and ivory, and floors that are covered in mismatched rugs that look like they belong in a model-family living room.

It is the strangest place I've ever been in.

The more time I spend taking it all in, though, the more I find its lack of order oddly appealing. Comforting, almost. But that still doesn't change the uncomfortable fact that I have no idea how or why I ended up here.

I sit up, and realize that I have been lying on yet another table, but one that has been turned into a makeshift bed, piled with foam cushioning and flannel blankets. "How did I get here?"

"I carried you," Seth says, plopping back into a nearby chair and—finally—giving me more space. "And got strange looks from every person on the street who I didn't manage to avoid, because apparently a strapping young lad like myself carrying a half-unconscious girl through the city is actually more creepy than chivalrous."

"Carried me?" I try to hide the mortification in my voice.

"I didn't have much choice. It was that or leave you hanging like ten stories off the ground, until you'd either unconsciously rolled off the edge of that sign yourself or until some other CCA creep came and finished the job."

"The job of killing me off," I think aloud, my eyes

drifting to a half-finished painting propped on a chair in the corner. An amateur work in watercolors, depicting a parklike setting framed by dogwood trees. It looks vaguely familiar, somehow. Like one of the dozens of places that Catelyn pointed out to me on one of our trips through Haven, though I can't remember why she thought I should know about it.

"Yeah, I didn't really see that part coming," Seth says. "But I'm not entirely surprised; the clone-hate has been reaching kind of alarming levels at headquarters these past few months—more alarming than usual, I mean. I had a feeling someone was going to get hurt. Because I'm smart and observant like that, you know."

"And modest, clearly."

He nods, as though I am being perfectly serious. "And I figured that clone attack last night would send at least some of them over the edge, which is why I tried to tell you that you'd be better off leaving. But you're like those girls that end up getting killed first in every horror movie ever—the ones who run upstairs when the ax murderer is trying to break in through the front door, instead of just going out the back door?" He leans back far enough in the chair that the front legs lift off the ground. "You probably haven't seen any of those movies, though," he adds thoughtfully. "So I guess you get a pass this time."

"I wasn't running," I point out. "Just getting some fresh air."

"The air was pretty refreshing out there on that sign," he agrees. "I probably would have really enjoyed it if I hadn't been so concerned about plummeting to my death as I tried to carry your unconscious deadweight back inside."

"How did you even find me out there?"

The front legs of his chair crash loudly back to the floor. He suddenly looks uneasy, and his voice is noticeably quieter when he says, "I saw you fall."

Quiet as they are, the words seem to expand, looming large and filling the already-crowded room. "How? Where were you?"

Hesitation, and then: "When you didn't meet me in the city, I came back—I was waiting, just in case you changed your mind. I missed you somehow, but I saw Josh and the others come outside. And at first I let them go, but then, I dunno. . . . I had a bad feeling, so I tracked them up to the roof. I couldn't get to you and Josh in time, though."

"Because the others got in your way." The memory is suddenly surprisingly clear edged and bright. "I heard fighting behind us. That was you, wasn't it?"

He doesn't deny it, but he doesn't really answer me either.

"There were six of them. One of you. You're lucky they didn't throw you over the roof right behind me."

Of all the ways he could reply, he laughs.

"They were armed," I say, annoyed by his lack of concern, and at how I suddenly feel the need to justify why I ended up being thrown off the building when he didn't. It makes me feel weak. And I don't know why, but I can't stand the thought of him thinking I'm weak.

"So was I," he says, more to himself than me. Which is

fine, because I am tired of talking to him anyway. Silence settles between us, and I go back to examining the things around me with distracted interest. In the next room over, I can hear movement, someone—that woman from earlier, I assume—rummaging through things. I get to my feet. The noise makes me anxious for some reason, desperate for movement myself. I head for the only other door in the room, the one opposite of where the woman is rummaging.

"You can't leave," Seth says.

Now it's my turn to laugh. "Stop me. I dare you."

He stands as well, as if he plans on doing just that, and I want to laugh again. But I can't. Because another memory opens suddenly in my mind: We've been here before, haven't we? When I tried to run past him back at headquarters, and he caught me. Somehow, he caught me. Something about him, whether it is his distracting mind games or otherwise, slows me down. Knocks me off guard.

"They'll be looking for you," he says. "And for me, too, and I'm not going to let you just waltz out of here and give away the location of this place that easily. Besides, you were messed up when I brought you here—you should probably take it easy for a bit until we're sure everything is functioning like it should."

"And you're staying here too?" I ask, ignoring his latter concern. "Hiding from all of the CCA? Some of them may be creeps, but you're the son of their president."

"Adopted son," he reminds me.

"All the same—you can stay away from her? Even after

everything she's done for you? What about Jaxon? Him too?"

"It's not that simple. And it's probably better for both of them if I'm not there, anyway."

"I don't think Jaxon believes that."

"Yeah, well, he can be a little thick in the head sometimes, can't he?"

I don't return the cynical smile he gives me. I can still picture how upset Jaxon was while we were in his room, trying to contact Seth. Which, of course, reminds me of the whole reason I'd been in that room to begin with: Catelyn.

It's then that I notice my communicator is gone.

"Where is it?" I demand, shoving my empty wrist toward Seth.

"I got rid of it."

"That was my property."

"It was CCA issued. It would have been way too easy for them to trace."

"I want it back. Now."

"Can't do it," he says. "Sorry." But he doesn't sound especially sorry at all. And suddenly this place feels less like a comforting living room and more like a cleverly disguised prison. I am cut off from the few familiar things I had. Confused. Cornered. And that violent hum I am becoming so familiar with lately is almost palpable as it gathers around me, surging a little stronger with every deep breath I take.

Another blackout is threatening, and despite how Seth

annoys me, I don't really want to lose control right now.

"I'm leaving," I warn him. "And you need to get out of my way."

"There's nowhere for you to go, Violet," he says, and this time he does sound almost sorry, and somehow that's worse.

And it's the last challenge I can take.

I charge toward him, reckless, mind abandoned by any thought other than the need to knock him down hard enough to keep him down, and then to get out of this place. To find a way to contact Catelyn, to go back to her and something I recognize. I refuse to believe that I can't go back to her.

Seth manages to catch hold of me, to keep himself from falling all the way back, though the momentum of me is still strong enough that we slam into a table and send it—and everything on it—toppling to the floor. His arms brace against mine. I manage to heave him away from me, but it takes more effort than I expected. It throws me off balance. I fall sideways, awkwardly catching myself on one hand and hitting hard on my right knee. I recover quickly, bouncing up onto the balls of my feet. The muscles in my legs tense, preparing to spring.

My eyes lock on to his.

They're the last thing I see before a rush of heat consumes me, and everything flashes to black.

This time, when I feel my senses coming back to me, I open my eyes immediately. I see Seth a few feet away, holding the side of his head. I wonder what I've done. What I don't remember.

How those flecks of blood got on the floor between us.

I look up, and we stare at each other for a long, uncomfortable moment.

"You should have just moved," I say. "I could have killed you."

"Not swinging like that you couldn't have," he replies. "Maybe I should teach you how to fight while you're here."

My mouth opens to snap back at him, but then I see those dots of blood on the floor again, and I stay quiet. I move to shove myself back to my feet instead, and my fingers land on the edge of a handheld computer that fell from the knocked-over table.

It's coincidence, really, that I happen to look down at this computer. And only for a split second—just long enough to see the symbol branded in the corner of its lid. An intricate, partially encircled letter *H*.

Huxley's symbol.

I grab the computer and stand the rest of the way up. My blackout is forgotten for the moment, because at my feet are more of those *H*s, emblazoned on folders and on the letterheads of papers spilling from them.

"What is this place?" I ask, eyes wide and more closely searching the hoard around me.

Before Seth can reply, the woman from earlier appears in the doorway opposite my escape route, looking slightly frazzled. "What in the world was all that commotion? I told you to . . ." Her eyes light up as they fall on me. "Oh! I thought I heard an extra voice in here—and you're up and moving around, too. Good." Her smile is warm.

But this room seemed that way at first too.

I take a backward step toward the door, not taking my gaze off her.

"Wait a second," she says, lifting her hands as if in surrender. "Before you leave—I know you have to have questions. At least give me a chance to introduce myself, how about?"

She moves closer, hands still raised slightly. Her step is careful, body bracing a little with each movement, as if she is trying to hide a limping injury, or maybe battling the stiffness of arthritis. Probably the latter, I decide after glancing over her gray-streaked hair, which is pulled loosely back from a face grooved with wrinkles and laugh lines.

Not much of a threat either way, my brain decides as she reaches me. Though the way she is studying me so closely, so openly, is making me increasingly uncertain.

"He's told me a lot about you, Violet," she says with a nod at Seth. "All good stuff, don't worry."

Should I have been worried?

She extends a hand, and I cautiously take it. It feels like soft, well-worn leather. "My name is Angela," she says, and then her eyes drift back to Seth. "He probably hasn't told you much about me, but I'm his mother. And it's nice to meet you."

CHAPTER TEN

The door seems closer. More inviting than ever before. Because it feels as if I've stumbled into yet one more thing that makes no sense—or been carried into it, rather. And my carrier is uncharacteristically silent.

"I didn't think you had a mother," I say to him, still edging toward the door and thinking of bolting. "Other than President Cross."

"It's complicated."

"And not especially important at the moment, in light of other things," says the woman who introduced herself as Angela. "I only mention it because I thought it might make you more comfortable."

I keep my focus on Seth. "Why did you bring me here?"

He hesitates, picking up the table and straightening a stack of folders against its top. "Because I knew Angie would be able to help you."

"Because she knows about clones." I gather some of the scattered papers and hand them over, my eyes lingering on one of the letterhead logos. "Because she works for Huxley."

"Worked for, rather," Angie corrects, kindly but firmly. "But you're right about the other part—I'm no stranger to cloning technology. Which is a good thing, because it looks like you smacked the back of your head pretty hard on something during that fight. And a bit too close to your sensitive brain-hardware stuff for comfort, at that."

Sensitive brain-hardware stuff?

That hardly sounds like the technical term for it.

My gaze finally shifts to her. Who is this woman, truly? How much does she honestly know about Huxley? About cloning? She isn't how I pictured a Huxley employee looking; not that I have encountered or personally seen many, but for some reason I already had an image of them all in my head: scientists in stiff white lab coats, their expressions sterile and postures proper. But when I look at this woman—with her bright aqua-colored glasses and hair consisting mostly of flyaways—"proper" is the last word that comes to mind.

I realize that I am staring and quickly look away. The jerk causes a sharp, pulling pain along the back of my head, and when I lift a hand to it, I feel a layer of gauze taped there. I peel it off in annoyance. Underneath it is a tiny, clean-edged cut. Surgically precise.

"I did that," Angie says. "So I could get a scope in there to check for possible driver damage that might end up causing memory loss. A bit of a primitive method for checking that sort of thing, but as you can probably tell"— she gestures at that messy hoard around us—"this isn't exactly my former laboratory. Proper equipment's a little scarce around here."

My body tenses, and skepticism floods my voice. "You cut me open just so you could have a look?" There are plenty of advantages to having what is essentially a supercomputer for a brain; having to worry about whether or not people have hacked or reprogrammed it is not one of them.

"Exactly," she says. "There was no funny business. Promise. You're still the same Violet you were when you came in here. I briefly overrode the autohealing program so I could keep things open to enable me to poke around in there, but it's been rebooted and should be taking care of that cut and any pain it might be causing soon."

I've been only vaguely aware of that pain since I woke up, but now that she mentions it, it's all I can think about for a moment. My eyes close as I feel it radiate from the base of my skull, around and up into my jawbone.

"Give it a few minutes," Angie says, voice softening. She starts to reach forward, hand half raised as if to comfort. But thankfully she thinks better of it. "The program is working. Just a little slower than you're used to, probably."

"It . . . aches." And it's strange. I know what pain feels like, but I'm used to quick sparks of it, lasting only as long as it takes the simulated pain receptors in my brain to recognize and respond to its cause.

"Well, healing and aching can feel a lot alike sometimes." She leaves the room and reappears a minute later with a bowl of water and a washrag, the latter of which she hands to me. "Part of the normal human experience," she says.

"I'm not human." I don't know what makes me so quick to say it, just that with every piece of the past forty-eight hours that flashes through my rebooting brain—from the fighting, to the faces of those clones on the bridge, to the way Emily looked at me as I stood between her and them—this part of my reality, at least, feels more and more clear. I'm not human, and not even a normal clone, either, between the blackouts and everything else.

Angie nods toward me and the rag, but touches a hand to the back of her own head. So she is observant enough to have noticed that I don't like being touched, at least. "Looks like human blood to me," she says. I absently copy her hand's movement with my own. The rag comes away from my skin tinted lightly with red. Blood.

Human blood, clone blood . . . She's right, I suppose, in that they both look the same. But what about how they're made? I know basic human anatomy. I have what a lot of people would see as a strange fascination with it, really—a fascination that has led to me pouring over encyclopedia files and diagrams late into the nights when I can't sleep. So I know about platelets and plasma, about bone marrow and all the ways bodies like Angie's continuously create and pump blood cells through her body. But as for my own blood? I am not sure how the ones who created me managed to simulate the process. All I know is that it's simulated. An imitation of the real thing. My blood may technically be the same in the end, but I can't ignore where it came from.

We're different.

And more and more I find myself wondering what that means. How I could ever fit in, anywhere, and what I would have to do to make that happen.

I finish cleaning the blood from my skin as my eyes find Seth. He's abandoned our conversation and moved instead to a computer station set up in the corner with several mismatched monitors, one of which he is studying intently.

Speaking of things that are different from what I thought at first.

He is still more silent than I thought he was even capable of being. What is that silence hiding? If this woman is truly his mother, what does that mean? Who is he, really?

"I need you to explain some things." I don't realize I've vocalized the thought until he throws a quick, expectant glance my way, and I have no choice but to continue. "You brought me here so she could help me, but why do you care? Why did you interfere with Josh and the others? Why did you care so much about making me leave the CCA the other night?" I've forgotten about the door for the moment and moved toward him, instead. "And if you dare answer me with 'It's complicated' again, I will make you sorry for it."

The last part causes an almost-grin to twitch his lips. "Well," he says without taking his eyes off the largest of the monitors in front of him, "it *is* complicated." My face flushes with anger as his hands fly over the computer's keyboard, filling the room with a clicking and clacking that drowns out all of my hanging questions. "And it's about to get a lot more complicated," he adds after a moment. His attention darts to Angie. He says nothing, but the look in his eyes must mean something to her, because she nods in an understanding way and then rushes to my side.

"I need you to come with me," she says. And I may not be particularly good at reading people, but it's obvious that something has changed. Dramatically.

"Come with you to where?"

"We need to hide. Quickly." I can tell she's struggling to keep her voice reasonably calm.

"I'm not hiding from any—"

"Just go already!" Seth seems to care less about appearing calm as he jumps up from the computer and rushes around cutting off all the lights, until the only thing illuminating the room is the soft whitish-blue glow of the computer screen. He goes to the cabinet beside the computers next, and starts jerking an assortment of other electronic equipment from it. I'm so busy watching him, trying to figure out what purpose each piece of that equipment might serve, that when Angie grabs my arm it actually makes me jump. I stare at her in stunned silence as she drags me toward the other room. I realize how easily I could jerk free of her grip, but for some reason it doesn't occur to me to actually do it.

Once in the next room, Angie lets go of my arm

and—with the aid of a small flashlight—kneels down beside one of several faded throw rugs tossed over the floor. She flops a corner of it back and reveals a metal hatch that was hidden beneath. I stand in the doorway looking back and forth, between her as she pries the hatch open, and then Seth as he finishes collecting things from the cabinet and heads for the exit.

"Where is he going?" I ask.

And for once, I get a straightforward answer. "Those computers are part of a makeshift security system we set up. We've been fortunate to have this safe place for most of the past few months, but we've had a few . . . incidents lately, with some of the people who would like to interrupt my nice and quiet little existence here." She gets the hatch open and lowers herself down into the floor. I have no idea what the space might have originally been used for, but it is deep enough that once her feet have thunked against its bottom, only her shoulders and head are left sticking out. "I'm going to have to find a new hideaway soon. But for now, at least this old warehouse has several of these stowaway spaces. An old friend of mine—his father owned this place, and he created these spaces during the war. Just in case. I think his paranoia was a little over the top, but then, I'm benefitting from it, aren't I?"

"Who are you hiding from?"

She doesn't answer right away, focusing instead on resituating the hatch and its concealing rug. I almost think she hasn't heard the question, but then I take a step toward her and she looks up at me with a small, weak sort of smile. "Just some old demons," she says.

"But not demons that you're afraid to let Seth face alone."

"You already have me figured out, do you?" The question is challenging, but not especially unkind; I am starting to think she might not actually know how to inject anything like harshness into her voice. "But you apparently don't know him as well as you think you do, because if you did, you'd know it's useless to try to talk him into just hiding with me." Her smile wilts even further. "He can take care of himself, at least. Even if I don't especially want to think about that."

Doubt gnawing at me, I turn to look at the screen Seth had been monitoring. From this distance it's hard to see what's on display, but it looks like a large, open room, with several bay doors lining the wall the camera is facing. The room is empty now. But who did he see before?

He can take care of himself.

Just like he took care of himself before, when he was outnumbered by Josh and his gang. And just like he took care of me, even though I never asked him to and never would have. If anything, it should be the other way around right now—between the three of us, it should be me who is rushing off to secure this hiding spot, to protect it from whatever intruders may be out there. Even as I'm recovering, I am still a superhuman compared to them. Still stronger. Faster. Smarter.

Right?

I keep going back to that moment at the CCA. To how easily he caught me. Stopped me. Maybe he can take care of himself. Maybe . . .

"You said you used to work for Huxley, didn't you?" A rush comes over me as my mind starts to pull up impossible possibilities and explanations. But Angie is much slower to answer.

"Years and years ago," she finally says.

"What did you do for them, exactly?"

". . . I'm afraid that's what we call classified information."

"But Seth knows, doesn't he?" I ask, looking back to her.

"He knows most of it now. I've made sure of that."

"Now? What about before now? As long as I've known him, President Cross has been his mother, and he was a member of the CCA. This?" I thrust a hand toward her hiding spot, and then sweep it back to the mess of Huxley-labeled folders and equipment in this front room. "This is all wrong. This is not who he is."

These are not the facts my brain assigned to him. Not the files it saved for me to so easily access when I needed a picture, an understanding, of Seth. Angie swears there was no funny business, but it still feels as though someone has gone in and deleted and rearranged that vital information, replacing it with broken images and corrupted data. Because it must be corrupted. The only explanation for the strange thoughts and conclusions my brain is racing to is that something has glitched.

Something is rewriting my truths into lies.

"Maybe you should talk to Seth directly about this when he comes back," Angie says, the corners of her mouth finally giving in and falling into a frown. "As far as who he is . . . Well, his life is his own. It's not for me to give away." I start to argue, but just then we hear voices, echoes of shouts in the distance. We listen for a moment.

They sound like they're moving closer.

The computer screen goes black. Slipping into sleep mode, I guess. As my eyes adjust to the room's deepening darkness and the voices grow louder, I find myself wishing I had stayed asleep.

"Come here." For the first time since I met her, there is a sharpness to Angie's words—enough of a razor edge that I consider listening to them. I could hide with her. Maybe she could shut my brain down somehow. Wake me up again when this is all over. That might be nice.

I would never let her do it though.

I know too much to sleep soundly anymore. And I have much more to find out—which is why I ignore Angie's pleas to join her in the shadows beneath the floor, and instead set off in the same direction Seth disappeared in.

Outside, I find myself facing down a long hallway, which is lit only at the far end by a flickering emergency light. Its weak blue beams barely reach me. There are several doors along the hall—or rust-framed empty spaces where I assume doors used to be, at least—and the rooms behind them are as dark as everywhere else. No signs of life. The voices from earlier are no longer shouting, either. I still hear them, but they sound much farther away. Distant and ghostlike. I wonder if I made them up. If I'm making all of these things up inside of a mind I no longer trust.

I walk toward the light, my footsteps lonely and eerie against the smooth floor.

From the end of the hallway, I can see them in the room beyond: the group those voices belong to. Four people huddled together, their faces partially lit by the communicator one of the women is holding to her lips. I make myself as small as possible against the hallway wall.

"Target number two has been spotted," I hear the woman say. "Building has been secured to prevent escape. We're about to begin the search and sweep of the east wing. All teams should—"

A high-pitched *crack!* interrupts, and in the same instant the woman convulses, grabs her throat, and falls to the ground. The other three spin around, weapons drawn. Their guns are equipped with scope lights that they circle with, illuminating every corner of the vast room. But there is no one for the light to find.

Another *crack!*

Only two of them are left standing, now.

The gun lights bounce more frantically. They dart to the high ceiling, searching the lofted storage spaces and thick metal beams for hiding places. There's an abrupt exchange over a communicator.

A cry for backup.

A confirmation.

Things begin to happen impossibly fast after that. The called backup floods into the room. More and more lights bouncing around, and then one finally finding what they were all looking for: Seth, armed and perched in the claw-like apparatus of some sort of machine attached to the warehouse's ceiling.

The shots, from seemingly every direction at once.

But when Seth falls to the ground, I would swear the world slows back down, all the way to a crawl.

CHAPTER ELEVEN

He didn't fall.

He jumped.

From what must have been at least twenty feet up.

As the world quickens again to its normal pace, I realize that almost instantly—in the same moment that he jumps again, only forward this time, and lunges straight at the person nearest him. And the next thing I realize is that he didn't even need the gun that is now strapped to his back. Because all it takes is one hit from his fist—one so fast that Seth is literally a blur as he makes it—and that first person is down. Not moving.

The other two of the backup group try to aim their guns, but Seth doesn't hesitate long enough for them to manage a single shot. In a few more wickedly quick flashes of movement, he disposes of them the same way he did the first.

It would all be very impressive, except for one thing: He's forgotten about the original group. The two of whom are still standing a safe distance away, their guns still at the ready. With the others down, they now have a clear shot at him and him alone, and they have plenty of time to take it. Even he isn't fast enough to cross this huge room in time to stop them from shooting.

I am much closer than he is, though—and I owe him for saving me after that fall, even if I didn't ask him to.

And unfortunately for the two in front of me, I hate owing people.

I focus on the one on the left first. Her grip on her gun seems much less secure. Like a dart launching, I fly across the room and slam an elbow into her lower back, while my other arm reaches for and wraps around her gun. I jerk it out of her grip, and in the same motion shove her toward her companion. She collides hard enough with him to knock him partway to the ground. Shoving my newly acquired gun into his face makes him drop the rest of the way down, his hands lifting into the air.

"How many more of you are there?" I demand.

He laughs weakly. "This building is surrounded—you aren't going to make it out of here. And the one you're trying to hide? We'll find her, too."

"Let me clear this up for you." I press the muzzle of the gun deep into his chest. Just in case he isn't taking me seriously enough yet. "I am not hiding anybody. I have nothing to do with anybody in this building—I'm only passing through, and I'll be leaving soon, so I need you to tell me the quickest way out of here and to see to it that your friends don't interrupt my exit."

He opens his mouth to answer, just as I feel a gush of wind pass between us. An actual dart this time. It lodges in his chest, just above the tip of my gun. He chokes on his words, swallows hard, and starts to sway as a thin trickle of drool escapes the corner of his mouth. I pull away and let him fall to the ground. Still breathing—as are all of the others, however slow and shallow they're doing it. Tranquilizer darts, I realize. I'm not surprised. Seth never struck me as the killing type.

He is next to me a moment later, gathering the weapons of the unconscious and slinging them into the collection already across his back.

"I was having a conversation with him," I say.

"Well, wait here then," he says, walking away. "He'll be coming around in about twelve hours or so, and you guys can pick up where you left off."

"Where are you going?"

"To lock these up somewhere," he says, giving the bundle of weapons a little shake, "and then to figure out how to get rid of the rest of our intruders."

"Or to get killed by them? Like you almost did just now?"

He glances back at me with a smirk. "Key word there is 'almost.' Nothing wrong with almost dying. I do it all the time here lately."

"Then I should have just let you carry on and not interfered."

"Yeah, but thanks for interfering all the same," he says, and then—of all the things he could do as we're standing here in this cold, dark room, surrounded by unconscious bodies—he actually winks at me.

Idiot.

"I only did it so we would be even," I say. "And because I still want answers from you, which I won't be able to get if you're dead, now will I?"

Those are the only reasons, right? The cold, calculated, and logical reasons. It used to be the only kind of reasoning I was capable of, once upon a time.

I wish it still was.

He is still walking away, and typing something into a small scanner device, when he calls back: "That's a good point."

He's hardly paying me any attention, in other words. And I am finished with being ignored. I wait until he reaches the small door in the corner, pries it open, and starts unloading the guns into the room behind it.

Then I move.

He turns as I reach him, but not quickly enough; I grab him by the arm and pin him roughly against the wall.

"Violence is not the answer," he says.

"Then what is the answer to this?" I ask. "To you? Who are you, exactly?"

"You really did hit your head hard during that fight with Josh, didn't you? You know who I am."

I shake my head. "You aren't the Seth Lancaster I thought I knew. Not the same one that Cate and Jaxon and everyone else at the CCA knew. You . . . I don't know who you are. All I know is that you shouldn't be able to do the things I've seen you do."

I feel his body stiffen in my grip, and he does his best to avoid my prying gaze as he says, "I don't know what you're talking about."

"Just now. You fought how many people at once? And how many of Josh's gang at once?"

"So I know a thing or two about hand-to-hand combat."

"You fell at least twenty feet down from the ceiling without getting hurt."

"Acrobat skills. When I was younger, I ran away and joined the circus for a while—that's where I learned that."

I tighten my grip on his arm, fingernails digging into his skin.

"Um, ow?"

"That didn't hurt you. If a fall from twenty feet didn't hurt you, neither did that."

"You are an incredibly violent person," he says. "Has anyone ever told you that?"

"I can be much more violent than anything you've seen so far. Trust me."

"I do trust you. Still, though, at least this is how I wanted to go."

"What?"

"Death by beautiful girl. Somehow I always knew this is how it would happen, too."

"This really is all a big joke to you, isn't it?"

He doesn't answer right away. We're both silent for a moment instead, listening to the sudden hiss of a voice over one of the communicators, which is still lying beside its unconscious owner. "No," he says with a sigh, finally turning to look me directly in the eyes. "This is very serious, all right? More of them will be coming soon. You need to let me go."

"Not until you tell me who you are. What you are."

He laughs softly, shaking his head. "Come on, Violet," he says. "We both already know, don't we? You just don't trust yourself enough to believe you're right."

I don't know what to say to that. He takes advantage of my stunned silence to work one of his arms free, and then reaches into his pocket, pulls out a knife, and flips it open. Before I can protest, he jerks the blade across his face, leaving a shallow gash that quickly wells up with blood.

But the blood hasn't even dripped past his chin before the cut starts to heal itself, his dark skin knitting back together as I watch.

CHAPTER TWELVE

Healing technology.

Clone. Healing. Technology.

"Satisfied now?" he asks.

"You . . . you are not the real Seth Lancaster."

"I am the only Seth Lancaster, as far as I know. Have been. For years."

I loosen my grip on his arm and sink back a step. "I thought I was the only one at the CCA. Why didn't you tell me? Why didn't anyone tell me?"

"I haven't told anyone else. President Cross—and now you—are the only ones from there who know for sure. Not even Jaxon knows. Although, after everything with Josh and them, that might change soon. We'll see if they're smart enough to figure it out."

"The president knows? But how—"

Voices over the communicator interrupt us again, and Seth's next words are more urgent. "I can't explain all of this right now. Just . . . listen: All these people? They're from Huxley, and they're looking for Angie, and I can't let them find her, all right?" He pushes me away, and I'm still too shocked to put up much of a fight. "So I can't do this right now. Maybe later. This is more than they've ever sent before, though, and I don't know how things are going to go down, but if—"

"If I help you, will you tell me the truth? About everything?" I don't know what makes me say it. Because even if he agrees to it, I don't trust him to tell me anything. Yet I still find myself holding my breath. Hoping. Even though I've never been the hopeful type.

"Help me how, exactly?" he asks, closing and resecuring the door that he's hidden the weapons behind. "No offense, but I'm used to being a one-man show. I'd rather you just go back and hide with Angie."

"Give me your jacket."

"What? Why?"

"It has a hood. I'll pull it over myself, hide my face, move a little more clumsily—they only know you and Angie are here, correct? So we'll trick the ones still conscious into thinking I'm her, and lead them away from here. And we'll have to hide the bodies of the unconscious ones so the others don't find them, of course."

"I should have known I'd end up hiding bodies when I started hanging out with you."

"You don't want the others to linger here, right? So we'll lock them up somewhere. Steal their communicators, send a message that makes the others think they've already moved out. And then come back for Angie before they wake up."

"That will never work." He starts to jog away from me. "You look nothing like her. You're taller than her, you—"

"I'm five foot eight inches. She's approximately five

foot seven." I may not be able to read people's emotions very well, but I have a talent for memorizing what Catelyn would probably call useless details: physical characteristics, mannerisms, faces. . . . I never forget what people look like. And I know my body could pass for Angie's—at least from a distance.

"So you're similar heights. That's hardly enough."

"And what's the alternative, then?" I ask, catching up and grabbing him by the sleeve. "I'm happy to fight and be as violent as you would like to be, but you have no idea how many more we might be facing once we're outside."

"This isn't the first time I've done this by myself. She's been staying here for months."

"I am not going back and hiding."

"Then go somewhere else. I don't need your help." He pulls himself free of my grip. Easily. I wasn't prepared for that strength—somehow I have already forgotten he isn't as human as I thought he was, and that he isn't trying to hide it anymore. Maybe because it all still seems impossible.

"If you don't let me help, then I will go find as many of Huxley's people as I can, and I will lead them all directly to you."

"No, you won't."

"Yes." I run in front of him, cutting off his path to the nearby door. "I will."

"You're an awful person."

"Blame it on the programming."

"Fine," he says with a humorless snort. "Whatever. I

don't have time to argue about this anymore." His eyes still watching the door, he jerks the weapons from his back, strips off his coat, and tosses it over my head. I scramble to get it situated, pulling the hood over me and tucking my hair into it, then shifting the whole thing up as high as it will go—until only the bridge of my nose and my eyes are visible—and securing it with the hood's drawstrings. I take a deep breath and inhale the crisp, clean smell of soap with a hint of something woodsy; I've never bothered to notice his scent before, but now that it is quite literally suffocating me, I can hardly help it. So at least it's a nice smell. Kind of.

We make quick work of hiding the bodies, and then he hands me a gun and motions for me to follow him toward the exit. "You'll have to watch how you move once they've spotted us," he says, "but for now, try to keep up."

He races into the next room, which is long and narrow, full of conveyer equipment and more claw apparatuses like the one hanging from the ceiling in the room we left behind. But the ceiling here is too shadowy and high to see where those claws attach. What I do see is a supervisor's catwalk stretched over the center of the room, a metal-grate pathway leading to a window-lined alcove on the second floor. Seth leaps from one piece of equipment to the next until he reaches it. He makes it look easy, not even hesitating between jumps—like he is intimately familiar with every inch of this building and doesn't have to think about it. Like he's done this before.

In the recess, he moves to a square of the window that's

obviously been cleaned recently, and motions for me to join him.

"I don't see anybody yet," he says, eyes scanning the ground below, "but this is the main entrance that most of them will probably come through. They'll be wondering about the others who disappeared this way." He points at a patch of roof one story down, diagonal from us and about fifteen feet away. "We should be able to get their attention from there while still keeping enough distance to get away. But we need to get there before they're here to see us make this jump, which Angie wouldn't be able to do."

"Through the window?"

"Through the window. We need both of these panes out of the way—"

He swings for the top. I hit the bottom. Glass shatters around us, tiny shards of it slicing into my fist and arm. The pieces of it crunch beneath my feet as I get a running start and leap into the cool night air. We both hit the roof and roll to the edge in one fluid motion, staying low as we scan the path leading to the rusted bay door below, which we now have a direct line of sight to. I can't help but take a quick glance at Seth's hand. Streaked with blood, but, like mine, the skin is already smooth again. It's strange. Almost as strange as the fact that he isn't even winded from the jump, either.

He told me to keep up with him.

But I'm still not used to anyone being able to keep up with me. I don't know how it makes me feel; all this time

I thought I was alone—that there were no other clones outside of Huxley's control—but now here he is, and he's been here all along. I was just too blind to see it.

What else have I missed?

"There they are," he says suddenly.

I give my head a little shake, reminding myself that now isn't the time to try to make sense of this strangeness; there will be answers at the end. Assuming, of course, that we manage to pull this off.

I shift my gaze to the group gathered near the door below. "We have to make it seem like an accident, or they'll know we're baiting them."

"Over here." I turn, and he is crouched beside a steel utility ladder that's hooked over the edge of the roof. "This thing is barely hanging on to the building," he says.

I nod, understanding. We drop the ten feet or so to the ground, and together pull the rickety ladder down with us, making sure it slams—as noisily as possible—into the pavement. Into plain view of the group by the door. And then, just to be on the safe side, I make a show of pretending to have gotten caught up in the falling ladder. Once I'm certain they've seen me, I duck around the corner and out of sight. Seth follows a second later, and we both press against the wall and listen.

There is dead silence for a moment. Then the whole group starts talking at once. The beeping of communicators follows, and then another hush. Then footsteps.

We run.

Although it feels more like crawling, since I have to

move slowly enough to make them believe I'm Angie. And that is almost maddening, when all I can think about is how easily I could lose this group.

This group that feels close enough now that I am surprised I don't feel their breath warming the back of my neck.

To keep one step ahead of them at this slow pace, we weave the most confusing trail we can away from the warehouse. Every other block or so, we pause to make sure they're still following, and to "accidentally" let them catch a glimpse of our retreat. I don't know where we're running to, or how far Seth plans on going, but I can't see much with this hood pulled up so tightly around me. So I have little choice but to trust his sense of direction.

Even if I can't see, though, I can still hear. And after a few blocks, it sounds as if the voices shouting after us have increased in number. Hard to say, though, whether it's still the group that surrounded the warehouse or just the few people we've passed on the street—people who have to wonder what is going on when they see us, especially since it must be past midnight by now.

Without speaking, we both decide to risk speeding up a little, until the voices behind us grow more distant.

We turn a corner and I'm blinded by headlights. I stagger out of their beams, nearly tripping on a curb as my eyes adjust to the brightness. Once the spots in front of them clear, I see a truck parked in the middle of the street and at an odd angle. Like it just pulled in there, expecting us.

There are more lights, too, I realize—flashing blue lights coming up behind us, and more at the end of the street ahead.

"The police?" I pull the strings of my hood tighter and tuck the long strands of hair that have flown loose back into it.

"And knowing our luck, they probably aren't on our side," Seth says, and I nod, because I know you can't trust anybody in this city. It was the first thing Catelyn warned me of before I left headquarters for the first time; both the CCA and Huxley have members in all sorts of occupations throughout Haven—from police, to government officials, to teachers and everything in between. It's impossible to know who is working with an ulterior agenda and who isn't. So it is simpler—safer—to just assume no one is on your side.

Not that I ever assumed that, anyway.

The truck doors open. Two people jump out.

"New plan," Seth breathes, placing a hand on my arm. Before I can even ask him what he thinks he's doing, he's got another hand on my lower back, and then he lifts me into his arms in a single easy motion.

"This is not okay."

He responds by pulling the hood farther down, completely hiding my face.

"I will murder you."

"Okay, but it will have to wait," he says. "For now, we're going to pretend you're an old, weak human, and you need me to help make a quick escape. So brace yourself."

It's muffled by the hood, but I hear the garbled sound of a man's voice, telling us to stop where we are. To surrender. Seth doesn't say anything back, he just bolts from his spot so quickly that it takes my breath away. I hear that same man's voice shouting something as we blur past him, but we're moving so fast that I don't have time to make out any of his actual words. Within seconds they've faded into the night. All I hear after that is a barrage of city noises, coming and going just as quickly as those words.

It's unnerving to not be able to see what's making the noises. To not be able to see where we're going. I try to focus on the movement, on each turn, each jump that Seth makes. On anything and everything except the way my body is crushed so completely against his.

Our escape takes less than a few minutes, but it's easily the longest I have ever been in such close contact with somebody. My skin is crawling. Burning in the worst possible way. The second he stops, I push away so quickly that, between that and still not being able to see through this stupid hood, I end up landing hard and awkwardly on my side.

"Nice job," Seth says in between attempts to catch his breath. "But you can stop acting like a weak, clumsy human now. We lost them, I'm pretty sure."

"Be quiet," I say, springing back to my feet and yanking the hood off.

Even with it out of the way, it's still dark. We're in what looks somewhat like the Electronic Transport Shuttle car that I rode in with Catelyn once, except it looks like no one has been in this particular car in a very long time. There are rows and rows of cracked leather seats behind me, stuffing exploding from some of the bigger tears across their backs. Most of the windows above the seats are broken or else missing entirely, but on one of the few bits of intact glass, I see a faded sticker advertising a yearly pass for the Inner City Light Rail. So this is a relic left over from the public transportation system that existed before the ETS system they have now, I guess. There are other cars scattered around us outside, all in varying degrees of rustiness and decay, lit by the only two street lamps in the area not burned out or shattered.

"Where are we, exactly?" I ask, sliding into one of the seats and using the sleeve of Seth's jacket to clear a patch of condensation off the window. In the glass's reflection I see him typing something into a communicator. Its screen goes black, and he waits until it lights up again—with a reply to his typed message, I assume—before he answers me.

"Close to the southern city-limits line," he says. "In the neighborhood known as Newbrook. A charming place to commit a murder, or to get mugged, or participate in a drug deal. If that's what you're into, I mean."

"Nice choice of hiding place."

"We're not staying here long," he says. "Just until I'm sure we're not being followed. There's a safe house on the outskirts of town that we've been working on setting up for a while, with the help of some old friends of Angie's."

"More former Huxley employees?"

"Some of them, yeah. More of the good ones. We've

been planning to move Angie there for a while, once every-thing is all set up. I wish we'd already done it, obviously."

"Were you messaging her just now?" I ask, nodding to the communicator still resting in his palm. I feel strangely nervous about his answer. Much more invested in the fate of this woman I barely know than I should be.

"Yeah."

"She's okay, then?"

He nods.

Good, I think. But at least I manage to keep myself from saying it out loud. I still don't quite know what to do with all these sudden attachments I seem to be forming to people, and until I figure it out, I at least want to keep them to myself as much as possible.

There is a long silence between us then, one bursting at the seams with all the questions I want to ask him. It's hard to choose the best one to break that silence, but in the end I settle for, "Why would they send so many people after just one rogue former scientist?"

"She isn't just any scientist."

"By which you mean?"

He tries to go back to the communicator, but I grab his arm and jerk his attention back to me. "We had a deal. I helped you, so now you're going to start giving me some answers."

He stares, eyes hard and searching me for something—for a sign of weakness, maybe, a chance that he might be able to get away with ignoring me one more time. I sharpen my gaze and make sure there's no chance of him finding it.

"She was one of the head scientists in charge of designing the program that allowed Huxley to remotely control its clones," he finally says, each word dragging slowly and reluctantly from his mouth.

Any concern I had for her well-being disintegrates in a flash of white-hot anger. "So she's the reason for all the brainwashed clones? The reason I have to worry about my own thoughts being reprogrammed into plans and purposes I want nothing to do with?" I jump to my feet, nearly hitting my head on the train's low ceiling in the process. "And what about you? Why are you helping her? What has she done to your brain to make you want to do something so—"

"That program was disabled in my brain a long time ago," he interrupts, far too calmly, "after she'd realized her mistake, and right after she took me and the only perfected version of that program and ran from Huxley. Trust me: She wishes she hadn't created it either."

"That's what she's told you, is it?"

"She came out of hiding to tell me about it." An edge has crept into his voice. "And she's almost gotten herself killed several times because of that."

"Why come out of hiding now?" I lean back against the seat and fold my arms across my chest, unconvinced. "What changed?"

He shakes his head. I refuse to let the question go unanswered though, and I glower at him until he finally stops seething long enough to say, "I wasn't safe where she'd left me anymore."

"Where she'd left you?"

"Yeah." He goes quiet again, and something in his tone—something I don't understand, something I don't want to understand—makes me hesitant to push him this time. He eventually continues on his own, though, and without looking at me, he says, "It wasn't an accident that President Cross found me that night in the park. Because apparently she and Angie are like . . . BFFs or something, from the time they spent working together at Huxley. Which is why the president took me in as a favor to Angie. And probably because she felt obligated or whatever."

The way he says "obligated" almost makes me cringe.

Had she felt obligated to bring me back too? Is that the only reason I am alive—because of some sort of misguided attempt the president was making to atone for her sins?

"Anyway," Seth continues, "they've kept in touch, just the two of them, and so Angie knows about all the crap that's been happening at the CCA lately. She was worried that things were getting out of hand there, so she decided it would be a freaking brilliant idea to show up and try to convince me to leave the city and run someplace far away with her."

"But you didn't think it was a freaking brilliant idea?"

He gives a short laugh. "Look at you, figuring out how to understand people after all."

"You aren't what I would call subtle." His emotions have always been loud and simple, and maybe that's part of why I liked him better than most of the people back at the CCA—because I prefer loud and simple.

What now, though?

Now he doesn't seem so simple at all, but full of quiet, unspoken things I can't make sense of, things that are making his eyes glaze over and his usual confident posture slump as he says, "What should I have done? Just left the city, and the only two people I'd ever thought of as family, without knowing what might happen to them? I don't remember anything about the time I spent with Angie before the president found me. We were close, apparently. I have her last name—but what the hell am I really supposed to do with that?"

"You're asking the wrong person about family," I point out. But my stomach gives a strange lurch as I say it, because even though I don't want to, now I'm asking myself the same questions as Seth.

Because I share Catelyn's last name too. There is precious little else of what we were in my time before this life, but there will always be that, and I'm fairly certain she will never stop reminding me of it—as though I could actually forget it. I may not fully understand family, but I know enough to realize that she is the only thing I have that comes close.

And, just like Seth, now I am wondering what might happen to her if I don't come back.

Seth is watching me closely, curiously, as if he is thinking about asking me what is going through my head. But thankfully he doesn't. "Yeah," he eventually says with a slow nod, "I guess you're even more screwed up in the family department than I am, aren't you? I should pick better, more useful friends."

"I am not your friend."

He sighs. "Case in point."

"So what now?" I say. "Do you plan on spending the rest of your life trying to hide Angie from Huxley? And what about Jaxon and the president? If you're worried about what's happening at the CCA, then what are you going to do about it? You have to go back there, right?"

He runs a hand through his hair, lets it drop in a defeated sort of way back to his side. "You have greatly overestimated the degree to which I have figured things out," he says.

"Perhaps because you tend to act like you know what you're doing, always. All the time."

"It's called faking it until you're making it," he says, pulling up the communicator again as it beeps.

"Are you sure it isn't called arrogance?"

"Whatever you want to call it, I'm really good at it."

I frown. "And what are you going to do if you don't make it?"

He pauses, his fingers hovering over the communicator and his eyes staring at a crack in the window for a long time before he answers.

"No idea," he says, and his voice sounds oddly small and choked, and for the first time since I woke up all those months ago, I think I feel something like fear.

CHAPTER THIRTEEN

After traveling some twenty miles more—mostly in silence—we reach a run-down shack of a building on the edge of a meadow buried deep within the woods outside of town.

I feel as if I am on autopilot, my mind more concerned with trying to make sense of everything that's already happened than with paying attention to what is happening now. There is a blur of introductions between me and the four people inside the house, and I am vaguely aware of the suspicious looks that most of them fix me with, but that's really all I notice about them for now. What little bit of focus I can manage is on Seth. I watch him move through the house with intent and purpose—more of his "faking it," I suppose—as he checks monitors and all the other alarm and safety measures they've equipped this house with, and then as he pulls one of the four people aside and has a quiet, heated discussion with him in the corner. Once they've finished, the man heads outside, and a few minutes later Seth follows.

I sprint after him.

"You're leaving already?"

"Angie is waiting for us." He stops, but doesn't turn

around, just motions to the man he'd been talking to, who is now sitting expectantly behind the steering wheel of a gleaming silver car. "And so are a few other people who are going to help us out, back in the city."

"And what about me? What am I supposed to do now?"

"I don't know. You can stay here if you want. Or, hell, leave and go to California for all I care. I thought we'd already established that I really don't have this all figured out? I got you out of trouble at the CCA. I just wanted to make sure you were far away from that place, for your own sake and to maybe, hopefully, calm things down a bit there—but that's as far as I've got with my grand master plan."

"I never asked you to get me out of anywhere. Or to be a part of any of your plans."

"Yeah, I realize that."

"Maybe you should have just left me there."

He turns back to me uncertainly. Expectantly. I don't know how to explain this to him, though—how I don't know exactly what to do, now that I've paused to catch my breath, and my head is clear, and the only life and city I've ever known has faded out of sight. Now that I don't have specific expectations. A set role to play. I thought I didn't want those things, but in its own way, this freedom is almost more frightening than a lifetime of following orders.

Because following orders is what I knew.

That girl who was so obedient to the president for those first months . . . she was who I knew.

This Violet Benson? I don't know this Violet Benson. This girl that is standing in the middle of the woods, surrounded by so many huge and complicated things. I don't know what she is supposed to feel about those things. What—if anything—she is supposed to do about them.

It feels like I'm meant to do something, though, now that I'm here.

But what if I end up doing the wrong thing?

Seth is still staring at me. To avoid speaking a little longer, and because I'm tired of wearing it anyway, I slide out of his jacket and fling it back to him. He puts it on slowly. Shoves his hands, one by one, into the pockets. "Things are more complicated for you now, aren't they?" he guesses. His voice has softened the tiniest bit, but that doesn't make me feel any better—it sounds too much like pity, which I don't want or need.

I don't say anything back.

"It sucks, doesn't it? Being caught in between like this." He pulls the jacket's hood up and turns to leave again. "Sorry about that. I figured this would be the best thing for you, but who the hell knows in the end?"

"I want to talk to Catelyn." The words come out of nowhere. Just like thoughts of her so often do—surfacing when I haven't tried to make them, or even when I've tried to stop them. In this case, I think she is the only sane reason I can come up with for why I care about having been ripped so unceremoniously from my life at headquarters. She is the only reason I would ever have for going back.

Is she safe? I wonder.

"Not happening," Seth says.

"Why?"

"Because I don't trust Catelyn, and I don't trust you to not tell Catelyn everything that's happened since you left the CCA. And the fewer people who know about this place, about Angie and everyone who's helping us, the better."

"I won't tell her any of that. Why would I?"

"Because she is annoyingly good at getting things out of people? She would get you to talk."

"Have you actually met me?"

"Yeah, and you aren't as difficult to crack as you think you are. Especially when Catelyn is around."

My face burns. I feel like I've just been insulted somehow. "You can't keep me from contacting her. Besides, don't you care at all about what's happening at the CCA right now? What about Jaxon?"

"Of course I care," he snaps. "But I can only focus on keeping one person alive at a time, all right? So just . . . I don't know. Stay here, I guess? We'll work something out when I get back, assuming you can go the whole time I'm gone without beating anyone up or violently setting anything on fire."

"We'll see."

"I've told them to shoot to kill if you get unruly."

"Then I'll be sure to destroy their guns before I set the fire."

"Good-bye, Violet."

"Good-bye, Seth."

• • •

Inside the house, I'm met with the same suspicious looks as before. But it isn't as if I've never encountered this sort of thing before; if anything, I just feel like I'm back to my familiar life at the CCA. So I ignore the stares, and I sink down into a ratty old armchair that smells like dust, and I close my eyes.

Sleep, I think, and I file away everything else and bury it deep in my mind.

Within moments, though, I sense someone in front of me. I don't open my eyes. That someone remains anyway, and then makes the mistake of touching my shoulder. My hand darts forward, grabbing a bony elbow in the same instant my eyes flash open.

They meet the shocked face of a woman who looks like she may be a bit younger than Angie. I recognize her from the earlier introductions; she is the only one of the four whose appearance I somewhat bothered with committing to memory—mostly because she is hard to ignore, since she's so . . . bright. Silvery-blue shadow dusts her eyelids, and the only thing demanding more attention than that is her hair, which is equal parts vivid purple and a pale blond that's been bleached recently enough that I can still smell it. There's a small ring hooked into her pink-stained lips, which part slowly, uncertainly, as I stare at her.

I notice the others have risen to their feet, and then I realize how tight my grip on her arm still is.

I let go.

She keeps staring at me.

"Can I help you with something? . . ." I trail off, realizing I don't have a name to address her with. I search my mind for one, knowing that my brain likely heard and stored it even if I wasn't paying full attention earlier. She answers me before I find it, though.

"Leah," she supplies, relaxing and suddenly looking much more cheerful and confident than the rest of her companions. "It's Leah, and no, not really anything in particular, I guess. I was just hoping you might talk to us."

The way she watches me reminds me of the way the president did when I first woke up, though Leah's eyes are a bit kinder; it's the same, intensely interested gaze of a scientist waiting to see how an experiment plays out. I consider lashing out at her again—and I think she must anticipate that, because she draws back a bit—but in the end I decide she isn't worth the effort, and I let my attention drift instead to the computer screen nearby.

Now that I've let go of Leah's arm, the other two in the room have gone back to this screen and huddled around it, same as they were when I walked into the room and interrupted them.

"I'm assuming you weren't paying attention to anyone else's introductions either," Leah says. She refuses to let me ignore her as thoroughly as I want to, stepping back into my line of vision as she points to the curly-haired woman seated at the computer. "So, that's Tori, who's sort of our security specialist and the reason we can call this a 'safe' house. And next to her is James." At the sound of his name, the man glances over and gives me a cautious sort of half wave, but his eyes are drawn almost instantly back to the screen.

Partly because I'm curious about what's on that screen, but mostly because Leah is still much too close and I need to move, I get up and wander toward James and Tori. My gaze fixes on the computer between them.

It's a newscast being streamed, and I realize immediately why they're both having a hard time looking away from it: because the headline scrolling along the bottom reads CLONES MISSING: SUSPECTED CCA INVOLVEMENT, and behind the live reporter is a small brick building that serves as a CCA meetinghouse—one of the many public spaces the group has scattered throughout the city, mostly to help distract people from its actual headquarters. Nothing terribly important actually happens in any of the buildings like this, but it gives reporters like this one something to focus their cameras on.

The reporter cites her source for her story—a Huxley representative—and it makes Tori sigh. "Of course Huxley ran straight to the news with this," she says. "Like they're perfectly innocent in this or something. I mean, I'm assuming that the CCA did have something to do with the disappearances, but how much do you want to bet that it was Huxley, again, who sent those clones to mess with the CCA in the first place?"

"But why?" I meant only to listen and observe, but suddenly I find myself glancing between Tori and James, anxious to understand. Tori shivers a little at the sound of my voice, and her gaze slides away the same way I've seen so many others do, so often: as if looking at me might strike her with some sort of curse.

Though maybe, for her, I am a curse, or a reminder, at least, of all those cursed things she worked on at Huxley. One she would rather not look at.

James is a little braver. He meets my eyes, but his expression is strange, like he doesn't think I have any reason to be asking questions. "Because this is basically just part two of the same story that played out at the CCA headquarters a few nights ago, isn't it?" he says. "More clones directly targeting the CCA's operations. And all of them for the same reason, most likely—at least based on what Seth has told us about the things happening within that organization."

"And that reason is because . . . ?"

"Because they see an opportunity." There is a hint of impatience in his voice, I think, as he tries to keep watching the newscast.

I ignore it.

"The CCA is dividing," he reluctantly continues as I step between him and the computer. "Weakening, and Huxley just wants to take the time to make sure it breaks completely. So they send clones to cause a bigger mess of things there, and throughout the rest of the CCA's operations in the city, and then they do things like tipping off this reporter"—he nods to the screen—"to get the public rallying against them too. Because believe it or not, there are still people in the city who are skeptical about Huxley being the bad guys, and they think the CCA is fabricating most of the horrors and rumors you'll hear about them."

"Though to be fair," Leah chimes in, crossing the room to join us, "the CCA has done plenty of that in the past."

"Personally, I think the world would be better off without either group," Tori mumbles, her wide eyes still fixed, unblinking, on the screen.

Leah chews on her lip ring, but says nothing.

"Maybe," James says. "Bottom line, though, is that said world doesn't really know all the facts about either of these organizations. And the Huxley people are using that to their advantage, trying to get some sympathy on their side."

"And you think they're managing it?" I ask.

"Well, they've managed to make this reporter sound plenty biased, at least," he says. "Because, sure, the missing ones are clones, but they also belonged to families in the city."

"'Belonged'? . . . " The word lodges itself in my brain.

Belonged, as in the way property belongs to a person?

Or as in the way important pieces fit as part of a whole?

Could it ever truly be the latter?

"Yeah," he says. "And playing that up is probably stirring up people on both sides of the cloning debate. It's good for their ratings, I imagine."

The four of us fall silent then, and we stay that way until the newscast draws to a close. Then James turns to me again. "So, you fared better than most clones at the CCA at least, huh?"

"You could say that," I reply, though what I am thinking

is that I was only a tool there—almost certainly in the property category—and I don't know if that is any better at all. Huxley may not have been able to control me, but the president managed to, and even now, it still doesn't feel as if I am in control of myself. I don't know how I got here. Why I am breathing the same air as these three, or why they are staring at me like they expect answers, some sort of insight into the CCA or cloning that I don't have. I am as clueless as the rest of the city when it comes to the truth about these things. It doesn't seem fair, to be caught in the middle, squeezed so tightly between these two organizations that each had a hand in my creation, and still not be able to find meaning in either of them.

Maybe monsters aren't meant to have meaning.

I can hear the voices of Josh and his gang. I can see their faces in my mind, lips twisting around the word "monster." And then, as if I needed another reminder that control is a luxury I don't have, that buzzing begins in the back of my brain. It floods warmth forward, a burning that shakes my vision and makes me feel clumsier than usual as I take a step away from the others.

"What's wrong?" I hear Leah ask.

I'm too busy focusing on moving my fingers, one by one to the count of ten, to answer her.

"I only asked you a simple question," James says. I shake my head but don't look at him, not trusting myself to take that focus off my fingers. But for some reason he sees that as a challenge, and keeps pushing me. "Sensitive, aren't we?" he says darkly. "Still missing your friends back at the CCA?"

I manage to laugh at his assumption.

It is the only response I give him though, and he doesn't seem to understand why I find him so amusing. And as it so often does with humans, that lack of understanding just makes him angry. Even without looking at him, I can feel the waves of that anger rolling off him as he asks, "Why are we sure we can trust her to be here, anyway?"

My eyes flash his direction, and my hands go still.

"She's not the same as Seth," he says, skipping right over me to exchange a look with the other two. "Angie was responsible for his programming, at least."

"Leave her alone, James." It takes me a moment to break through the buzzing and realize that this small, uneasy voice belongs to Tori.

"All I'm saying is that we don't know what Cross has done with this one," James continues, ignoring her. "She could be dangerous."

"Could be?" The challenge slides out with a small smile before I can stop it, and I would be lying if I said some part of me didn't enjoy the way it makes him shrink away from me just the tiniest bit.

If I can't entirely control myself, I think, at least I can control this much of others.

I remember Seth's words from earlier, though—his lack of faith in my ability to not turn violent in his absence—and for whatever reason, I want to prove him wrong. So I close my eyes and force a deep breath. Over and over I force myself to breathe, even as James continues to talk, and I do everything I can to ignore his words, because I realize by now that he has nothing good to say.

He is loud, though.

And Tori's voice is quiet in response, but the fear in her words—fear of me and what I might do—is still deafening, and I know that nothing I could ever do would completely silence it, and the thought of that makes me want to run away from them all.

At least until I remember, again, that I have nowhere to run to.

My head is caving in, splitting right between my eyes and collapsing into that violent sea of droning noise. I feel trapped, cornered, because I can't fight these people, and like it so often does when I start to feel this way, my mind begins to flicker to black.

Back away. The words claw desperately to be heard between flashes of darkness. *Back away, before you do something you regret. Something you won't even remember.*

I see Leah step toward me. Her lips are moving, but there is no sound coming out. Her hand reaches for my arm, but there is no sensation of touch. She must be holding me back, though, because when my eyes find the door to outside, and I try moving toward it, I get nowhere.

Nowhere.

Nowhere to go, and everything is turning black, black, black—

When the light comes back, I am lying on the ground. Leah crouches down beside me a moment later.

"Well, that isn't normal," she says.

Her face is just inches away, and my muscles coil in response to her nearness, and they spring me to my feet and push me away without any conscious thought. My back slams into the nearby sofa. I grapple behind me for the sofa's edge—for something solid to grab hold of—and glaring at Leah, I say, "Not much about me is normal."

"I know," she replies, not moving from her crouched position. "But I mean, what exactly happened to you just now? Your eyes looked strange, and then it was like you were fighting with yourself, and then you just sort of . . . collapsed."

I scan the floor around us. No flecks of blood this time. But then, I hadn't been thinking of hitting Leah—the person closest to me—before my consciousness slipped completely, so perhaps that's why.

I still shake my head at her questioning gaze though. "I don't know what happened, exactly," I say. "I . . . I black out sometimes."

"Sometimes? Like how often is sometimes?"

Too often, I think, but I don't want to admit that out loud, so I just stare at a knot in the wood floor instead.

"It happens when you get upset, when you feel threatened, that sort of thing, maybe?" My eyes jump back to her, but I still don't answer. It doesn't matter, though, because she already realizes she's right. "I can fix it," she says.

"Fix it?"

"It sounds like something is off with the prefrontal cortex controller. And god knows what else—several of the

CCA used to work at Huxley, yeah, but it's not like first-rate cerebral programmers were a dime a dozen. And I feel like this should probably be obvious, even to you, but human brains aren't exactly simple to replicate. I know President Cross's background, and I have an idea of who she has working for her, and I have to say: I'm sort of surprised you're as functional as you are. No offense."

There is a hint of arrogance in her tone, enough that I could see Catelyn not liking this woman, but overconfidence doesn't especially bother me. I almost like her better for it. "I'm assuming you consider yourself one of these top-rate programmers, then?"

She smiles. "I learned from the best. The 'best' being Angie, if you were wondering."

"But Angie didn't say anything about fixing it before," I say. "The other night, when Seth brought me to her, she checked everything out in there—wouldn't she have noticed if something was wrong with this . . . controller thing?"

"Probably?" She stands, walks over, and offers me her hand. I don't take it, but I do rise to my feet and meet her gaze as she adds, "But I also doubt she would have wanted to touch it if she had. Angie's sort of sworn off messing with that sort of thing since she left Huxley. She may have checked you out to make sure nothing was critically malfunctioning, probably as a favor to Seth, but I doubt you could talk her into making any real changes in your programming."

"But you would make those changes?"

"Only if you want me to. No sense in letting my talents go to waste, right?"

I'm still skeptical, but some of the tension seems to be rolling out of my shoulders on its own, even as I ask, "Why should I trust you?"

She shrugs. "You don't have to," she says. "Just thought I'd offer." And with that, she turns and starts to walk away.

I feel the word "wait" rising in my throat, but I manage to swallow it. At least at first. Because at first, I am the same me from six months ago, still hesitant, distrustful of everything in the room, and even more loath to accept help from anyone—much less someone I've only just met.

Because what will I owe her if she helps me?

What will she expect from me then?

But then all of a sudden I realize: *I am not exactly the same, am I?* There is something bigger than that loathing inside me now. There is a desperate need for something like control, and a realization that I may have to rely on someone else if I am going to achieve it.

So I find my voice. I make Leah stop. And when she turns back to me, and she explains what we have to do to fix me, I hesitate only for a moment before nodding and agreeing to let her try.

CHAPTER FOURTEEN

Seth keeps his promise. It is almost a full day before he comes back—accompanied by only Angie now—and one of the first things he does is pull me aside and hand me a small computer.

"I brought this back from the warehouse. It's been rigged to be untraceable, and you can use the Connections application on it to create a straight feed to Catelyn's communicator. You remember her number?"

"I never forget numbers. Or anything else, really."

"Right. Computer-brain and all."

"Just like yours."

Or, something like his, at least. I still don't know—and maybe don't want to admit—exactly how alike we are. I imagine we're becoming more similar, though, now that Leah has had a hand in programming my brain, same as her mentor programmed Seth. I suppose it remains to be seen whether or not she did as seamless a job as Angie did; it's something I had been trying to figure out a way of properly testing, up until the moment Seth reappeared.

"So you remember, then," he says, "what I said about not telling Catelyn anything that's happened?"

"All I want her to know is that I'm alive."

"Right." He still looks less confident than usual as he guides me into one of the three small rooms off the house's main living area.

"Are you planning on hovering over me the entire time I make this call?" I ask.

"Why do you think I wanted you to wait until I got back for this?"

"You really trust me that little?"

"I really do."

It takes him a minute, but soon he has everything configured, and a video player with a green connecting bar pops up on the computer's screen. It flashes three times before Catelyn's face appears in the player.

"Oh my god. Violet!" She moves closer to the camera, squinting, like she can't believe she is seeing me. "Where are you? What's going on? And what are you calling from? What happened to your communicator?"

"Long story." My mouth is oddly dry all of a sudden. I expected her barrage of questions but not this difficulty I would feel when facing them. There is so much I can't tell her, but I didn't think I would care about that. Now that I see her, though, not being able to tell her everything is somehow causing an actual, physical aching in my chest.

"Violet? Are you okay?"

"Yes." I force a smile and a nod. "That's why I wanted to call you. Just so you could see for yourself, so you wouldn't do anything stupid like trying to come find me."

I know that look she is giving me now, the way her eyes are narrowed and her lips are pressed into a tight frown;

it's the look she gets when she thinks she is being lied to, and she is trying to see past it to the truth. I get lucky this time, though, because at that moment Seth leans into the frame and distracts her.

"Seth? What the hell are you doing with her?"

"I convinced her to run away with me and become my lover," Seth says. "We robbed a bank and now we're heading to Mexico, so this might be the last you hear from us for a while. Is Jaxon there?"

I lean away from the screen. I still don't know what else I am supposed to say to Catelyn, so for now I don't mind letting Seth take center stage; besides, it will be interesting to watch him talk to Jaxon, knowing what I do now.

How can he keep a secret as big as Angie—and as big as his own identity—from this boy he calls his brother? That he has always treated as his brother? They may not be biologically related, but I can't help but have noticed how quick Seth was to ask about Jaxon. I don't think not trusting me was his only reason for wanting to sit in on this call. A fact that becomes all the more obvious once Catelyn disappears and then comes back in a huff, dragging Jaxon into the video feed with her, and Seth's entire body seems to sink at the sight of him. Relaxing, as if just seeing Jaxon alive and well is enough to give him a heavy, overwhelming peace, if only for a moment. Even I can see that.

I can see the relief in Jaxon's eyes too—though it's clouded a bit with exasperation and possibly lack of sleep, judging by the bags under both his and Catelyn's eyes.

"What's up, man?" he asks. "What the hell are you doing? Mom is going crazy, you know—I'm going to have to tell her I've talked to you."

I glance at Seth. He reacts to the mention of President Cross as his "mom" in the same way he always has—by not reacting at all. The lie rolls over him, easily and effortlessly.

Tell him the truth.

The thought crashes so violently into my head that I don't know how I manage to keep from blurting it out. I'm tired of all these secrets and lies. Lately it feels as though this whole world is made of nothing except secrets, stitched together with nothing but lies.

Tell him, tell him, tell him.

Could Seth ever tell him, though? Is it any different from all the things I keep filed away in the deepest compartments of my own mind? The things that I refuse to open, even for Catelyn? All my uncertainties, all that indifference I feel toward the man who is supposed to be my father, and toward the memories that belonged to the Violet Benson I was before?

Suddenly it feels as though there is much more than just a computer screen and a few miles of the dark and sleeping city separating me and my "sister."

Maybe there will always be too much separating us.

"There was another attack here yesterday," I hear Jaxon say, which pulls me away from thoughts of Catelyn and makes me think of my conversation with Tori and James.

"I saw a report yesterday," I say, "about more clones going missing from the city. Was it actually something the CCA did, then? Retaliation for this latest attack on their main headquarters?"

"I don't know."

"Because the clones that went missing weren't anywhere near those headquarters, according to that report. Did they even do anything? Or were they just guilty by association?"

Jaxon doesn't seem to be able to look at me all of a sudden. He lets his gaze fall to the safer, more familiar eyes of Seth, instead, and he says, "Remember when we used to know everything that went on in this place? And everyone, and what they were doing? . . ." He hesitates, glances at me for a breath of a moment before finding Seth again. "Yeah. It's not like that anymore. Mom only authorized people to protect the base, to deal with the clones that were actually attacking us. I have no idea what happened to any of the others. And Mom won't admit it, but I don't think she knows exactly what happened either. There are rumors flying around that Iverson and that committee he's formed were involved, and that they've all been doing a lot of other shady stuff outside of our main headquarters, but . . . I don't know what—or who—to believe around here anymore. Because that's not even the craziest thing I've heard this past week, you know. Not even close."

Something about the way his tone changes toward the

end makes it impossible for me to let the statement be, even though Seth suddenly looks as if he's ready to turn the computer off.

"What else did you hear?" I ask. But Jaxon doesn't answer. He just keeps staring at his adopted brother, waiting. Seth is suddenly the king of silence, though, and when Jaxon finally breaks that silence, he still doesn't look at me, or acknowledge that I've asked anything at all.

"You should come home," he says to Seth. "I don't want to talk about this stuff over a stupid screen."

"I'm going to," Seth replies slowly, carefully. "I just . . . I can't yet. I have to figure some things out first." His voice wavers a bit when he says it, and I wonder if it was the word "home" that did it. Because where is home for him now? Is it the place where he's lived the longest? Or is it here with Angie, where he doesn't have to keep such impossibly big secrets?

"You both need to come home," Catelyn says, interrupting the uncomfortable quiet that's threatening to settle. I need to come back to her, is what she means. As though home could be a person as easily as it could be a place.

And for a moment I am tempted to tell her I will come back, because that aching in my chest isn't going away. It's only getting worse, the longer I look at her, and the deeper this conversation sinks into its permanent place among my memories.

There was another attack.

Is she safe there, without me?

Home should mean safe, I think.

"Violet?"

I meet her eyes again but I can only shake my head. I say nothing. Because I can't go back there. Not now.

She refuses to take a simple "no" for an answer. Nothing surprising about that.

"Why didn't you come back to my room that night?" she presses. "What exactly happened in that meeting with President Cross, anyway?"

I am still silent to this, but mostly because, with everything between now and then, I'd almost forgotten I even had that meeting. What did happen in that room? What has happened to the president since then? I try to think back, and all I remember, at first, is how tired and strange she seemed when I cornered her in her room. How she admitted that she didn't want to talk to the other CCA members. And those marks on her shoulders, her back. . . .

"She seemed . . . strange," I think aloud. I haven't forgotten the way she insisted I keep quiet about her scars. But I am sure Jaxon must know about them—and if he knows, then Catelyn most likely does too. I never asked to be the president's secret keeper, anyway. And I would much rather talk about her, because it steers the conversation away from all the questions surrounding Seth and me.

"Strange?" Jaxon repeats.

"Strange and tired. And I saw marks on her back, ones she didn't want me to tell anyone about." Jaxon recoils a bit, but I was right—he doesn't look especially surprised;

it's more as if I've poked at a sore memory that he would rather have kept covered.

"Virus scars, right?" Catelyn asks quietly.

"She said not everyone knew about them," I say, nodding, "and that she wanted to keep it that way. And something else . . . something about how they had to do with why she was involved with Huxley in the first place."

This last part does make Jaxon's eyebrows lift a little. "She talked to you about her time at Huxley?"

"Not in detail." I frown, thinking about the way the president had avoided giving me any real answers that night. It was remarkably similar to the vague way Angie had answered my questions back at the warehouse. No wonder they were—as Seth put it—BFFs. "Dodging questions seems to be a skill of all former Huxley employees," I say. And then, without really thinking about it, I glance at Seth and add, "Angie did the same thing."

I realize my mistake even before Catelyn asks: "Who?"

"Should I know who that is?" Jaxon asks.

Instead of answering him, Seth reaches for the computer's power button, and the screen collapses to black with a high-pitched click.

"What do you think you're doing?" I reach for the computer, but he slams it shut and jerks it back, tucking it securely under his arm before dancing back out of range of my fists.

"Seriously," he says, shaking his head at me. "You had one job."

"It was just a name! It means nothing to them, and I wasn't going to say anything else."

"When did you see those scars, anyway?" he demands. "How did you see them? As long as I've known her, Cross has been going to ridiculous lengths to make sure they stayed covered up."

"I broke into her room. Caught her off guard, I think."

"You did what?"

"Get Catelyn on that computer again, and give it back to me."

"Not happening."

"What exactly did you think you were going to do, anyway? Did you plan on keeping Jaxon in the dark about all of this forever?"

"No." The word is clipped with annoyance. "But it would have been nice if I could have kept him in it a little longer, until I actually figured out how to answer anything he might have asked, and—"

"He already knows more than you want him to. Those strange things he mentioned hearing? How much would you like to bet that they're rumors about you? Because what did you think was going to happen after you fought with Josh's gang? Did you think they would keep your secret? Tell everyone that a normal human managed to deal with all six of them single-handedly? There is no telling what sort of things Jaxon has been hearing about you, you know."

"I don't care what he's heard."

"Liar."

He walks over to the bed in the corner and slams the computer down onto the foot of the mattress. And without another word, he collapses back on the bed himself, grabs a pillow, and folds it over his face.

"The least you could do is admit why you can't go back," I push. "Tell him at least one truth: You're a clone, things are even worse for our kind back there as long as Iverson is stirring things up, and so you're afraid—"

"You think that's what this is about?" He lifts the pillow off his face just enough so that his glare can meet mine. "Seriously? You think I'm afraid of Josh or any of those other idiots?"

"I suppose something about the way you're hiding under a pillow strikes me as cowardly."

He flings the pillow aside. "I'm not afraid," he says, sitting up. "I'm pissed. I can't go back and see the president, because she didn't tell me about Angie, and now all I can think about when I see her is what else she hasn't told me about my own life. And now—you're right—there is no way Jaxon hasn't figured out the truth about me, and I wish I'd never agreed to tell him such a huge lie in the first place, because what do we do now? I can't just go back and act like everything's the same. Even if things weren't getting so crazy there, I still couldn't do that."

"You could at least tell him all this," I say, frowning, "instead of telling me."

"I'm only telling you because if anybody knew about not having a home to go to, I thought it would be you."

"We are not the same." The words come out harshly, and the way he sinks toward the wall a little—as if those words are something physical, pushing him back—almost makes me wish I could take them back.

I can't, though.

So instead, I do something that I usually don't bother with; I've never much cared, before, whether or not people understand me—but this time, at least, I try to explain myself for him. "I was somebody before I was reborn at the CCA," I say, "and this city is full of people who know who that somebody was, who expect me to be the girl who came before even if they won't claim that out loud. Your memory was as blank as mine when you woke up as Seth, maybe, but Angie wasn't there. And I know you're angry about that, but at least you had a chance to become who-ever you wanted to be because of it. You didn't have a house full of things people told you were yours. You didn't have photographs of people who looked exactly like you that you didn't remember taking. You didn't . . ."

Stop, I command myself sharply. *You've made your point. You don't need to talk to him anymore.*

Why do I want to keep talking to him?

"Catelyn told me you were only six when the president found you," I say, voice almost a whisper now. "You've had nearly a dozen years to make a life full of things that actually belonged to you. So don't try to tell me we're the same. Just . . . don't. And perhaps you should actually try thinking for once, before you throw away all those things you've made, just because you're angry with the people you made them with. With the family you made them with." I hear the bitterness slinking into my tone toward the end, but I can't stop it any more than I could stop talking. I don't know where it comes from, even—just that it's there. And I expect Seth's reply to be an equally bitter, *Why don't you mind your own business?*

He continues to be full of surprises, though.

"I'm sorry," he says instead, and I know he isn't apologizing for anything he's done, because from the way he is looking at me, it's obvious that I am the only thing he's thinking about just then.

"Don't be," I say, averting my eyes. "Just forget about it."

But in true Seth form, he doesn't manage to stay quiet. "I wish those things were still yours. Some of them, at least—like the photographs and stuff. I really do."

"Keep your pity," I say. "I don't want it."

It's just one more thing that I don't understand or know what to do with.

He does manage to be silent for a minute then, long enough that it grows well past the point of uncomfortable. I turn away and move for the door, more than ready to be finished with this room and conversation.

"Everything from here on out is yours though, right?" he asks, before I can make my escape. His voice is close to timid in a way that seems completely out of character for him. "Your past might not be yours, but everything that happens from now on is all you, right? You don't have to follow the president's orders out here, and Huxley doesn't have control over you. And that's . . . I mean, most clones don't have that. So it's got to count for something, right?"

I stand in the doorway, letting the things he's saying sink in. But I don't look back before disappearing into the hall. And I avoid eye contact with everybody I pass on my way outside and then head straight for the solitude of the woods.

Seth doesn't follow me. Only his words do—and one of them in particular.

Control.

I find myself thinking, again, about a way that I could possibly test the reprogramming that Leah has done. Because so long as she has fixed that malfunctioning bit of me, then Seth is right, isn't he? I have control. We both do. It's how he managed to stay hidden in the CCA for so long, and it's what brought us together while setting us apart from the brainwashed clones that plague this city.

Does it matter, though, as long as those brainwashed clones still exist?

It seems we'll forever be lumped into that majority—guilty by association—and that my life will never manage to be all me, as Seth put it. Not unless something in this plagued city changes. Something in the clones, something that puts an end to the CCA and Huxley's warring.

Something drastic.

An idea flutters in the back of my mind, quiet and small and impossible at first. But just like the conversation I had with Seth, it refuses to leave me alone. It only grows louder. Bolder. I spend the next several hours alone with it, walking the edge of the woods until that idea becomes a plan, until I have turned that plan over and over and imagined all the ways it could possibly go both wrong and right.

And by the time I head back into the dark, quiet house, I am almost ready to do something drastic.

CHAPTER FIFTEEN

There is no one in sight aside from Leah, who sits watching a system of computers similar to the setup Seth had back at the warehouse.

"You all right there, clone-girl?" she asks with a yawn. "How's your head feeling? Any more crazy spells to speak of?"

I still haven't really tested it. But I have an idea, now, of how I might be able to create the sort of violence I need to try to prompt a blackout reaction from my brain. It will have to wait for Seth, though, assuming he ever decides to come out of that room again. But still, just the thought of it—along with the excitement of another, grander plan that is thrumming through my veins—makes me feel positive enough to answer Leah's question with: "So far so good."

"Awesome." She pauses, leaning back in the computer chair and rubbing her eyes with the heels of her hands. The quiet stillness between us borders on amicable—instead of the uncomfortable silence I'm used to causing most people—and maybe because of that, I venture a few steps closer.

"So, I should thank you, I guess." It's premature, I

suppose. But she asked me if I was all right, and for some reason I almost feel as though I should thank her just for that.

She lets her hands fall back to her lap, and her gaze trails up to the ceiling. "You're welcome, I guess." She looks like she tries to smile then, but something stops it. Drowsiness, maybe. A glance at the clock above the doorway tells me it's well past midnight. I frown; I didn't realize I'd lost track of time quite as much as I apparently did. And I don't want to wait until morning to figure out the details of my plan.

"Is Angie still up?" I ask.

Before she can answer, we hear a whistling sound coming from the kitchen area.

"In there," Leah says, closing her eyes and sinking a little more deeply into her chair. "She doesn't sleep much these days."

I don't find that hard to believe. I can think of several things that probably keep her up at night.

The source of the whistling turns out to be a kettle. Angie is taking it off the stove when I walk in, and she doesn't let my sudden appearance interrupt her tea making. She only smiles a greeting at me—as if she fully expected me to walk in on her at one in the morning for an impromptu meeting—and offers me a cup. I decline, even though it smells wonderful. Like vanilla, and the spoonfuls of honey she is tipping into the cracked teacup. It's the same scent I first noticed back at the warehouse.

"This is nice, isn't it?" She takes a seat at a small,

rickety-looking table, and uses her foot to push out a second chair for me. "Very homey, much cozier than that warehouse—I think they did good picking this new place out. I'm crossing my fingers that it lasts."

"You have to move often?"

"I enjoy a change of scenery now and again, anyway."

"Doesn't it get tiring? Not having an actual home?"

She shrugs. "Home is something you carry with you, I think." She takes a sip of her tea, closes her eyes, and breathes in the steam rising from it. "A house—or a warehouse, or whatever the case may be—is just a shell. It's the people and things inside it that count. Like tea, for example. I can be at home anywhere as long as I have a good cup of tea."

This isn't really what I wanted to talk to her about, but her words make me think of the time I spent with Seth in that train car the other night. He'd seemed so angry then, about the way Angie had reappeared so abruptly and confusingly into his life. And it's not like me to be angry on other people's behalf, but my hands are suddenly shaking all the same. "And the people?" I ask. "Seth is one of those that count for you now?"

"He's always counted," she says quietly.

"Then why did President Cross find him alone and abandoned and have to take him in herself?"

"He was never alone. I was always watching from a distance, and I made sure that Jacqueline found him, because I knew she would take care of him. She had growing power with the CCA, more ability to protect him from the past we were both trying to escape . . . and who would think to look for a clone anywhere close to her? I thought he could be overlooked there. Forgotten about."

I move to the chair she pushed out for me, and I sink slowly down into it.

Could he have continued to have been overlooked, I wonder, if I hadn't been brought back there? If the president's decision about me hadn't made people start questioning her, and all the other decisions she'd made—including the one to take Seth in?

"Things are much more dangerous there now," she says, as if reading my thoughts, "but at the time, I thought his life would be more stable with her. I didn't want this for him—this running and hiding constantly, and having to worry about me."

"But how did you know you could trust her?"

"I would trust her with my own life." She takes another slow sip of her tea. "We were very close, once upon a time. She was with me when I first found Seth, when he truly was alone and abandoned, and a very sick orphan."

"So you're not actually his mother either?"

"I didn't carry him inside of me, if that's what you're asking." She looks up from her cup and fixes me with a hard look. "There would be no Seth without me, though. Because his origin was nearly dead by the time we brought him back to the lab. And there was no one else who cared enough about him to try to keep his life going. Even at the lab, everyone else was afraid to do what I did so aggressively—we hadn't perfected the cloning procedure at that point, and there was still a lot we didn't understand. But I had to take a chance on him."

"And he was the perfect candidate to take chances with, wasn't he?" I say stiffly. "A dying orphan who no one would miss."

"I didn't see it that way. Neither did Jacqueline. She was one of the few people who supported my growing attachment to him, and she helped me push our team to do what we had to do to create a new, healthy and thriving version of Seth. This was a different Jacqueline Cross from the one you know, of course. This was back when she believed she still had her own personal stake in making cloning successful."

"Because she was sick."

If she's surprised that I know this, she doesn't show it the way Seth did. "Yes. Sick, and a new mother to a son whose father made it all the way to the last days of the war only to die in a plane crash on his way home. So the future was more than a little uncertain for her. Cloning offered her control that none of us seemed to have back in those days."

"What happened to make her change her mind, though? Why did she start the CCA?"

Her eyes, so open and warm up until now, cloud with sudden reluctance. "Well, we didn't really have the control over cloning that we thought we did, did we?" She is staring at the cup in her hands, as if she expects it to answer her. "We thought we'd worked everything out, and she was more desperate than most for that certainty that we wanted cloning to offer. So Jaxon was part of the group of newborns that we used to create what should have been the first successful 'batch' of clones. That was our idea of success, you know: to be able to create a clone who started life and grew with its origin, so that they would be a truly interchangeable copy."

"Well? What happened? Why did you say this group 'should have been' successful?"

She grips the cup more tightly. "There are differences, complications, when you try to clone a baby that has yet to be born, as we did with Jaxon's group. Complications that you don't encounter when taking your 'materials'—if you'll forgive my use of that word—from an older child such as Seth's origin. The clones we made of these newborns didn't develop the way their origin counterparts did. They mutated strangely, and their bodies rejected the artificial minds we'd built them. . . ."

She trails off, and every other noise in the room—the humming from the ancient refrigerator in the corner, the wind gently rattling the screen of the window, the steady rise and fall of Angie's heel in a slow, rhythmic tapping against the floor—sounds infinitely louder.

"So what happened to them?" I ask, even though I know I won't like the answer.

Her eyes are shining when they meet mine. "Gone, now," she says.

I squirm uncomfortably under her gaze.

"And losing your child in the horrific way we had to lose those children—even if they were only copies—is enough to make anyone start rethinking their choices. To drive them to some extreme reactions. So let's not judge her too harshly for the choices she's made or the things she's created since then." She rises to her feet, starts to clean up the mess she made from brewing her tea. "I went to my own extremes after that too. It was after that when I began to work obsessively on perfecting the programs that I hoped would give us the control over any new clones that we didn't have with that first group. And Seth doesn't remember all the ways I used him to help my research, but that doesn't change the fact that I did it. It doesn't change the fact that the boy you know is yet another version of Seth's origin, another new body 'born' after that horrific incident with the first group of newborns. I could have left him alone. He was developing well enough at that point; there was no reason to recreate him—except to benefit my own obsessive research. I wanted to study his early development again. I told myself I could create a more perfect clone, that I was pursuing something bigger, something that would benefit so many, and I—"

"The clone that was already developed 'well enough'," I interrupt. "What happened to him?"

"Stasis." She says the word very carefully, as though she might break herself getting it out. "And then I don't know. I heard a rumor that the body was destroyed some years later."

It was more than a body, I want to say.

But I can't find my voice. Not as I am sitting here in the third version of my own body.

She finishes washing her cup and the teakettle in the sink but keeps the water running, staring absently at it long after she's put the dishes aside to dry.

"Seth told me you thought he was being stupid for helping me, for trusting me," she finally says, walking back and sitting down across from me again. "And so I'm glad you came to talk to me—I hoped you would, and I thought explaining all of this might help you understand why he does trust me, but you know what? Honestly, I think I agree with you. I only came out of hiding to make sure he was okay, and I guess because some selfish part of me wanted him to know I existed. I had this idea that maybe he would leave with me, and we could go someplace far away, start over someplace new. But I forgot, somehow, that he already had a home here. He doesn't need to start over. He doesn't need me."

"You were right about him needing to leave the CCA, though. Whether to run away with you or someone else."

"I appreciate you saying that."

"I'm not saying it for your sake," I assure her. "Only stating facts."

She laughs softly. "Fair enough," she says. "I'm not sure I've made things any better for him; he won't leave the city, and as long as they know I'm here, Huxley is going to keep after me. And for reasons I'm not quite sure I understand, Seth has decided he needs to stick around to protect me."

"Because you're his family," I say, surprising myself.

"The reason he's alive, at least. For better or worse." It sounds like something Catelyn would say, not me.

I am still carrying pieces of her with me, it seems, even though I never really meant to.

"For better or worse," Angie repeats slowly. She doesn't look like she quite believes the words, and I'm not sure I do either, but neither of us tries to take them back. We sit in silence and give them a chance to sink in instead. I let my mind shift back to Catelyn. I know she would readily believe the silly, sentimental thing I just said. It's why I had to contact her, after all—because I would never be able to convince her, I don't think, that I am not her family, regardless of how I got here. So she will always worry, just as Seth worries about Angie.

Family is a messy thing no matter how it's put together, I suppose.

And she may not be Seth's actual mother, but I'm still convinced, now, that the messy bond between the two of them is reason enough for me to trust her.

"I need your help with something," I say.

"Oh?"

"I had an idea. But it is . . . it won't be easy. Impossible, maybe."

"They told us the same thing about cloning," she says with a little smile. "And then about the mind-control program I was writing, and then—"

"That program is what I wanted to ask you about, actually."

Her smile disappears.

I hurry on before she can try to derail the subject. "Would it be possible to create something that . . . rewrote it, somehow?"

"Like a virus, you mean?"

"Something like that, yes. One that disables the program, maybe, the way you disabled the program in Seth, and the way it's been disabled in me, so that Huxley can't control us anymore. It would have to be something that acted on its own once it was introduced into the host brain of the other clones we were trying to free, but that should be doable, right?"

She considers it for a long moment. "Theoretically? Yes. Between me and Leah, we could likely manage to write something like that." She still looks skeptical, though—as if she is waiting for me to tell her I am kidding about all of this.

Instead I ask, "But would you?" That excitement that was humming in my veins earlier is filling my voice now, almost overwhelming it to the point that my words tremble. I can't remember ever feeling anything like this before.

And Angie looks cautiously intrigued at least, if not entirely optimistic. "I don't know, Violet," she says quietly. "It's been a long time since I've done anything like that. A lot of sleepless nights wondering how things would have been different if I never had."

"But if it's for the right reasons—"

"That's the difficult thing, though, isn't it?" Her fingers are splayed out on the table in front of her, and all of her focus seems to be on the spaces between them. "We can't see the future, how the choices we make will eventually play out. So how do we know what's right and wrong?"

It is the exact same uneasiness that has made me so unsure of myself since the moment I decided to confront President Cross. An uncertainty that I thought was thanks to my short life and strange beginning, but now I'm not so sure, because here is a woman who has had at least fifty years to overcome this uneasiness but hasn't managed it yet.

So maybe it never goes away, and maybe part of being human is doing things even in spite of uncertainty.

"You regret what you did, don't you?"

She doesn't take her eyes off her hands.

"This could be your chance to undo it. To undo Huxley, the CCA—all of it."

The last part makes her look up at me, at least. "You weren't joking when you said this idea was likely impossible, were you?"

"I'm not really the joking type." She chuckles a bit, nods, and then starts to stand. But she freezes halfway up. She braces her arms against the edge of the table, and with her eyes staring straight ahead, she says, "You would have to find a way to upload this hypothetical virus into each of the clones' brain."

"I know," I say. "I'm working on it. I have ideas."

She nods again but doesn't press me for details.

I don't know if that means she is agreeing to my plan or not, but I remind myself that there is a limit to how much a human brain can absorb at once; I've seen it with Catelyn, who is stronger under pressure than most, I think, but who would likely still look just as overwhelmed in thought as Angie does right now. So I don't say anything else. She hasn't really agreed to help me, maybe, but for now, the fact that she is clearly thinking about it is close enough.

And there is one more person I need to focus on convincing, anyway.

CHAPTER SIXTEEN

At the edge of the woods, sitting in the shadow of an oak tree with my back against its trunk, I am waiting.

And in my peripheral vision, I see him arrive within an hour of my being out here: a lone figure in the almost-twilight, walking toward the house. A dense fog rolled in earlier, following a late afternoon thunderstorm. It lingers now and obscures his features, but I don't need to see his face to recognize him. My brain has memorized the way Seth moves, the same way it has memorized every other detail about him.

He left sometime in the night, before I had a chance to talk to him about everything I discussed with Angie, and he told nobody where he was going—so I have been waiting all day for him to come back, mind racing, body teeming with anxious energy.

Twenty minutes after he disappears into the house, it's started to drizzle. My eyes are closed—helping me focus more completely on the calming sensation of the fine mist stinging my skin—so I hear Seth before I see him, in slow footsteps sucking in and out of the mud until they finally come to a stop a few feet away from me.

"Leah said you were waiting to talk to me?" He sounds more tired than I expected. For a moment I consider waiting until later to attempt to test my blackouts, and letting him be for now. But then I look up. I see him staring down at me through eyes wide awake, and wearing his usual half grin. "Also, I don't know if you noticed," he says, "but it's raining. You probably could have waited inside."

I stand and stretch. "Not enough room inside."

His head tilts sideways, questioning.

I answer by launching myself at him, my fist drawing back and punching. He catches it just centimeters from his face, but the force of it is still strong enough to send him sliding and stumbling backward in the mud.

"What in the actual hell do you think you're doing?" he demands, shoving my fist from his face and then twisting just in time to avoid my follow-up swing.

"I want to test something."

"Are you testing to see if you're insane? Because if so, congratulations"—he grabs both my arms, clenches them in a bracing, stopping grip—"you are. You pass with flying colors."

I jerk out of his grip with some difficulty, back off, and narrow my eyes at him. It looks as if this might be harder than I thought. He glances toward the house. I step around him and block his line of sight to it. And then, because I know he's no better at turning down a challenge than I am, I say, "Afraid to fight me, Seth?"

His smile is as relaxed as ever, but the muscles in his arms and chest—more visible thanks to the rain soaking his shirt against them—tense, just slightly. "I don't hit girls," he says.

"I suppose I'll just have to kill you, then."

"Are you flirting with me?" He cocks an eyebrow. "Casual death threats . . . it's a bold strategy, but I think I like it."

My fist connects this time. It just grazes his jaw as he attempts to roll out of my path, not a hard hit, but he's still holding the side of his face when I dive after him again, and maybe he's still stunned, too, because this hit also lands: a solid punch straight into his stomach.

His smile looks a lot more strained all of a sudden, and a dark, dangerous irritation flashes in his eyes.

Perfect.

Because if this is going to work, I need to convince my mind that he poses some sort of threat.

When I dive at him this time, he's more prepared. He catches me by the arms as before, only this time, he holds tighter when I try to break free. We push against each other, a deadlocked struggle of inhuman strength, feet scrambling for traction and kicking up flecks of mud.

We're evenly matched enough that this pushing could go on indefinitely.

It doesn't, though.

Because he flinches.

Just a split second—but it's long enough.

I throw him off, hurling him toward a nearby boulder. He hits it and bounces back, quick and smooth, as though the stone were made of rubber. Too quick. I can't dodge, and next thing I know, he's hit me hard enough that I can't keep my footing in the slick soil. I land on my back. I taste blood on my lips, feel it warming a path down my chin. The ground I sink into is cold, and I expect burning in my mind—that searing, deadening buzz of noise—to counter it. But it doesn't come. Not yet.

Seth looms over me a moment later, looking entirely too much like he thinks he's won.

I hook a foot around his ankle, and jerk. He drops like a cat landing on its feet, his hands catching him lightly against the ground. "Seriously?"

"Seriously."

He springs up and back in the same instant I spring forward. He's fast enough to deflect my next attack, but I'm the one with the momentum now, and so he doesn't manage more than deflecting; over and over again my fists meet his hands as they catch my strikes just in time to spare his face. I don't let up. I keep him moving backward, and the two of us are a violently graceful blur as we press deeper into the woods, navigating through trees and over roots without missing a step.

A crash of thunder distracts me for a moment, and he finally manages to escape my driving attack. He ducks, and then lunges behind me, and by the time I spin around, he's somehow already disappeared into the fog.

The rain is pounding down now. Even under the canopy of trees, enough of it pours into my face to near blind me. I start to reach up to block it, but decide I'd rather keep both my hands free, and so I close my eyes and focus my other senses instead.

And I can focus them, I realize in an exhilarating rush. Even with the taste of blood on my lips, and with the fog pressing in and making me feel trapped, vulnerable, as anxious as if that gray and rolling mist were a solid wall. Even as my muscles throb, and violent twitches clench and unclench my fists, anticipating. Ready for a fight, as they always are.

But it's different this time.

This time, I am not afraid of myself, or of what I might accidentally do if my mind were to slip into that black and empty place.

Because my mind isn't slipping, no matter how hard I try to push it.

And the feeling that I am completely in control for once causes a surge of something incredible; some beautiful combination of relief and happiness and . . . power. And it makes me even more sure of the plans I discussed with Angie, just as I hoped it would.

I focus my senses even closer, just because I can. Just because there is nothing in my way now. Soon I hear quiet breathing. A too-fast heartbeat, a foot lifting quietly, cautiously from the mud.

There.

To my left.

I turn just as Seth explodes through the fog.

I don't bother to evade this time; I just let him hit and push me against the trunk of the nearest tree. He's drawn a tranquilizer gun from somewhere, and he presses the tip of it against the hollow of my throat, while his free hand braces against the trunk and he leans in closer. The added threat of the gun doesn't trigger even the slightest tingling in my brain, and even his closeness doesn't seem to be bothering me as much as it normally does. "Enough," he says. "I don't know what sort of frustrations you're trying to work out here, but we both know how violent confrontations tend to end for you, and I don't particularly want any part of my body broken today."

But he's so perfectly wrong this time that I can't help but laugh.

A genuine laugh too—one that, for once, isn't laced with contempt, which makes it feel foreign and strange in my throat. Seth must find it equally strange, because the pressure of his gun slips a little. "Oh my god," he says.

"What?"

"I was kidding before, but it's true, isn't it? You really have gone insane. Completely out of your mind."

My smile turns to a scowl as I grab his wrist and twist the gun away from my neck.

"That's better," he says, wincing a bit as he tries to pull his wrist free. "That kid-in-a-candy-store grin you had going on was really freaking me out."

"Don't you understand?" I say, exasperated. I slide out from beneath him and step away, pacing several feet before turning to see him still giving me a confused look.

"Clearly I do not."

"It wasn't going to end the way it normally does." I rush back, grab his gun too quickly for him to protest, and press it against my throat again.

"Insane," he repeats.

"This? This didn't even faze me. And it could have been something much more deadly than a tranquilizer, and I don't think I would have lost control over it, either." He's still just staring at me, so I spell it out as clearly as possible: "Leah fixed whatever was causing those blackouts. So if I break any part of you now, it's because I want to."

". . . But you don't want to, right?"

"Not at the moment. Though it could change."

"Right. So, maybe give me my gun back? Just in case." I roll my eyes but throw the gun at him—hard enough that he has to draw back to catch it. He holsters it at his hip and pulls his shirt back down over it. "There was probably an easier way to test this, you know. A more normal way."

"Well," I say, smirking, "so much of my life is already easy and normal, I thought I needed a change."

My sarcasm brings his easy smile partway back. "Understandable," he says, tilting his face back and letting the rain wash over it. He sweeps away a streak of mud across his cheek, revealing a dark purple bruise underneath. I cringe a little at the sight of my handiwork, even knowing that he likely barely feels it and that it will be healed within hours.

"That looks terrible," I say.

"My face never looks terrible," he replies, and then turns and starts back toward the house.

I follow without really thinking about it, in a silence that feels simple, more comfortable than anything I'm used to with him. It's so strange that I almost have to stop, to try to process and understand it. The second I slow down, though, he glances back and says, "Angie said the two of you had an interesting conversation last night. Told me I should ask you for the details. Is this what it was about?"

"It's related."

"Well?" He glances over at me. "The suspense is killing me."

I feel suddenly . . . hesitant. Nervous? Something about the way he is watching me makes me worry that I haven't thought this plan through enough, that I won't be able to convince him. And as much as I hate to admit it, I don't want to do this without him.

So I have to try.

"You said we were the same last night," I tell him, "and we aren't completely, maybe, but there is something that sets us apart from Huxley's clones, isn't there? You managed to spend the past twelve years at the CCA because Angie had disabled the mind-control program in your brain, and so you could control your actions, make yourself human enough to fit in. And that's the difference."

"The difference?"

"Between humans and monsters. It all comes down to control. Free will."

Everyone has monstrous thoughts, but it's what you act on that makes the difference.

"Have you been reading Angie's philosophy books or something?"

"That's what makes Huxley's clones so terrifying,"

I say, ignoring his attempt to turn this into yet another joke. "They aren't choosing their actions for themselves. Some of them fight the mind control, but most can't break it at all, and so their constant existence is just like me in one of those blind rages."

Seth gives me another sidelong look, but doesn't seem to think I've said anything particularly revolutionary. My mind is racing again, though, all the parts of my ideas and plans popping up almost faster than I can compute them. It's a long, confusing moment before I manage to slow my brain enough to continue our conversation.

"But what if that wasn't the case?" I ask.

He stops walking then, his interest looking a little more piqued—though still tentative.

"Imagine if they were completely in control," I say. "Like you. Like . . . like me now." The end of my sentence trails off, my voice turning almost anxious in a way that makes it sound like it isn't my own; I think I've some-how managed to frighten even myself with this ambition I am feeling, with the thought that maybe this is who this Violet Benson is supposed to be.

Because I am already picturing it now: a world where people actually can't tell the difference between someone like me and the other, normal members of that family I was supposed to help put back together. I could exist in that world. Freely. Unafraid. And without violent clones urging it on, maybe the fighting between the CCA and Huxley could stop—at least enough that I could avoid get-ting caught up in it.

"I can imagine it, I guess," Seth says slowly, "but what are the chances of that ever actually happening?"

I cut in front of him and force him to stop. "This is what I talked to Angie about. She can do this—write some sort of program that could disable the mind control in the clones, same as she did you all those years ago, minus the memory wipe." The look he gives me is wary, uneasy. But I'm used to making people uneasy, so I don't back down. "So those clones will be what Huxley actually promised their families: stronger, healthier humans. Not remotely controlled machines."

We reach the edge of the yard in silence, and then the porch in silence, and then the front door still in silence, before I finally lose my patience. I grab the sleeve of his shirt and pull him around to face me. I expect him to fight, but he doesn't. He just looks at me.

The porch creaks. Through the old wood planks with their barely intact joists, I can feel his weight shifting from foot to foot.

"There are a lot of ways it could go really badly," he finally says. "You realize that, right?"

"But what if it goes really well?"

He holds the door open for me and then follows me inside, to where most of the safe-house group is gathered around the kitchen table. Their conversation stops abruptly. Angie's eyes rove over the bruise on Seth's face, the mud on his clothes, and then to the trail of dirty footprints he's tracked in.

And she may not be his actual mother, but she still looks as if she is considering grounding him.

"What in the world?"

"She started it," Seth says with a nod at me, before slumping down into a chair in the corner.

"I thought you two were going to *talk*," Leah says.

"We did."

Angie clears her throat purposefully. "Perfect," she says, throwing one last stern look at Seth before turning to me. "So you've told him your idea?"

I nod.

"And I've told everyone else, so now we're all on the same page."

"Are we?" James says, frowning. "I don't think we landed on the same page at all."

I somewhat expected him to disagree with anything I might have come up with, just based on the way he acted toward me before. But I'm a little surprised to see Tori—who struck me as more reserved—agreeing so quickly and enthusiastically with him.

"We were done with this sort of thing, Angie," she says. "You said it yourself: no more playing god."

"People come out of retirement all the time," Angie says with a dismissive wave. She seems much more cheerful, much more confident, than she did last night—though her eyes are still distant, not really meeting anyone else's.

"But what if something goes wrong?" Tori argues. "These are sentient brains you're talking about messing with, whether for their benefit or not. What if you end up doing irreversible damage?"

She is looking at Angie, but an answer surges out of me before I can stop it. "I would rather be damaged—I would rather be dead—than a mindless slave in Huxley's army."

"And what makes you think you get to speak for all clones?" James asks.

I don't feel a blackout coming, but I have to move my fingers to the count of ten all the same, trying to come up with a civil answer. In the end I don't have to say anything, though, because Seth answers for me.

"If anybody in this room is allowed to speak for them," he says quietly, his eyes shifting toward James, "it would be her."

He leans back against the wall and folds his arms across his chest, but James doesn't say anything to that. I don't really know what to say either; I'm not used to anyone other than Catelyn sticking up for me. And I may be getting more and more used to Seth doing things like this, but I still avoid his gaze, and I turn back to Tori instead.

"Something has already gone wrong," I say. "I . . . I'm proof of that." Somehow I manage to keep my voice soft—because I haven't forgotten the way she was so quick to jump at my every move when I first arrived. And because, this time at least, I actually care about not making an enemy. We're going to need all the people on our side that we can get.

Tori's frown doesn't budge. But at least she manages to meet my eyes—even if she says nothing when she does. It might be a silent understanding passing between us, I'm not sure; I don't know her well enough to read her.

"So, I still vote we go for it," Leah says, interrupting that silence. "Because she's right: I don't know if things can get much worse than what Huxley's already done."

"There are plenty of worse things that Huxley can do—particularly to us," James says. "Even if we did manage to pull this off, what do you think Huxley's retaliation will be? Do you think they're going to give us a medal for helping them see the error of their ways?"

"Of course I don't think that, idiot."

"I would have thought that you of all people would know better than to do anything to make them angry again."

I don't understand what he means, but the words make Leah jump to her feet. "Shut your mouth," she warns, and she looks like she might be thinking of shutting it for him—but Angie steps between them first.

"Enough," she says. "Both of you."

James doesn't argue with her; he just turns and leaves the room. Tori hesitates for only a moment before following him.

"They'll come around," Angie says to no one in particular. "They always do."

Leah is still breathing hard, whatever enraged her making her face flush even brighter than her wild hair and makeup. I find myself wanting to distract her, to calm her down somehow. Maybe because she took my violent rages away first. I don't know. But whatever the reason, I hurry to pull her away from her anger and back into the conversation. "Angie said she thought the two of you could write the virus," I say, "but then we'll need a way to spread it. What do you know about the way Huxley manages to remotely control its clones?"

She grabs on to the question like a drowning person who's just been tossed a life preserver. "A lot," she says, taking a deep breath and bracing her arms against the computer desk before continuing in a rush. "Huxley has its own secure network, hosted on controller servers spread throughout, and in between, all the cities it operates in. And all those controllers are linked together to provide uninterrupted access to the clones. Think of each clone as like an access point—a node on the Huxley wireless network that these controllers host. Because Huxley had to be able to access them constantly for their mind-uploading sessions. . . . Or, that was the original reason for the extensive network, at least."

"So if the virus was unleashed on this network, there's a chance it could spread to each of these . . . access points?"

She doesn't immediately dismiss the idea, but she doesn't look especially convinced, either. "It won't be that simple," she says. "Even if you could somehow break into that network, there are a lot of security measures in place, in each individual clone computer-brain, that this uploaded virus would have to outsmart."

"It's lucky for us, then, that you're one of those first-rate programmers from Huxley, right?"

She stares at me for a long time, almost as if she is

surprised that I was listening when she said that the other day. A slow, wry grin starts to spread across her face. "I learned from the best," she says, exchanging a look with Angie. Then she sighs.

"So, I guess we'd better get started, then. This could take a while."

CHAPTER SEVENTEEN

The day after the meeting in the kitchen, I corner Seth as soon as he steps out of his room. "You can't avoid Jaxon forever," I say.

"Actually, I probably could."

"I know you're worried about him."

"I still have contacts at the CCA. I know he's fine."

"Are you sure you don't need to see that for yourself?"

He scowls at me. But then he gets lucky, because Leah sticks her head around the corner and calls for him, and so he manages to slip away.

On the second day I try a more honest approach, and I tell him the real reason I want him to contact his brother.

Because while Angie and Leah are working on their part, I argue, Seth and I should be figuring out other details—such as what we're going to do after this virus has done its job. Because once we manage to successfully free the clones from Huxley's control—assuming we do—that won't change all the years that came before. This city is stained with violence, marred with the fear and uncertainty that's come from living in the shadow of its unpredictable clones. If there is ever going to be a chance for me to live a normal life here, the people of Haven will have to be convinced of what we've done, shown that they don't need to be afraid anymore.

And this is where we need Jaxon to help us. Jaxon and his mother both, if we can convince them to trust our plan. Because the CCA has the resources, the public reach, we need to help transition the city toward peace.

It seems obvious and worth trying, to me, but the entire time I'm attempting to make my case for this part of the plan, Seth doesn't move; he stays the same as I found him on the front porch: leaning back in a wicker rocking chair with his feet propped up on the splintered porch railing, the hood of his sweatshirt pulled up and down over his eyes.

He's silent. So frustratingly silent that I find myself considering how fragile his position is, and thinking about how easily I could knock that chair out from under him.

Almost as if he anticipates that, though, he finally glances up at me. His eyes are just barely visible from beneath the hood. "You're a strange mix of violent cynicism and hopeless naïveté," he says. "Did you know that?"

And then he tells me to go away so he can take a nap.

But on the third day, all I have to do is walk up to him with a purposeful look on my face. And then this particular game is over, and I've won. "Oh my god," he says. "Fine. If it will make you happy, I will call him and set up a warm and fuzzy family reunion right the hell now."

"It would make me happy."

"Well, you know I live for your happiness," he mutters, and goes to retrieve the computer.

It takes the better part of the morning and afternoon for him to get in contact with Jaxon, but just as the kitchen clock blinks past five, Seth returns with details.

"Seven o'clock tonight," he tells me. "And Catelyn is coming with him. Though you probably could have guessed that last part."

I could have, because I know there is no way she would have let Jaxon leave her behind. And I would never admit it to Seth—I kept my face perfectly impassive at his words, as usual—but for once I am grateful for that stubborn streak in Catelyn. Grateful that even if I don't quite understand why, she is finding her way to my side yet again.

It's a matter of efficiency, is what I tell myself. My brain is a machine, and it hasn't been able to function at full capacity since I saw her face over that computer screen a few days ago. Too much of its processing power has been taken up with replaying that conversation, scanning it for anything I might have missed, for subtle signs that might reveal things she didn't want to say about what she has really been experiencing at headquarters.

Too much of me is weighed down, worrying, again, about whether or not she is really okay without me there.

"I hope she asks you lots of awkward questions and makes this reunion just as uncomfortable for you as it will be for me," Seth says.

"She usually does," I assure him, which makes him smile a bit.

He pulls up a map of the city on the computer, and points to a place called Lakewood Park, which they've decided on for our meeting. It's a small patch of green among the buildings of the Northside Business District, and Seth explains that it's usually frequented only by office workers on their lunch or smoke breaks, so we can count on it being mostly empty by the time seven o'clock rolls around. The only downside is that it is almost as far from the safe house as we could possibly get while still staying in the city.

"That car I took the other day was Tori's," he says, "and she'll be gone for the rest of the day, so that mode of transportation is out."

"So we're going by foot?" The distance isn't much of an obstacle to us, but it will take time—which we don't have much of. And I'm not especially in the mood to deal with the stares and commotion we'd cause by running at our full speed.

"We could," he says, "but I have a better idea."

There is a mischievous gleam in his eye that makes me want to question him, but then, I don't want to give him any reason to change his mind about this meeting. So I just follow him as he leads me out of the house and through the woods to the edge of town, and I don't argue.

At least not until we start approaching the nearest ETS station. The station that is far too crowded for my taste, overflowing with people eager to start their commute home from work or to wherever else they may be heading for the evening. I grab Seth by the arm and jerk him into a nearby alleyway.

"I don't really do public transportation," I remind him.

For those few trips I took into the city with Catelyn, we borrowed Jaxon's car almost every time; I don't know what I thought Seth was planning, but he should have known better than to think he could get me on that shuttle. That he could surround me with people who might recognize my face, and then trap me in that giant metal box where I couldn't even escape from them.

"I know that," Seth says, pulling free. "Just trust me on this, all right?"

"No."

He laughs quietly, his gaze shifting toward the street. "I'm going to show you a better way to do public transportation," he says.

"What are you talking about?"

"Wait here. I need to check something first."

He's gone before I can protest further, and I don't want to fight through the surging crowd to catch him. So I stay, drawing as far back into the alleyway as I can while still managing to watch him. He pushes all the way to the lines forming at the station's entrance turnstiles. Once there, he studies the large screen suspended above those turnstiles— the one that shows route information—before turning and shoving his way back to me.

"We've got only a few minutes to get into position," he says. It's the only explanation he gives me before telling me to hurry up and come with him, and then he skirts around the crowd, moving away from the station's entrance. And I don't especially want to blindly follow him, but I also don't want to stay where I am; the crowd is flooding back toward my safe alley now. People are starting to notice me, staring as if trying to place my face.

Seth is jogging toward more open space, at least.

When I catch up to him—after I'm almost sure I've heard at least one person in the crowd whisper the name Violet Benson—he sees the questioning look I am giving our increasingly empty surroundings, and he meets it with a partial explanation. "We have to get to a stretch of track with as few people as possible around," he says, nodding to the ETS tracks rising over the buildings to our right. "Preferably with no people."

He darts down a street that leads to a more residential area, where the houses grow increasingly spaced apart as we get closer to the bridges that stretch over the part of the Neuse River that winds through Haven. There are three bridges, total. One narrow, two-lane path that now serves the few personal cars that exist in the city, and about a half mile from it is the huge suspension bridge that closed not long after new, strict environmental regulations phased out most of those personal cars in favor of mass-transit solutions such as the ETS. Too expensive to keep up, I remember Catelyn telling me, but also expensive to tear down. Which is why the third one—the one used by those electronic transport shuttles—just runs parallel to the boarded-up suspension bridge.

Now that the number of people and houses is thinning out, Seth picks up his pace a bit, heading straight for the old suspension bridge.

"I'm guessing you have some sort of plan?" I ask.

"Of course I do. I've done this like . . . well, at least once before."

I slow almost to a stop as he leaps over the boards and no-trespassing signs across the bridge's entrance.

"I mean, just in this particular spot, I've only done it once," he calls, glancing back and slowing a few steps himself. "But jumping shuttles? I do it all the time."

"Jumping . . ."

"And timing is kind of critical, so you'd better get out here before we miss our ride. I mean, unless you're afraid you can't keep up with me."

My eyes narrow, but he's already turned back around and raced on, so he doesn't see it. Not like he needs to see it, though. I'm positive he was counting on this exact reaction when he said it. He can predict me now, and I would probably take a moment to loathe myself for that—except that, just then, I hear the metallic whir of the shuttle approaching in the distance.

I sprint to the middle of the bridge, where Seth is stopped with one hand braced against a tower, the other holding one of the cables suspended from it.

He takes a deep breath as I approach, and says, "So the tricky part—"

"You mean aside from not dying?"

"—is that we have to wait until the very end of the shuttle, because the last few cars are just for storage and automatic controller boards—no windows on them, and no people inside them who might hear our landing."

"Do you remember the other day, when you called me insane?"

He points to a section of the bridge some twenty feet ahead, where the thicker, horizontal suspender cables droop to their lowest point. "It's thick enough to run on," he says. "I did it last time."

I shake my head at him, but he just smiles.

"If you miss," he says, "you probably won't die. But still, brace yourself, because that water below is probably pretty dang cold."

The front of the shuttle roars past.

Seth turns and breaks into a run. Slower at first, while watching almost the entire first half of the shuttle slip past, but he's a blur before he leaps onto the cable. I can't keep my eyes on him after that, because I need to focus on running myself. There is no way I am going to back down. No way I'm going to miss.

Not in front of him.

I hit the cable fast and hard. The sting of my landing shoots up through my legs, but I push through it, leaning forward to help my balance as I climb the slope of the suspender up and farther up—

And then suddenly I am as high as I can get, almost horizontal to the bridge, and I know that a second's hesitation will mean losing my momentum and falling.

So I spot the flash of silver below and to my left, and I jump.

The moment I spend in the air, arms and legs reaching, mind racing to calculate every possible outcome—how to brace for the impact of landing in water, on the tracks, or by some miracle on the top of the car—probably lasts only seconds. But it feels like an eternity before I hit something solid again.

The surface beneath me trembles. Wind rushes into my face. My hands find an edge of warm metal and clench it so tightly I'm surprised I don't crush it.

The shuttle. I actually managed to land on the shuttle.

I roll over onto my back, struggling a bit against that wind barreling around me, and close my eyes. This ranks very high on the list of stupidest things I've done during my short life, but somehow, I don't regret it. My heart, even with all its artificial enhancements, is still fighting to keep up with me—a frantic drumbeat, pounding violent proof that I am alive, alive, alive.

I am still considering killing Seth for this, though.

My eyes shoot open as I crane my neck, searching. But they don't find him. And though I didn't think it was possible, my heartbeat skips up to an even faster beat. I'm determined not to let myself get too anxious about the thought of what might have happened to him, but somehow my body is already moving on its own, crawling along the grooved top of the shuttle until I am close enough to cautiously peer over the back lip of the last car. I scan the tracks behind us, squinting, even though I know it's really pointless—this thing is moving so quickly that the bridge is already almost out of sight.

"No . . ."

I'm embarrassed that even this tiniest bit of my anxiety

has escaped my mouth. And then it gets worse. Because out of the corner of my eye, I suddenly see him hoisting himself up from the side of the car. Just a few feet away.

How did I not notice him there?

I sigh, already knowing what's coming from the stupid grin on his face.

"You look worried," he says.

"Only because I wasn't sure of what stop to get off at, so I needed you to be here to tell me."

His grin doesn't waver. "So, on a scale of one to ten, how devastated do you think you would be if you lost me? Like an eleven?"

I lie back and close my eyes again.

Moments later I sense him settling down next to me, his body close but not quite touching. But I keep ignoring him, concentrating instead on the wind rushing around us, whistling in my ears and sending bumps rising across my skin. It's at least a full five minutes before Seth speaks again.

"That was kind of insane, wasn't it?" he asks, as if he just now realizes what we did.

"I believe that was the exact word I used before you did it," I say without opening my eyes.

"Yeah." Silence, and then: "Do me a favor and don't tell Angie about this, all right? She'd go nuts."

"Maybe I will, maybe I won't."

"I love being able to count on you."

In spite of myself, I feel a smile threatening. It doesn't quite reach my lips, though, because now I am thinking about Angie, about the rest of the group back at the safe house, and remembering the tension and uncertainty we left behind there. Tori was coming around some, maybe, but the tension between Leah and James hadn't improved much by the time we left. And I wouldn't care, normally, about a quarrel between two people I hardly know—but in this case it seems to be distracting Leah from the work she should be doing on the virus.

As the shuttle slides through a tunnel, and my eyes open to orange ceiling lights flickering past just a few feet above our faces, I find myself thinking of their argument in the kitchen.

"What did James mean the other day," I ask, "when he said Leah of all people should know better than to make Huxley angry?"

Seth props himself up a bit on his elbows, bringing his head close enough to the top of the tunnel that it makes me flinch. He gives me a curious look—probably because he finds it as strange as I do that I'm suddenly interested in other people like this. I can't really explain it; I just haven't been able to get the image of Leah, so flustered and upset by James's words, out of my mind.

Because she's crucial to your plan, I try convincing myself. *So you need to know everything you can about her.*

Whatever the reason, I find myself growing impatient for Seth's answer.

"Well?"

"I don't know all the details," he says. "Just that she had a daughter that died. And, same as most people involved with Huxley, she of course had a backup clone there in the labs—but the death was after she'd already left Huxley. And it was apparently a really ugly breakup between them, so Huxley has been like. . . holding her daughter's clone hostage. It's crazy."

I feel sick, suddenly.

Is this what it feels like? That empathy thing Catelyn was always talking about? She would probably be so happy to hear about it finally catching me like this. But just as I assumed I always would, I hate it, and I do everything in my power to try to force that sickness away, to focus on the task that lies ahead of me and nothing else.

I can't force it away fast enough, though, and that horror I feel toward Huxley must show in my face, because Seth's eyes widen a little bit.

"Oh, man," he says.

"What?" I ask, against my better judgment.

"First you're prematurely mourning my death, and now you're worried about Leah? You realize you're sort of turning into a compassionate person, right?"

"Shut up, or I am going to compassionately shove you off this shuttle."

"Fine by me," he says, rising into a crouch as we emerge from the tunnel. "We're almost to our stop, anyway."

"I'm guessing the way off also involves jumping?" I turn my head so I can see the city rushing past us: a blur of drab colors occasionally broken up by shimmers of glass and golden sunset.

"Unless you want to explain what you were doing to the

stationmaster at the end of our route, then yes," he says. "I'd rather avoid that mess, though, since we're sort of on a schedule here. Right before our route's official stop, there's a stretch of track that goes through the place where they store and work on malfunctioning shuttles—no public access there, so we should be able to make a fairly clean getaway. Some people might see us, but there won't be enough of them to stop us or anything."

I sigh, but it's really more of an automatic reaction to him at this point; I don't completely mean it.

It's odd—insane, as we've established—but I think some part of me is looking forward to jumping. Because I can jump, with him. I can leap from bridges and buildings and crash through the world at my full, blinding speed, and I don't have to hold back. I'm not strange to him.

And I think I finally realize, maybe, why he wanted to help me escape the CCA. Why he has been so reluctant to see Jaxon again. It's because of all the years he had to spend holding back too. It's because of his past, the twelve years he stayed hidden behind everything he could to throw people off—whether it was behind jokes, or man-made weapons to convince people he was weak enough to need them, when really he was so much stronger than all of them.

What happens now? I wonder.

Now that he can't go back to the way things were.

"What do you think Jaxon is going to say when you tell him the truth?" I ask.

The question startles him, maybe; his balance slips a

bit, and it takes him a moment to steady himself in the driving wind. "No idea," he says. "I think you were right, though—I doubt there's any shortage of rumors about me flying around the CCA now. He's probably already put at least some of all this together." He inches toward the edge of the shuttle, to where he can peer more easily at the upcoming tracks, before adding, "So maybe that will make it easier."

He doesn't sound especially convinced of this last part. But I nod as if I agree anyway, and we watch the world speed past, together in our same strangeness, until it's time for us to jump.

CHAPTER EIGHTEEN

We reach the park ten minutes before seven, but the two of them are already there, waiting.

As we approach the bench they sit on, paranoia starts itching the back of my neck. My senses take over on their own, eyes and ears focusing as that instinct-driven part of my brain—that part that cares more about survival than anything else—snaps to life.

Because there are other people here, of course. Jaxon and Cate won't have come alone. Even if they wanted to, the president wouldn't have allowed it, not with all the unrest the clone activations and disappearances are causing the city, and not when there are CCA members turning against the president herself, and possibly plotting rebellion or revolution from somewhere outside their headquarters.

So Jaxon and Cate have bodyguards.

I can't tell how many, but I know they're here.

"Who did you bring with you?" I ask Catelyn. I don't like not being able to see them.

Although, even if I could see them, and even if I recognized them, there would still be no way of knowing whether or not they were worth trusting.

Catelyn doesn't seem concerned about it either way. Instead of answering my question, she stands and flings her arms around me, insisting on a hug that lasts entirely too long—until I fix a firm grip on each of her shoulders and push her away as gently as I can manage.

I'm fairly certain I hear Seth snicker beside me, probably happy to see that it's taken only seconds for this reunion to become much more "warm and fuzzy" than I care for, but I ignore him. Because something strange is happening in my mind: a rapid, unexpected shift from that paranoia, from that focus on all the uncertainty and possible threats against my existence to . . . her.

Just her.

I still haven't taken my hands from her shoulders, I realize.

My eyes do a quick glance over her, and I force my mind to handle this situation in a way that feels safer, more familiar to me—by analyzing her appearance, searching for solid facts that I can infer from it. The still-there circles under her eyes tell me she hasn't caught up on her sleep since we talked over the computer that day. She's lost weight too, and together with those dark eyes, it suggests anxiety.

But she is still in one piece, I observe. All her frail human skin and bones are unmarked and solidly together, and so I can conclude that she has been safe enough without me.

I feel relief rising in me, forming a sigh that I hold in as I let Catelyn go and draw slowly back. I'm grateful when Jaxon gets to his feet, because it pulls her attention away from me.

As his brother's eyes meet his, Seth attempts his trademark confident grin. It falls flat, though, and he doesn't bother to try to recover it; he just frowns, shoves his hands into his pockets, makes some stupid comment about the weather, and then about school—about lots of pointless things—until Jaxon finally interrupts with a single, quiet question:

"Is it true?"

I don't think I have ever seen Seth look less confident than he does in this moment.

"I won't believe it until I hear you say it," Jaxon says.

And then it happens, much the same way as it did between me and Seth that night in the warehouse. Seth finally sighs and gives in. Instead of healing technology, though, this time he proves it with his inhuman speed and strength—by kicking up a rock at his feet with incredibly quick accuracy, snatching it from the air and then crushing it to dust in his hand.

Catelyn sucks in a breath. Jaxon only stares as Seth unclenches his fist and lets the light breeze scatter the shining dust from it.

"Neat trick, right?" he says, once his hand is empty.

"Why didn't you tell me?" Jaxon asks after a long pause, still staring at the gray-dust-streaked lines in Seth's palm.

"Because," Seth says, "your mom swore she'd send me away if I told anybody. And I . . ." He pulls his hand back, wipes the rock residue away on the side of his pants. Jaxon finally meets his eyes again, and Seth quietly finishes, "I didn't want to go away, all right?"

"So what changed?" Jaxon's voice is strained.

"A lot," Seth says, and it is obvious from his tone that he realizes there is no more putting this off.

The next fifteen minutes or so are a confusing tangle of explanations—about Angie and the others, about what happened the day I left the CCA, and finally about the plans we've been making. When I mention our need for President Cross's help, though, Jaxon shakes his head.

"She's kind of got her hands full at the moment," he says.

"We didn't get a chance to go into detail the other day," Catelyn elaborates, "but things have been getting worse back at headquarters, and not just because of these recent attacks. The president was already making enemies, you know, from bringing Violet back—people calling her a clone sympathizer or whatever, and calling themselves purists, because they didn't think the CCA should have anything to do with any clone, whether it was under Huxley's control or not. And they were looking for whatever else they could pin on her to gather some more support for their side—so when Josh and his gang started talking about what happened with Seth, and the possibility of him being a . . ." She hesitates, unable to bring herself to say "clone" even now, I guess. She is staring at Seth's hand as though she expects him to reveal the original, uncrushed rock—for him to explain how a human performed what must have been a sleight-of-hand trick. "Well, you know," she finally finishes, her gaze darting away. "It just added more fuel to the fire."

"I should have pushed them all off the building when I had the chance," Seth says, shaking his head.

"They're just a bunch of stupid kids," I argue. "Surely the president's word means more than whatever rumors they were spreading?"

"It's not just the kids who were spreading those rumors, though," Jaxon says. "Their parents are all in Iverson's inner circle, and the possibility of Seth being a clone fit their agendas perfectly. So they played up the credibility of whatever Josh and the others were saying, I'm pretty sure."

"People already had doubts," Catelyn says. "I guess they were glad to have something like Seth to prove them right, to justify their feelings. Because now even some of the ones who were on the fence before are joining these so-called purists. It's hard to say for sure, but there are probably as many of them now as there are of the president's loyalists."

"So, yeah," Jaxon says, "getting involved with this save-the-clones plan of yours probably isn't going to help her regain any support. Especially if these attacks on headquarters keep happening along with everything else."

"Don't you see though?" I take a deep breath, focus on letting it seethe slowly back out, trying to keep my frustration from getting the better of me. "That is exactly what Huxley wants. They see the CCA cracking, and they're doing everything they can to try to make the situation worse, to make sure that the biggest obstacle to their operations completely collapses before this is all finished. They're encouraging this civil war. And then as soon as the CCA has destroyed half of itself, Huxley will be able to come in and destroy the other half with ease. So it isn't just about saving clones—it's about the CCA saving itself, too."

"And you think that disabling the mind control in the clones is going to undo everything that's already happened?" Jaxon asks. "Somehow miraculously put the CCA back together?"

"Maybe, maybe not. It will stop the attacks, at least. And with no more of that particular fuel being added to said fire, I'm sure your mother will have an easier job swaying people back to her side, and this revolution might manage to die out before it becomes entirely catastrophic."

Jaxon's mouth is set in a hard, unconvinced line, but he seems to have run out of arguments, for now.

So Catelyn picks up where he left off. "You said this virus thing could take months to complete," she says. "I don't think we have that kind of time, Violet. There may not be a CCA left to help with your plan by the time you're ready for it."

"What if we helped make sure there was?" Seth says, and all three of us turn to him with a questioning look. "I was just thinking of a little quid pro quo," he explains, leaning against the lamppost with a thoughtful expression on his face. "Of ways a couple of clones could prove useful to them. I mean, after all, that's why the president kept us around in the first place, right?"

"That's not the only reason Mom kept you," Jaxon says quietly.

Seth seems determined to ignore the comment, one way or the other, and continues in a rush: "You said the other day that you thought some of these purist creeps were taking their business to somewhere outside the CCA, right?"

Jaxon nods, still looking uncertain.

"And we know that Iverson started a lot of this, with that committee he set up and everything—so at the very least, Violet and I could follow the jerk, and maybe some of those committee members, too. See what they're really up to. See who all is meeting with them, and where, and find out exactly what they're meeting about. And then we can pass that intelligence on to the president and the ones loyal to her. We help them out, and maybe we all end up on the same side in the process, right? One big, happy family that can eventually cripple Huxley's plans for world domination together."

"We don't know exactly how many Iverson has already recruited," Catelyn says, frowning at him. "If one of them catches you, there's no telling how many others you'll have to deal with."

Seth rolls his eyes. "And I could crush all of their dumb little heads, same as I did that rock earlier."

"So could I," I point out.

The look Catelyn is giving me clearly says *I wish you wouldn't*. She stays quiet, though, only shifting her weight from foot to foot as if trying to find her center, as if all the things we've said here tonight have knocked her away from it.

Jaxon, too, is quiet for a long time. But then he and Seth exchange a look that I can't decipher, but that, for some reason, causes the first genuine grin I've seen from Seth since we got here. "I know you're going to do whatever you want," Jaxon says. "So all I'm going to say is this: Mom is not going to be happy about you doing this."

"Well," Seth says, his eyes dancing in the lamplight, "between the two of us, I was always the problem child anyway, wasn't I?"

CHAPTER NINETEEN

The communicator around my wrist vibrates and lights up for the third time tonight. I double-check to be sure the audio is set to my earpiece instead of the speaker, hit accept, and Seth's voice fills my head.

"Majestic Firebird to Ice Queen," he says, "how are things looking at the main exit?"

"I told you I wasn't answering to that ridiculous nickname," I say, my gaze sharpening, focusing even more closely on the exit in question. I have been in this position for almost two hours now, and not a single person has gone in or come out of the elevator, which is normally the most-used method of transport between the CCA headquarters and this parking garage.

"You could have picked your own, nonridiculous handle," Seth replies. "I gave you the opportunity."

"Would it kill you to take this a little more seriously?"

"It very well might."

"I think Zach might have mixed up his days," I whisper, trying to bring the conversation back to business. "That, or he isn't as trustworthy as you thought."

"No way," Seth replies. "Zach is one of the good ones."

I want to believe him. And not just him; Catelyn and

Jaxon both vouched for Zach too, when we were trying to find someone to discreetly keep watch on Iverson's comings and goings around headquarters. Zach swore that Iverson usually disappeared from the CCA around this time on most Saturdays, though, and so far there's been no sign of him.

So either Zach is wrong, or worse: Iverson has caught on to the fact that we're watching him, and is now trying to throw us off.

I press closer to the cool cement and shut my eyes for just a moment, swallowing my concerns about Zach's reliability in favor of keeping as quiet as possible. Seth fills my silence by offering me other, equally absurd nicknames. One of them—Ninja Kitten—comes dangerously close to making me laugh, until movement in my peripheral vision stops it.

"Quiet," I breathe into my communicator. "I see someone."

It's not Silas, though. It's his son.

And Josh is all alone this time.

I rise from my hiding place without really thinking about it, every muscle in my body suddenly tense and eager to move. To carry me, soundless and deadly, to that space behind him.

I could snap his neck before he even started to turn around.

I could finish what he started, and then he would never hurt me or Catelyn or anyone else, ever, ever again.

I watch him glance around the parking garage. He

doesn't see me, somehow, but I want to think he still senses me. I want to believe that it is me making him hesitate and look uncertain every few steps. Because there is no mistaking it: He looks uneasy. And I'm glad for it. He should be frightened. After what he did on the roof, and the way he even dared to mention Catelyn's name to me, I am the last person he would want to meet in a dark parking garage. He should be completely terrified.

My lips part and I breathe in deep, as if I could taste his fear across my tongue and savor every morsel of it.

I imagine it would taste sweet, the way they say revenge does.

He walks faster. I creep after him, darting beneath shadows cast by stairwells and graffiti-covered signs, and by the time he reaches the street, I am no more than fifteen feet behind him. *How long would it take me to clear that distance?* I wonder.

One second?

A half second?

His gaze shifts. First to the left, then to the right. But never behind him. Never to me. He lifts his communicator, taps it a few times, and then studies it for a moment. My breathing stills, quiets even further. My fingers choke around a support column to my left. I squeeze the column, and I swear I leave fingertip indents in it when I pull my hand away. In my mind, I see everything from that day on the roof through my memory's cursed clarity—so painfully vibrant, so near, that the same violence from back then surges through me all over again.

I am not the same as I was back then, though.

Because if I were, then this would likely be the moment that the vicious images in my mind and the heat in my blood would make my world flicker to black.

But none of that happens.

Instead, I center in on his every movement, on every breath that makes his chest rise and fall, on the curves of his neck and the exact points on his body that I would need to hit to break him completely.

I slink a few more steps forward.

My communicator vibrates.

Only the tiniest bit of noise, but I still dive and roll into the shadows out of an instant, instinctual drive to not be seen. Josh is out of the garage and into the street in the next moment. I fall back against the wall and absently press the accept button on the communicator.

"You all right up there, Ice Queen?"

I give myself a little mental shake, trying to make sense of these past couple of minutes. What was I doing? What was I thinking? I don't have the blackouts to blame now, but I still almost lost myself just the same.

What is wrong with me?

The communicator vibrates again.

"Okay, fine," Seth says, "are you all right up there, *Violet*? Just answer me, please."

"It wasn't Silas," I say. "It was Josh, though." I push away from the wall and start for the street. Josh isn't hard to spot once I'm there; he is one of only a handful of people walking about. I manage to zero in on his red jacket just as he turns the corner a few blocks ahead of me. "I think I'm going to follow him," I tell Seth.

Seth hesitates for a moment, and then all he says is: "Violet . . ."

My stomach flips at his tone; he sounds . . . concerned? Anxious? As if he just spent these past minutes up here with me, watching me come so close to attacking Josh, and now he's afraid of what I might do next. "I'm not going to pick a fight with him," I say, in my best attempt at a reassuring tone. "I just think chances are good that wherever he's going, his father—or at least some of his father's followers—won't be far away." I manage to sound so confident that I doubt Seth can tell this thought is only just now occurring to me. Suddenly I feel even more embarrassed.

Attacking Josh would have been incredibly stupid of me, I realize. It could have given Seth and me away, made the tension within the CCA even more explosive than it already is, made the past few weeks' worth of work we have done completely pointless. And what would it have said about what we were supposedly working for? We're trying to free this city of clone violence. Murdering someone probably wouldn't rally many to our side.

Even if part of me still feels like he deserves to die.

Bigger things, I think as I break into a jog, trying to close enough space between me and Josh that I don't lose him. We have to focus on the bigger picture now. And Josh is only a bratty little cog within the larger operation we're trying to bring down.

Seth's voice is suddenly in my ear again. "Where is he headed? I want to come too."

"You really don't think I can handle this?" I whisper back, avoiding the gaze of two curious women who clutch their purses closer to them as I rush past.

"I do. I'm just bored. And my legs are cramping from hiding here so long."

I doubt this last part is true, because his muscles are as powerfully advanced as mine, but I don't bother pointing that out. "I'm approaching the intersection at Elder and Fifth," I say.

Josh just turned left at that intersection. I sprint after him. I slow to a stop as I reach Fifth Street, though, leaning against a building on the corner—a bakery, it smells like—and peering as casually as I can around it. I catch sight of Josh and watch as he dips into a small parking lot surrounded by a run-down chain-link fence. He emerges a few moments later pushing an electric jet cycle, which makes me curse.

"He's got a bike," I hiss into my communicator. "I'm going to end up losing him." I'd expected to be following someone in a car, which would have been slower on the narrow city streets and easier to keep up with, or perhaps for him to take an electric bus, or the shuttle—something with frequent stops and a predetermined route we couldn't lose. But the bike is faster, smaller. It's able to outmaneuver the traffic, even drive over it, in some cases, thanks to special bike lanes that the city created in hopes of encouraging people to use these more energy-efficient vehicles.

I can still keep up with it, of course.

But not without causing a scene that will likely catch Josh's attention as well.

"Relax," Seth says. "I've got a plan. I'll be there in a second."

"You don't have a second," I say as Josh swings a leg over the bike and starts it with a twist of the handle.

"Well, make me some seconds. Slow him down somehow, create a little chaos—you're usually good at that sort of thing. You'll just have to be subtle about it for once. Think you can manage that?"

"Of course I can manage that."

"I'm just saying. If he realizes you're the one causing trouble—"

"I've got this, all right? Just hurry up and do whatever it is you're planning on doing."

"Pushy."

I ignore this last comment, because suddenly there is no time to keep arguing, or to do anything except move. Josh pulls onto the street, and the second his eyes are fixed straight ahead, I start to run. Luckily, the traffic is heavy enough here that Josh isn't moving fast enough to require much more than a jog to keep up—even as he's darting in between cars and buses and trying to find a faster route.

But keeping up isn't enough.

Somehow, I need to get in front of him without him seeing me. And then figure out how to stop traffic while remaining equally out of his sight.

One thing at a time, I think as we approach another

intersection. His light has just turned red, and as he slows to a stop, Josh slides his bike toward the shoulder of the road. It's hard to tell from this side of the street, but it looks like there's a narrow stretch of empty pavement ahead of him. He leans forward, like he's sizing up the space and thinking about racing through it.

To my left, I see the opening of an alleyway. I dash toward it, picking up full speed once I'm in and there are buildings rising up on either side, concealing me. I leap a wooden fence at the alley's end and land in a pile of boxes and wooden pallets on the other side. I break through one of those pallets, and have to kick my way free of it before running on, clearing the rest of the building to my right and then careening around it to reach the intersection a block ahead of where Josh is still waiting.

Not waiting for long, though.

I haven't even had a chance to take a deep breath before the traffic he's in starts to move.

Focus, I command myself. And my brain manages it. It takes in the sight of everything around me and processes it at lightning speed, running every possible scenario, every possible—

There.

I've spotted it: a fire hydrant, no more than ten feet away. I pull the hood of my sweatshirt up around my face as much as possible, and I run to it. Probably too fast, but I don't care at this point—a few more seconds and I will have missed my opportunity.

I reach the hydrant. Pretend I've dropped something,

and go to pick it up. As I straighten, my hand falls on the nozzle pointing toward the road, and my fingers grip its cap as tightly as any wrench could.

I twist it free.

And in the same second, I turn and bolt from the scene, away from the sound of the pressurized water exploding and gushing onto the street. There's a screech of tires, and then the sound of metal hitting metal, and all of it muffled by shouts and honks and the *glug pump crash* of shooting water. I slow down just long enough to glance back, to see that I've managed to bring traffic almost to a standstill.

I don't manage to find Josh before someone gets a hand on my arm from behind.

I jerk loose, keep my face turned away with my other arm covering it, and I run for the alley.

Footsteps pound behind me. Once I clear the fence in a single leap, though, they abruptly stop; if the people following had been wondering if they were dealing with a clone before, they won't be now—but I'm hoping no one took enough notice of my face to connect it with my name. Likely they'll just end up pinning this on one of the multitude of Huxley clones that have been wreaking havoc in their city.

I circle back around to the intersection I left Josh at, slipping behind a bus that's pulled up onto the side of the street with its caution lights blinking. Seth's voice reaches me over the communicator a moment later.

"Got him," he says, and I am about to ask exactly how when I catch a flash of Josh's red jacket. He's past the intersection, weaving into the line of traffic that's started to pull around the mess I created, and he is slowly, steadily, moving away from me. I take a few automatic steps forward. My focus is so intently on Josh that when something grazes my elbow, I don't think to do anything beyond an automatic reaction; I just swing.

Seth catches me by the wrist, but lets me go the second our eyes meet. "Easy, killer," he says.

"What do you mean, you got him?" I say with a nod toward Josh, who is almost out of sight now. "It looks like he got away to me."

"Let's escape the scene of the crime first, how about? We need to keep moving, anyway; it won't matter if we track Josh to wherever he's going if we aren't around to see what he's doing when he gets there."

We move to a block parallel to the one we were on, and keep heading the same direction Josh disappeared into. Once we're out of sight of the mess on Fifth Street, Seth pulls a tiny, odd-looking little gun from his coat pocket. Or at least I believe it's a gun; there is a short barrel on it, and a button trigger on its underside; it has a screen across the top of it, though, and there is a map lit up on it, along with several blinking dots.

"Grabbed this as sort of an afterthought when we were leaving the safe house," Seth explains. "Good thing, right?"

I watch the screen more closely, following the yellow dot as it turns right just as it reaches the old library building. We turn right too, and pick up our pace a little.

"So, we're the green dot, he's the yellow?"

"Or his bike is the yellow, at least," Seth says. "I thought he might notice if I shot a tracker disk onto him. Hopefully he doesn't ditch the bike anywhere."

"He won't notice this disk on the bike?"

"It's, like, barely as big as the tip of your finger."

We follow the dot for the next fifteen minutes or so, and as I run, I am combing through the city map I've made in my mind's memory. These past few weeks we've been plotting out possible locations where the CCA insurgents might have been meeting, based on rumors and information gathered by Jaxon and Catelyn and a few other people they trust, and on our own knowledge—or Seth's knowledge, mostly—of the city's nooks and crannies and landmarks. And when I compare that map of locations in my head to the one in Seth's hand, I can already guess at Josh's possible destination.

"Do you think he's heading for one of the river buildings?" I ask Seth. It's a spot we pegged on the northwest corner of town—part of the old water-treatment plant there. Most of that plant is nonoperational now, replaced by the newer facilities a few miles upriver. One of the CCA women closest to Silas is in charge of keeping that old plant safe, and keeping the public out of it; that, combined with the relative seclusion of the spot and the dozens of buildings along the property, makes it seem like a distinct possibility for a meeting spot. A spot Josh has been heading steadily toward for the past five minutes or so.

"Seems like it." Almost as soon as Seth says it, though, he glances down at the screen, and then stops so quickly, I almost run into the back of him. "Or not," he says.

Because the yellow dot has turned around.

It's moving back toward us.

"Looks like he's changed his mind," Seth says.

I tense. "Do you think he realized he's being followed?"

"I doubt it," Seth says. "Maybe the idiot's just lost?"

We hide all the same, ducking behind a brick wall of a nearby apartment complex, and wait. Less than a minute passes before we hear him go by, the hum of the bike in sync with the little dot roving up the screen. He drives maybe a half a mile more before turning again.

"Is he . . . ?" I trail off, and we both watch closer as Josh slows and then makes another right turn. I still don't believe what I am seeing, though, or that he could actually be headed where I think he's headed—not until he actually stops right outside of it.

"Why in the world is he stopping at Huxley's old lab?" I ask, staring at the screen as though there is some way I might be mistaken.

But Seth sees it too.

"No idea," he says, "but I want to go find out for myself."

We break into a run, reach the metal fence that runs around the perimeter of Huxley's property a few minutes later, hop over it, and then immediately shoot behind one of the many construction Dumpsters set up as part of the ongoing cleanup of the crumbling lab.

Again, Josh is easy enough to spot. He hasn't dared to get too close to the ruined building; he stands outside that security fence, maybe fifteen feet from us, in front of the main entry gate.

And he is just . . . staring.

He is completely still and all alone, his eyes vast and empty as they take in what's left of the massive compound. I'm no longer concerned that he might notice us. Something tells me I could jump up and down in front of him, and in this moment, at least, he wouldn't see me. He would just keep staring past me, searching for whatever it is he is trying to find in the destruction left behind.

It's different from the anxiety, the frown I saw on his face as he left headquarters. And it is so far from that smugness—that arrogance of his that was so easy to hate, to want to destroy—that it makes me uncomfortable.

Or maybe it's just this place that's doing that.

"You were right," Seth says suddenly. I tear my eyes away from the awful emptiness on Josh's face and follow Seth's gaze instead. A truck is parked on the street a little ways back from Josh, and Silas Iverson himself is climbing out of it.

"Right?" I repeat in a daze, because suddenly nothing seems right at all, and I'm not really sure why.

"When you said we should follow Josh to get to his dad, I mean."

"Oh."

That's why we're here. We followed Josh. We're collecting intelligence for President Cross, because she's promised to help us if we do. We have a plan, just focus on the plan. . . .

And I try. But even as the details of that plan reopen in my brain and I run through them over and over, my stare stays frozen on Josh. He and his father are discussing something now. I could probably pick up at least some of their conversation if I could center in on it, but every time I attempt to, that uneasiness from before threatens to overwhelm.

A long few moments pass, and then Seth quietly says, "Is it just me, or does it sort of feel like we're eavesdropping on an intimate family moment here? I'm kind of afraid they're about to start hugging it out. Which I imagine will be incredibly awkward—like two evil robots embracing each other. Or like what I imagine hugging you would be like."

"I wouldn't hug you if my very life depended on it, so you can stop imagining that."

"I can't help it," he says. "Maybe if you wouldn't act so warm and overly friendly toward me all the time, I wouldn't have that problem."

Our voices are quiet, weak, but we're trying. Attacking the uneasiness, the uncertainty, with this silly banter that seems to have become our normal. But it doesn't quite drive those things away this time.

And Silas never embraces his son. He does grab him by the arm—but it's only so he can pull Josh away from the gate, which he does with so much force that it's almost painful to watch, because it is so clear, even to me, that Josh is not ready to leave whatever he came here for. Silas remains stern faced, though, as he directs his son into the passenger seat of the truck. Then he goes back and grabs the jet bike, loads it onto the bed, and gets in and drives away without so much as a glance beside him.

We follow the tracker in silence, and eventually find that our earlier hunch was right: We end up by the river. And we stay there for hours, observing every person that comes and goes out of an unassuming little cinder-block building, and quietly discussing ways we might be able to better see and hear—and perhaps even record—exactly what they're talking about.

Other than that, we don't say much. There are a few times when I think Seth might, but then he seems to understand that I am taking longer than normal to process this latest encounter with Josh, and so he leaves me to it.

On the way back to the safe house, though, as we're lying on our backs on top of a shuttle as it speeds along among the city's lights, I suddenly can't keep quiet anymore.

"What was he doing there, do you think?"

I don't have to elaborate; I know Seth understands my question, though it takes him a long time to answer. "Just trying to deal with old memories, maybe," he finally ventures.

"What memories, exactly? Was he there during the fight? During the fire?"

"No. I don't think so." He looks reluctant to keep going, but I can tell he has more he could say.

"You're keeping something from me," I say, frowning. "What do you know?"

"I know lots of things," he says. "I'm sort of a genius, if you haven't noticed."

"Don't make me force it out of you."

He gives me a sidelong glance. "Sorry, Ice Queen, but your threats don't work on me. You should know that by now."

I'm annoyed, but I'm also not one to beg. So I turn away from him and close my eyes. A few minutes later, though, he apparently tires of the silence, because he interrupts it again. "His mom was there," he says. "Her name was Michelle, I think."

I don't move. I don't say anything. I just take her name and I hoard it away with all the other words and secrets I've collected since waking up, all those other things I've felt like I should keep, even though I am not sure what to do with them.

We spend the next several weeks running more and more intelligence-gathering missions like these, until we know the name and face of almost every one of the CCA members who call themselves purists, until we have an idea of their fighting capability and their numbers. Numbers that reach at least a third of the existing CCA, by the time everyone is accounted for. Numbers that are enough to stage an uprising that might actually end well for them, if the cards fell just right.

Not once during all those weeks, on any of those missions, does Seth or I mention Josh. I keep replaying that conversation from the shuttle, though. And I don't sleep much—even less so than normal—but when I do, I keep finding myself waking up at odd hours of the night, my heart pounding, my skin glistening with sweat.

Nightmares, Seth guesses when I mention it to him.

But I don't remember what happened in them, any more than I remember the life of the Violet Benson who came before.

CHAPTER TWENTY

Almost exactly two months after they started their project, Leah bursts into the living room where Seth and I are sitting and breathlessly declares: "We've done it." Then she gives a little bow, darts back into the kitchen, and drags a much more calm-looking Angie back into the room with her. "Tell them," she says, which causes Angie to give a happy little sigh.

"She's right," Angie says, and I can tell she's trying to appear modest behind her smile. "At least as far as we can test it, I think. There are a few things outside of our control that its success still hinges on, but I believe we've given it our best shot."

"So, on to the next phase then?" I say.

"It's all business with you, isn't it?" Leah says with a soft laugh. "Personally, I'm going to celebrate for a few hours first."

I ignore her, walking over and grabbing the laptop from the desk in the corner instead of answering. I would celebrate, maybe—I'll admit that her words caused a rush of relief, and something like elation, to flood through me—but I don't have time to let these things carry me away.

I didn't much care, in the beginning of this, about what

was happening in the CCA. Not outside of how it might have been putting Catelyn at risk, anyway.

But with every name we've collected and given to President Cross, I've felt the tension between these people growing as if it were my own, and now I can't help but worry about that tension snapping.

Soon.

Exactly how soon is frustratingly hard to say, though. We haven't had any direct conversations with the president herself; she's being watched too closely now, with so many eager to find more of her weaknesses to expose. And the ones closest to her—including Jaxon, and Catelyn by association—are being scrutinized almost as closely. So we've been relying mostly on Zach, again, to quietly relay that information we've gathered. Our conversations with him are always quick and direct, though, for safety's sake. We've talked just enough for us to have gleaned that Cross is using our intel to launch investigations, and that several of the insurgents have been dismissed as a result of it.

I can't help feeling it isn't enough, though.

The violent clone activations are continuing in the city. Last week there was yet another attack on the CCA headquarters. So for every extremist Cross dismisses, it isn't hard to believe that another will rise in his place, spurred on by these things.

And part of my plan hinges on the president using her organization's power to help us, on there being enough CCA members left who we can possibly sway to our side.

So no, I am not wasting time celebrating.

"I'm still working on teaching her how to party," I hear Seth saying to Leah behind me. I roll my eyes as the laptop screen blinks to life. I navigate to the folder that contains the security diagrams of Huxley's former lab, which Tori obtained for us, and I open them. I don't need them personally, because I've already seen them once before; but it's easier to discuss things with the normal ones among us if we have pictures to point at.

"So, where exactly are we heading with this virus?" I ask.

Leah moves, somewhat reluctantly, to my side. "Let's see. . . ." Her finger slides along the screen. "I would try here first. It was a small computer lab, just used for minor record keeping and such; the information will have been backed up to some sort of remote server, of course, so they'll already have it—but this sort of thing wouldn't have been as vital for them to physically secure as, say, the original memory files for their clones. So they might not have moved the computers yet, and they'll likely still be wired into Huxley's closed network. Of course, that's also assuming that said computers weren't destroyed when so much of the building was."

"So, basically, there's like a five percent chance of us uploading and unleashing the virus this way?" Seth asks.

"More like a one percent chance, when you consider the number of people from Huxley still swarming around that place, the surveillance cameras they've set up, the teams they're sending in to retrieve and secure this stuff. . . . The building's not exactly what I'd call abandoned, no matter what the city officials are saying." She laughs humorlessly. "Oh, and there are those city officials to worry about too. They've marked the site as hazardous—got all their pretty and bright little no-trespassing signs stuck up all over the place, as I'm sure you've noticed if you've been by there."

"So, essentially, this is next to impossible?" I ask. Leah shrugs, that light her eyes held earlier diminished a bit. But Seth flashes me a small smile.

"Impossible games are my favorite kind," he says.

We wait until it is almost dark before we say our good-byes to the rest of the house. Or until Seth says his good-byes, at least. I just stand in the corner watching. He brings a blanket to Angela, where she sits on a beat-up old sofa in the corner, and reassures her one last time that we can do this. That he and I, with the help of the team back here and the loads of equipment they have set us up with, are more than capable of doing this.

She says she believes him, but even from my distant corner I can see the worry lining her brow, and the way she wrings the blanket over and over in her hands, unwrapping herself every time Seth tries to cover her up and make her comfortable. With my perfect hearing, I have heard every one of the five times that Seth has told her we have to go. And when she looks in my direction, and very quietly asks me to come here, I hear that, too.

I wish I hadn't.

I can't ignore her now, though. So while Seth double-checks our equipment one last time, I move to her side.

"Promise me you'll make sure he doesn't do anything stupid to get himself killed, will you?" she says. "I want you both back here alive."

I nod.

"Violet?"

"Yes?" I've already started to turn around, hoping I can escape before she asks me to make any more promises I am not sure I can keep.

"Both of you," she says.

Outside, the bitterly cold night air stings my cheeks and nose.

"What did she want to say to you?" Seth asks.

I shake my head, but he keeps talking anyway as we climb into the car Tori is loaning us.

"She thinks I'm going to get myself killed," Seth says as I pull the door shut. "The woman has no faith in me, I swear."

"She's just worried. That's how it's supposed to be, right?" I have never known anyone I felt like I could call mother, whether by blood or otherwise, but I still understand the concept. And after spending the past two months with Seth and Angie, I can see that however they got here, however unorthodox their circumstances, mother is exactly what they both see her as. For better or worse.

Which may be why I still feel the weight of her words, draped like a heavy chain around my neck, as we drive through the city.

I wonder how she would handle it if something really did happen to him?

I am glad, at least for a moment, that I don't have any-one to call mother. It's bad enough that I have to consider the weight of Catelyn's worry whenever I do anything; if I cared anything about the ones she calls "our" parents, then I think the weight might be enough to crush me into never doing anything at all. How do humans survive with all these ties to each other, tangling them up and tying them down? I'm better off with only eight months' worth of those ties, maybe.

For a moment I think that. And then it passes, and I hear Angie's voice in my head again.

Both of you.

It took far less than eight months for her to decide that I was worth worrying about. And the thought of that makes my stomach twist, because I don't know how I should have reacted to it, even after all these weeks I've spent living under the same roof as her. Because it calls for a human response, maybe—not one of those cold calcula-tions that I remain undeniably better at, no matter how much I interact with the "real people," as Seth jokingly calls them.

So many cloning opponents call us machines that can't be trusted, that could not possibly understand the intrica-cies and complexities that come with being truly alive. The truth, though, is that right now I wish I were a machine. I wish I could have stayed where I was during my first months, in my cave in the dark underground of the CCA, where I thought of no one but me and my days were more simple, mechanical.

But humans have this tendency to reach toward light, toward answers, and to those intricate and complex things. And for something created in a laboratory, I lately feel all too human.

We park a few miles from the burned-out Huxley compound, in the near-empty parking lot of an old elementary school, and walk the rest of the way. Even along this dark, poorly lit street, I'm still worried that someone might recognize me, so we move slowly, as casually as possible; as long as we don't draw any second glances, we hope anybody who sees us will dismiss Seth and me as two perfectly normal people, on our way home from dinner or shopping or whatever other perfectly-normal-people thing we might have been out doing.

We continue to look normal, right up until we reach the department store adjacent to the old Huxley compound. I've purposely stopped short of the front of the building, well out of sight of the main gate, where Josh stood that night, and Seth doesn't question it. There might be an easier way in on the other side, but we won't be going around to check.

The moment the sidewalk and street are clear of possible prying eyes, we jump to a window ledge, to a brightly striped awning, and then finally to the rooftop. We move on crouched legs across it until we find the vantage point that Leah pointed out to us on the old aerial photographs she pulled from a public data website before we left. Between that and the diagrams of the interior we viewed on the laptop, we have a clear idea of where the records room should be, and with the aid of night-vision binoculars, we can see it from here.

"It looks like it's still somewhat intact," Seth says.

He's right; the bricks around the record room's windows are a darker, burned-out shade of black, but compared to many of the other wings we can see from here—which range from only skeletal interior support beams, to some corners that have been completely demolished into nothing but ash and rubble—our target corner looks like it could be part of a brand-new building.

"Hopefully Leah was right about where we needed to go," I say.

Seth nods. "And hopefully they haven't moved things around since she left."

We determine that staying low along the rooftops is our best chance of going undetected, and will make for the best head start if we need to make a quick escape. The distance between the two buildings is too far for even us to jump, though, so we find a portion of the department store's overgrown rooftop garden area that looms above a reasonably stable-looking portion of Huxley's roof. While I keep watch for people in the dark alley between the buildings below, Seth digs out the specially designed grappling hook we packed. He aims it at a recess against Huxley's roof that, judging by the shattered glass around it, used to be either a skylight or some sort of solar-energy panel.

The gun fires and releases the cable coiled within it surprisingly quietly—which is a good thing, because it takes three tries before Seth manages to latch securely enough onto the recess. Once he's managed that, I cut and tie the loose end of the cable around the metal guardrail along this rooftop's edge, pulling it taut. We hook on and zipline across, two dark blurs descending silently onto what's left of the once-grand Huxley laboratory compound.

"This thing is cool," Seth says, pushing the gun farther back into his pack, better securing it. "It makes me feel like a spy." He then grabs a pair of cutters from the side pouch and snips the cable that carried us down here, letting it fall back against the department store and out of plain sight. The slap of it against one of the lower windows echoes through the alley and makes me wince.

"The world's loudest spy, apparently," I say.

We're both deathly quietly from that moment on, except for the words we risk to warn each other of dangerous bits of the path beneath us. There are places where the scorch-marked roof has started collapsing in on itself, where it looks as though one misstep might finish the job and take us with it. Other places have already been cleared, and these open spaces of the building are even more nerve racking because I keep expecting to see people in them, where all they would have to do is look up and they would have a clear shot at Seth and me. And while we see no people, at least for now, we do see the occasional camera that has obviously been installed to provide functioning security for the contents of the defunct building. We expected this—and so we have the transmission-jamming equipment to give us at least brief protection from it—but it still slows us down, because we have to make sure we see the cameras before they see us.

It takes an agonizingly long, tense amount of time to pick our way back to the room we came for. When we finally reach it, things don't look as promising as they did from the distance; the skylight above the room is blown out, scorch marks smudged on the roof around the rectangular recess. When we shine a flashlight into the space below, we see a soot-colored, alien landscape filled with hollowed and burnt and melted things.

It takes some searching, but eventually our light falls on a couple of computers in the corner that look like they have escaped most of the damage. Just two, in a room scattered with the remains of what looks like dozens.

We drop down through the opening. It's a high enough fall that we probably should have used a cable to climb down; my legs jar for a moment when they slam into the concrete slab flooring. Now that we're here in this concentrated space, the smells are almost overwhelming: acrid chemicals, old smoke. The lingering scent of burnt plastic and fried electrical wires. And all of it wrapped in a damp mustiness from recent rains and the lack of a proper roof above.

I give my head a small shake, as if I could shake all these scents out of my nose. As if I could throw off the eerie feeling that being in this burned-out shell, kicking my way through the ashes of things unrecognizable, brings with it.

There is something so . . . final about those ashes. A destruction so total that whatever it was can't be put back together again. Not even the way I was.

Fire would be a complete, uncomplicated way to go, at least.

"This is weird," Seth says, opening one of the two bags Tori packed for us and starting to pull things out of it.

"What is?"

"Being back here. Especially after what happened the last time we were in this place."

I pull my own pack from my shoulder and drop it at his feet. "You know I'll have to take your word for that."

"I know. And that makes it even weirder," he says. "That there's nothing, right? You don't remember a single thing about this place or what happened here."

The question annoys me—it always has, every time he or Catelyn or anybody else has asked it, thinking that maybe if they just kept prying, then maybe they could uncover my long-lost memories. As though I have never tried to do it myself. I am tired of explaining to people that the old Violet is just not there. That she never will be.

So I don't answer him this time; I just pull out the power-generating device that was in my bag, take it to the more intact-looking of the two computers left in the room, and start trying to turn that computer on. It takes switching out its power cord—which looks like it's been chewed in half by some sort of rodent—with another from an otherwise completely destroyed computer, and then wrapping that new power cord over several times with electrical tape, but then it finally happens: The small LED bulb beneath the monitor turns a faint, welcome shade of green. The top left half of the screen is cracked, and the display in that section is jumpy and covered in strange blots and lines of color. Other than that, though, it all works much better than we could have hoped for.

I take the video communicator out next, and Seth and I crouch down and position the camera so that Leah and Angela will have a clear view of the screen. I let him work out how to establish the connection back to them. He works at it in silence for a minute, but it's clear by the foggy look in his eyes that his concentration isn't fully on it.

"It's weird that you don't remember anything that happened here," he says, once he notices me staring impatiently at him.

"Yes. We've established that."

"But better, maybe." The words escape slowly from his mouth, as if he tried to hang on to them but didn't quite manage it.

Shock makes my words come even slower than his. "What did you just say?"

I don't think I have ever seen anything like regret on Seth's face, but the look in his eyes now comes close. They are filled with silent apologies, and I don't understand them any more than I understand what he said, and it makes me shake with anger and disgust.

"You think this is better?" I say. "My eight-month life, instead of everything I had before? Everything I lost?"

"You might not want some of those things, is all I meant."

"Well, lucky me then, right?"

"I never said you were lucky," he says softly, and those apology-eyes meet mine, and suddenly I can't stand to be so close to him anymore.

I rise up, brush the ashes from my knees and feet.

"Sometimes," he calls to my retreating back, "I think it would have been easier if all the stuff with Angie had never happened, if everything about me from before the president found me had been lost and stayed lost. I *know* it would have been easier, actually."

I don't want to, but I look back. "But would it have been better?" I ask.

And he has nothing to say to that.

"We are not the same," I say.

No one is the same as me, and no one ever will be.

Not even him.

"I'm going to go keep watch," I say, and then point him back to the computer. "Don't take all night about this."

CHAPTER TWENTY-ONE

It does take practically all night.

It takes so long, in fact, that several times I think I doze off without realizing it, because I keep snapping to attention and turning to see Seth in a different position, working on a different screen from the one I swear he was just at. It took hours to simply break our way into the computer. And now that he's in, with the guidance of Angie's and Leah's crackling voices over the old video communicator, Seth has already spent several more trying to bypass security walls that are keeping him from running our virus-containing program.

But finally, just after daylight breaks through the tiny opening in the ceiling above, Seth finally stops cursing at the computer. With a note of disbelief in his voice, I hear him tell the communicator: "It's installing."

"Perfect," Angie says. "Once it's done, you'll have to run it manually, but then you get the hell out of there. It should do the rest on its own."

He nods.

Things have gone much more smoothly than I thought they would.

I move to pack up the gear as Seth finishes with it, still

not looking at him. I haven't looked at him, or spoken more than a handful of words to him, since last night. I just want to pretend that conversation between us never happened. I just want to finish this, and get on with my plan, and then maybe cut ties with Seth and everyone else as much as possible, once this is all over.

Because I think I am better off alone.

I always was, and I am not sure what made me forget that. Life is so much less confusing alone.

My hand is reaching for my backpack when an electronic screech—one so loud I swear I feel it rattling my teeth—comes over the communicator. I jerk my eyes toward the screen.

Angie and Leah are both still there, but they aren't looking into the camera anymore.

Then something knocks the camera over.

Another squeal, and I decide it sounds like some sort of audio interference. Once my ears stop ringing from it, I hear their voices still, even though we can't see them anymore. They sound like they're getting farther away.

And I could swear I hear other voices too. Ones I don't recognize.

"What's going on?" Seth demands, picking up the communicator and pulling it right up to his face, as if it might bring their voices closer to him again. A jumble of voices and static is the only reply at first. Then a few words break through: his name, first. And then what sounds like, "Don't come back."

We both stare at the screen for a moment, holding our

breath. The audio goes silent. No voices. No static. No anything. Seth's fingers fly frantically over his own personal communicator, calling first Angie and then Leah. Neither answers.

"We need to get back." He starts shoving everything around him into his pack, not taking the time to look at any of it. "Now. We can try this again later, once—"

"Did you not hear what I did just now? They said don't come back. Are you just going to ignore that?"

"Yeah. I am."

"Wait a second!" I dive on his arm just in time to stop him from jerking the plug out of the generator. "We've already done all this." I jab a finger at the broken screen, which indicates less than five minutes left in the installation. "I'm not leaving until we run that program and at least give it a chance to work."

"Fine." He rips his arm free of the death lock I have wrapped around it, and backs away from me. "Stay. But I'm not waiting for you." And he is gone in the next instant, before I have time to argue, or even to ask him how to properly finish the installation job he's started.

The minutes crawl by. I pass them by staring at the video communicator, silently willing it to crackle back to life. It never does, though. By the time the computer finishes its task, my fingers are so unsteady, and my pulse racing so fast, that I can barely focus enough to figure out how to securely eject the external drive we loaded the program from.

I am not used to this sort of anxiety, and I don't like

it. Not the way it makes my movements so insecure, or the way it feels like it is edging closer to fear—which is an emotion I have never wanted anything to do with. Too many humans spend too much time being afraid of too many things, and fear too often leads to hate. I know it does. I haven't forgotten the fearful way so many of the CCA backed away from me on the day I woke up. I never wanted to become like those humans.

So instead of feeling fear, I force myself to think only of the movements required to pack up everything we've brought. Mechanical movements. Simple movements. One object after another, into the two bags, and then both bags over either of my shoulders. Then a glance at the building map Angela provided us. A route, memorized. The way back out.

There is no backing out now.

The thought chases me as I run. I can't escape it any more than I can escape that anxiety that is collecting in the pit of my stomach and making every step I take feel too heavy, too slow.

I am better off alone, I try telling myself again. Over and over, I am thinking that, trying to convince myself that I actually believe it. Trying to believe that if I wanted to, I could just forget them all.

But already I regret not leaving when Seth did.

Months ago I would have been glad for it, because then I could have run the other direction, as slowly and heavily as I wanted, without having to explain myself to him. Without having to explain to him how I am not anybody's savior. Now, though, I wish I were somehow already back at the house, that I could somehow know that Angie and the others are safe.

There is no more denying it: I want to be alone—to have never met any of them—but what I actually am is afraid. I think this fear is different, though. It isn't the hate-fueling kind I know so well.

So maybe fear doesn't always have to fuel hate.

And maybe how you handle fear is what determines whether you become a human or a monster.

I burst into the cold morning, into a steel and glass city alive with people. I turn heads as I run. I am obviously entirely too fast to be human, and even more suspicious looking in my dark clothes, with both overstuffed backpacks bouncing around me. But nobody tries to stop me. They just get out of my path, the way most people of this city have learned to do with clones.

I care more than I should about that—about the way they nearly trip over themselves to avoid me. I care about it more than I did when I first woke up. I know the people of this city don't realize what I have been trying to do these past few months. That they still don't realize that I am different from the clones that fuel their nightmares, so it isn't as though I could hold it against them.

Still, it makes me wish I had invisibility to go along with my super strength and speed.

And perhaps Seth wishes for the same thing, because when I run past that old elementary school we parked at, I see that he took the car, even though he almost certainly could have run a quicker, more direct route out of the city.

At least if he is driving, I should be able to catch up.

The city is a haze of early morning noise, a blur of shapes, as I sprint through it. I follow the landmarks I've memorized until I find my way back to the familiar gravel road that weaves close to the house, and then to the dirt turnoff that leads to the secluded grove Tori parks her car in.

The spot here is empty too, with still no sign of Seth.

I race on through the woods alone.

A quarter mile from the house, I hear vehicle doors slamming. Tires screeching. I see flashes of white through the trees a moment later—white trucks speeding away across the open field ahead. Clouds of dust billow up behind them. They come dangerously close to the woods as they race back onto the main road. I drop low, out of any possible sight lines, and then I creep the rest of the way to the tree line.

Once there, I wait.

Because from here I can see a half dozen more vehicles parked across the field. And just beyond where they've parked, down the hill, through more trees, is the house.

I swing wide through the field, far enough to avoid detection while still keeping the vehicles within sight. There are no people in them. No one outside them either. As I sneak closer to the house, though, I see where at least some of those people have gone: Two of them stand in the window closest to the front door, their faces obscured in a glare of sunlight. They are tense, unmoving. Waiting.

They must be waiting for us.

Why else would Angie have told us not to come back?

I move closer. Inch by inch, behind one wide tree trunk and then to the next, and the next after that, all the way to within just a matter of feet from the back of the house. All the while my instincts are screaming at me, warning me how stupid this is, getting so close when I have no idea how outnumbered I will be if they spot me.

But I am peering into the back window before I can talk myself out of it.

I see faces I recognize.

The faces of at least a dozen CCA members—members Seth and I have seen, countless times, at the revolutionaries' meetings throughout the city. I know all their names, because we gave them all to President Cross.

They're still in CCA trucks, though, and I'm not sure what that means.

The floorboards inside the house groan. Footsteps, coming closer. I slink back into the bushes on the far edge of the yard but don't take my eyes off the window. My hand reaches into the bag on my left, finds the gun there. I think of the ashes I swept from my clothing back at the old laboratory. That complete, total destruction.

Of how easy it would be to aim from here.

I see the house's old, splintering, dry wood siding, and I wonder how quickly I could send it up in flames. If it would be quick enough to turn everything and everyone inside into ash and nothingness. So many of them were among my worst tormentors when I was at the CCA, and I want those tormentors to become nothing, to be unrecognizable by the time I am through.

It seems like a fitting punishment for making me feel like I was nothing.

There is no way of knowing, though, what's happened to Angie and the others staying at the house. I don't see them from here, but they could still be inside. I keep hearing Angie's voice in my head, not just the warning she hurriedly gave us but all the words that came before we left the house. The last thing she said to me.

Both of you.

She cared enough to want me back alive. Trusted me enough to make sure Seth came back too.

Seth. Who I had almost completely forgotten about.

I edge back toward the front of the house, to where I can watch for him, too. And it's almost instantaneous: The second I look away from the house, I see a car materializing far in the distance, tearing its way off the main road and heading straight for the safe house.

That idiot.

I sprint from my hiding place, racing to intercept him. I don't have time to come up with a better plan. He has already been spotted; I hear the door of the house opening as I race past. Whoever comes out must immediately alert everyone else who was watching and waiting for us, because as I close in on Seth's car, two more cars appear behind him. They seem to come out of nowhere to block the exit back to the main road. Desperation surges through me, pushes me faster—and right into the path of Seth.

I'm lucky that his reflexes are as fast as my reckless decision making.

He comes to a screeching halt, creating a swirling storm of dust and dry grass. I choke on it until my eyes water, leaving me half blind as I yank open the door and shove and kick Seth over to the passenger seat. He is shocked enough that I manage to take control of the steering wheel from him. When he does start fighting back a split second later, I already have my foot on the accelerator. I slam it down and cut the wheel hard to the left, which sends him flying into the passenger-side window. He pushes off it and swerves and slumps back toward me, holding his head with one hand and still reaching for the steering wheel with the other. I cut the wheel again to throw him off balance.

He catches and braces himself against the dash. "Stop doing that."

"Sorry."

"Like hell you are."

I glance into the rearview mirror. Those two cars are still closing in, and more have joined the chase and are catching up in the distance. "We have to get to the trees," I tell Seth. "We can outrun them on foot if we have enough of a head start and we can get to the wider stretch of woods to the south. Get ready to jump out."

"As soon as I jump out, the only place I'm running to is straight back to the house."

I think about jerking the wheel again and trying to slam

some sense into his head. I don't believe it would do any good, though.

"Stop the car," he says.

"Not yet."

"Stop the damn car."

"She isn't even there!" The lie comes out so loudly, so fervently, that I almost believe it myself. Of course, maybe it isn't a lie. I don't know. I don't doubt for a second, though, that he will run right back to that house if he thinks Angie is still in it. And I promised her I wouldn't let him do anything so stupid.

"What do you mean she's not there?" His voice is quiet—starkly so, after my shouting and the chaos of the past couple of minutes.

I grip the steering wheel tighter and stare straight ahead. For a few seconds there is only the sound of the bumpy ground beneath us, the car slamming into occasional holes, wheels throwing up dirt and pebbles that ping against its frame. "I mean Angie is gone," I say. "They're all gone, and no one is there except more CCA members than the two of us could possibly fight on our own."

I slam to a stop, grab the bags at my feet, throw open my door, and jump out. Seth jumps out right behind me, but while I run straight for the woods ahead, he only turns toward the cars that are almost on top of us now. He has a gun lifted in his hand and a detached, crazy sort of gleam in his eye. I shout his name. My voice doesn't even make him stumble. I scramble to him, grab his arm, and jerk him aside just as one of the CCA members fires from the window of their car.

The shot whizzes past, just inches from our heads.

I tighten my grip on Seth's arm and keep dragging him toward the trees. Normally I wouldn't be able to overpower him as easily as this, but at the moment I am a lot more focused than he is.

I manage to keep him moving for at least a mile. Not as quickly as I would like to move, but still moving at least, and quick enough to shake our pursuers. The second I loosen my grip, he snaps out of his daze and is able to jerk the rest of the way free of me. He pushes me away a lot harder than necessary, considering I just kept him from getting his stupid self killed.

And then he just stands there, looking back the way we came, as if he is still thinking about running back toward those CCA members with guns blazing.

"We should keep moving," I say.

At first I think he is just going to ignore me. But then he turns enough my way that he can see me out of the corner of his eye, and he asks, "Why didn't you just let me go?"

"Because I made a promise to not let you do anything stupid. And she told us not to come back. You heard her."

"Now we have no idea what happened," he goes on, like I've said nothing. "No idea what they've done to her. What they're planning to do."

I quiet my voice to the same level as his. "We'll find out. Can we please just keep moving for the moment?"

"We should have been there. Why weren't we there?"

I don't bother trying to answer him this time because he is still not really talking to me so much as thinking out loud and pretending I am not even here. So I settle for watching the woods, listening instead for signs that we might still have people following us.

CHAPTER TWENTY-TWO

"I should never have gone along with your stupid plan."

The woods seem very quiet all of a sudden.

"I never said you had to," I say. "And spying on the CCA rebels was your idea, anyway—and we always knew there was a possibility we would get caught, and that they would come after us. I'm sorry that Angie ended up in the line of fire, but it isn't like this was part of my stupid plan." I keep talking, keep making excuses. Two things I have almost never felt like I had to do before now. I want to convince him, though. To convince myself that this isn't my fault. This can't be my fault.

How could I have known things would come to this?

Why couldn't I have known?

My brain can process things fast—so fast—so why couldn't it have run all the possible outcomes of my plan? Why didn't it see this exact scenario coming?

"It doesn't matter now, does it?" Seth says. "She's gone either way." His voice is still quiet. Still oddly calm. But his hands have started to tremble. I keep a wary eye on the gun still in the right one, wishing I had thought to take it. I take a cautious step toward him, thinking I might still try.

He backs away. Lifts the gun a little higher in his still-quivering hand.

"Give me that," I say. Not a request. A demand.

He shakes his head.

"I'm serious, Seth."

But he doesn't hand it over. He starts to walk away, then doubles back in a blind, frustrated rage and throws it at me instead. I duck just quickly enough to let it soar past and crash into a tree behind me.

"What the hell?"

"You," he says, thrusting a finger toward me, "you shut up. This is your fault."

I watch, not knowing what to say, as he wanders with heavy footsteps toward the tree he hit. He braces one arm and leans against it for a moment, his head buried in his free hand, and then he slumps down to the ground and reaches for the gun. He looks utterly defeated.

"I'm sorry," I say. And I mean it. I have been accused of lots of monstrous things in this short life, but this might be the first time that I feel like I truly, honestly deserve what I am being accused of. Like I should apologize for this. For being so shortsighted, so caught up in my plan that I didn't stop to think about what Seth was really saying, back at the beginning of all this. He warned me that things could go wrong. He didn't want to talk to Jaxon, or anyone at the CCA, about my plan—didn't want to drag these two different sides of his life together.

But I made him.

And apologizing for that doesn't make the sick feeling in my stomach go away like I hoped it would.

"I'm sorry too," Seth says after a long, awkward minute. "I shouldn't have thrown this." He holds up the gun and gives it a little shake. It makes a pathetic clattering noise, and the scope across its top looks as if it's moving more than it should be. "Because now I'm pretty sure it's broken, and I liked this gun."

"I should have just let it hit me," I say, matching his deadpan tone. "Would have been softer than the tree."

"If only I'd thrown it faster."

"Hindsight."

"It's twenty-twenty, they say."

He sits there quietly for a long while after that, staring at the gun like it's his tragically fallen best friend. I'm almost sure he's not really thinking about the gun, but that doesn't make him look any less pathetic. And I don't know how to deal with sad and pathetic. Mostly it just makes me terribly uneasy to see him this way.

I clear my throat. "Getting angry at me isn't going to help anything. And Angie could be fine, but if you keep sitting here, wasting time feeling sorry for yourself, then how are you going to find out?"

"I know." He leans back against the tree and shuts his eyes. "I'm just tired of all this. Tired of fighting. Tired of trying to decide which side is right and wrong and then inevitably ending up on the losing side either way."

I try to think of what it must have been like to have dealt with what I have for as many years as he has—walking

around in a secondhand skin, caught in the middle, play-
ing a role that feels like it was written for someone else. But
I can't fathom it. All I know is I don't want to deal with it
for as many years as he has. After only eight months of it,
I've already had enough. Which is why I can't stop now.
We have to find a way to end this.

I walk over and offer him a hand up. "I'm tired too," I
say.

He stares at my hand, debating for a moment before
grabbing it and letting me pull him back to his feet. Once
he gets there, he is slow to release his grip. "You're touching me," he says.

"So?"

"So you hate touching people."

"Oh." I did it without even thinking about it. "You
noticed."

"Something about the murderous look in your eyes
every time I got too close."

"Well," I say, drawing my hand back and shoving it
into my coat pocket. "People change."

"You think so?"

"Maybe."

Or maybe they just aren't always what you thought
they were in the beginning.

"Come on," I say, and I start to walk, as if I know the
path to take to escape all these things. But I don't even
know how deep these woods go. I don't know what lies on
the other side either, or what we could possibly do to fix
any of this when we get there.

And I don't know what that sound suddenly coming from one of the backpacks is, either.

It's a shrill *beep beep beep*, getting louder and louder—like a bomb ticking closer to its last seconds before it blows up.

"Give it here," Seth says, grabbing the pack and pawing through it. Before he can find the source of the beeping, though, it stops. New sounds distract us immediately: running footsteps. Gasps of heavy breathing. We think of bolting, but it sounds like only one, maybe two sets of footsteps. Few enough that we can easily fight them off if they do see us. So we hide instead. And from the middle branches of the closest tree, we wait, and we watch.

I see the shadow, stretched long by the midmorning sun, before I see the person it belongs to. They are coming from the direction of the house, though. A stray CCA member? Someone we might be able to force answers out of? I shift anxiously on my perch. There might be more coming; it might be smarter to just stay put, but who am I trying to fool?

I hate hiding.

They run beneath the tree. I drop one of our backpacks directly into their path, and the second they stumble and slow to avoid it, I launch. I hook an arm across their chest as I fall on top of them, sending them crashing to the ground and breaking my own fall against them. They struggle, legs flailing and hands flying up to protect their throat and face. But their hands don't fully cover their head, or the bright purple and blond strands of hair flying out from it.

The adrenaline that launched me from that tree settles abruptly as I actually take a close look at the person beneath me.

"Leah?"

"Please don't kill me," she gasps.

I think she is joking, but I still recoil, trying not to think about how many of her ribs I could potentially have broken just now. Seth drops to my side and helps her slowly to her feet. She manages to stand on her own after just a moment of leaning against Seth—but it takes her a painfully long time to catch her breath and start explaining herself.

"All my weapons have trackers on them," she says. "Including the one I loaned you and threw in one of those bags. So I locked on to its coordinates and followed them with this"—she holds up a device similar to the one Seth used that day we tracked Josh through the city—"hoping to find you guys. It should have been beeping a minute ago—I thought Seth would recognize the noise, and maybe realize it was me."

"You could have just answered your phone," Seth says. "That's how most people communicate, you know."

"Right, except that phone is with all the other stuff I had to leave back at the house. I only have this because it was in my hands when those CCA guys showed up in the doorway and started yelling orders and crap."

"What kind of orders?" he demands. "What happened? And where is Angie?"

Leah suddenly seems out of breath again as she

stammers for words. "She's fine. Well, she's alive, I mean. But she refused to cooperate with them when they asked where the two of you were. We all refused, mind you—but the rest of us got away before they got too upset. Angie refused to run, though. I think she thought she might be able to bargain with them, or at least buy the rest of us time to get away."

"And you just left her?" Seth asks.

"You know how stubborn she is, Seth." She falls back into her nervous habit of chewing on her lip ring for a moment before she adds, "Almost as stubborn as you, the way you ran back here like an idiot, even after she told you not to."

They're both silent for a few breaths, but I can sense another explosion coming from Seth, so I try to direct the conversation away from Angie.

"So the others are okay, then?" I ask hurriedly.

"As far as I know," she says. "We scattered when we ran, just in case we were followed. That way if I led any CCA to you, at least some of them might have separated and gone after the others. I think we're clear though." She glances over her shoulder, and then looks back at the device in her hand. "We're supposed to rendezvous with everyone else in Eastside in about an hour—at the old church on the corner of Eleventh and Main—and come up with a plan from there. Were you guys able to upload the program?"

I nod.

Leah looks relieved for a brief moment about this, but Seth only turns and starts to walk away without looking back. Because I imagine he is thinking the exact things that I am, even if I won't say them out loud: We took too long.

Even if every clone in this city and beyond became completely docile, completely in control of itself overnight, it wouldn't matter. The violence in the CCA has escalated too far to stop. Huxley's clones have already done too much damage to them and the city outside.

Everything seems to be hurtling toward catastrophe, and I don't know how to make it stop.

CHAPTER TWENTY-THREE

"I managed to reach Zach," Seth tells me as he walks in the room. "Jaxon and Cate are both fine for the time being. And, yeah, Angie is there; our purist friends have pinned some ridiculous accusations on her to justify keeping her there for questioning. Trying to get her to cough up information about me and maybe Huxley, too, I'm guessing. The president's trying to fight it, but she's getting overruled, and it's just making things more unstable there. Zach thinks things are about to reach a tipping point, and he's not the only one—apparently people are running away from that place left and right because they don't want to get caught up in it when these two sides start really throwing punches at each other."

"And what about you?" I ask. "What are you going to do?"

"It's obvious, isn't it?" His tone is sharp. "If the president can't get them to release Angie, then we'll have to go after her ourselves. I want her away from headquarters before things get completely out of control there. And Jaxon, too, while we're at it—though I'm probably going to have to knock that moron unconscious and drag him out before he'll leave his mom."

"Maybe he'll follow Catelyn if I can get her to leave," I suggest.

Seth nods, but the movement isn't especially confident. "Zach is going to organize a few people to help us out," he says, and the words are softer, duller now. "He said to give him twelve hours."

The others agree, one hesitant mumble after the other.

But I stay quiet, thinking and staring into the small fire we've built in this old metal crate we found in the church's basement. It's mostly dead now, because even with the windows open, it didn't take long for the smoke to start to overwhelm. Only a few glowing embers remain. Just enough to warm my hands over.

When I look up from the fire again, our little group has spread out. Leah is in the corner, wrapped in an old choir robe she found and bent over the computer one of the others stole on the way here, working furiously on something. Tori and James sit at the top of the steps that lead to the sanctuary, keeping watch. And Seth paces the length of the room, over and over, until I finally tell him it's annoying. Then he comes and sits across the fire from me.

"You don't have to help, you know," he says, stirring the smoldering fire with some of the tinder we gathered—a broken, ornately curved chair leg, it looks like. "I didn't really mean it when I said this was all your fault; it's at least as much mine, right? And I could tell by your silence earlier that you think me rushing into the CCA to save her is stupid, so you don't have to follow me. You can leave."

"Catelyn is still there," I point out.

"It's not like I'm going to leave her behind," he says. "I mean, as long as I'm saving the day and all."

I shake my head. "See, that's the other part of the problem."

"What is?"

"If you were to somehow, miraculously, manage to save the day without me, then your ego might actually get even bigger than it already is. And I'm not sure the world could handle that."

He doesn't say anything to this, but I think I see a trace of a smile—one close to what I used to see in my mind, whenever I thought of him. Just an association to remember him by, back then. That was all it was. Of course, now it feels . . . different. More complicated than it was before.

But better, I think.

"She wasn't like the others, you know?" Seth says suddenly. "With the CCA, with President Cross, I mean, I was always this big secret. I felt like this embarrassment, almost, that she could never let out. It wasn't that she didn't try to make the best of things, and she treated me fine, whatever, but I wasn't her son. My life was worth something to her, but with Angie, it wasn't the same." He flips one of the dying embers onto the floor and stamps it out with his foot. "If anything happens to her . . ."

"She'll be fine." I have no idea where it comes from, because I don't believe it at all.

I just told a lie to comfort someone.

What exactly have I become?

Whatever I am, though, Seth apparently agrees with it, because he nods. "You're right."

You have no idea whether I am right or not, I think. I manage to keep from saying it, though. Instead, with my eyes firmly fixed on the fire, I say, "I'll help you. Because, Catelyn aside, you'd probably end up getting yourself killed if I don't."

"You're probably right," he says, and then gets up and goes to the nearby closet, grabs a few more of the faded old choir robes like the one Leah is wearing, and tosses me one. If we had found these first, we probably wouldn't have bothered with the fire. I'm glad we did bother with it, though, because its smoky smell is a much more pleasant one to focus on than the mothballs-and-dust scent of these robes.

"So," Seth says, plunking down beside me, "truce, then? You help me rescue her, I won't throw any more guns at you." He offers his hand. When I don't take it right away, he extends his little finger instead. "We can just pinkie swear on it. It's a little juvenile, yes, but less skin-to-skin contact if that's what you prefer."

I finally give in and take his hand—his whole hand, because the situation seems a little more serious than pinkie swearing to me—and I shake it. "Fine. Truce."

"Good," he says, and then lies back on the floor. "And now . . . nap time. Since I'll be storming the CCA in about ten hours."

I stare at his closed eyelids, wondering how he manages

to talk and joke so nonchalantly even now.

He must feel me staring at him, because he cracks one eye open. "I know it's hard for you to do when you're around me, but please try to control yourself while I'm sleeping and vulnerable here. We're in a church."

"I've managed not to murder you yet, haven't I? So I'm not going to do it just after we've declared a truce."

"Murder isn't what I had in mind."

"I know," I say. "But it's closer to what I was thinking of."

In spite of everything, he laughs. And then he turns over and falls asleep. Or pretends to, anyway.

I don't sleep, not pretend or otherwise. I just listen to the whispered conversations of James and Tori, to the taps and clicks of Leah's fingers across the computer, and eventually to her snores as she curls over the keyboard and still-lit screen and drifts off.

The fire is long gone, along with its warmth and light. As it grows later outside, this lower room, with its few windows, is quickly swallowed up by shadows. There is an electric lantern in the bag at my feet, but I don't bother with it; I feel more relaxed in this near-silent darkness than I have in days. The proverbial calm before the coming storm settling in around me, I suppose.

The room is almost pitch dark when the storm starts.

Not with a bang of thunder but with a high-pitched ringing from Leah's computer. She jolts awake, and with a noise halfway between a yawn and a snort, starts sleepily mashing things on the keyboard.

A few seconds later I hear a familiar voice say my name over the computer's speakers.

Catelyn.

I trip in the tangle of choir robes as I get to my feet and race to the front of the monitor. And there she is, confined to a video player in the middle of the screen. The room around her is tiny, cramped and overflowing with metal storage crates. There is a door to her left, and at the moment her ear is pressed against it, her eyes closed in concentration.

What is she listening for?

"How did you access this computer?" Leah is staring at the screen in astonishment that matches mine. Catelyn doesn't answer right away, though, because at that moment she looks back into the camera and sees me, and all she seems able to manage is an odd little choking noise. Then she immediately clamps a hand over her mouth and glances toward the door, as if afraid someone might have heard it.

"How did you access it?" I repeat.

She forces her eyes back to mine. Swallows hard and composes herself, and then in a voice so low I can barely hear it, she says, "Promise you won't get mad?"

"No. I'm not promising that at all."

She frowns, but keeps talking anyway. "The president . . . helped. She doesn't need to track your communicator to know where you are. Because when she rebuilt you, or fixed you or healed you or whatever, we wanted to make sure you didn't go disappearing on us again, and without the regular memory uploads or any sort of remote access to your brain, we had to go with a different method."

"What method?"

"Um, they sort of embedded a microchip locator under your skin."

I stare at her, speechless and half expecting her to tell me she is kidding. I should know better than that by now, though. Of course it's true. Of course I never really escaped the CCA at all. I have been carrying them with me, everywhere I went since leaving.

And I am not supposed to be mad about that?

"You said we wanted to make sure," I say, somehow managing a calm voice. "So you've known about this all along, and it never occurred to you to tell me?"

"I just figured it was a harmless chip," Catelyn continues in a rush. "Anyway, so there it is, and it accesses the nearest network to function, to ping your location, and once I had the network address, I—" She cuts herself off with a sigh. "Look, I don't have time to explain this right now. There's a more important reason I went through all the trouble to reach you like this."

There's an audible *thump thump* from somewhere in the background on her end, a knock on the door, maybe, muffled and unclear through her computer's standard microphone. She hears it clearly enough, though. It makes her talk even faster. "President Cross isn't the enemy here. You know that, right? We don't know who managed to hijack your tracking information and find their way to where you were staying, but obviously we didn't mean for it to happen."

The next *thump thump* from Catelyn's side seems even louder.

"What is that noise?" I ask.

She turns toward the door, and for the first time I notice the gun she is holding in her right hand. She lifts it and wipes the sliding button on its side. It starts a low, barely audible humming. Charging. "They'll figure out that electronic lock soon," she says, more to the gun than us.

"Who will?" I ask, even though I could probably guess.

Seth and I are the ones who collected their names and faces, after all.

Catelyn lifts her eyes back to mine, but all she says is: "It's started."

"You need to get away from there," I say. "Now."

"I think I might have waited too long for that."

"Well, I'm coming to get you then."

"No!"

It's not a thump that interrupts us this time but a low screech: the sound of a blade whining against steel. Apparently whoever is on the other side isn't bothering with figuring out any locks. They're simply going to cut their way through.

"No," Catelyn repeats frantically. "That's why I had to reach you, to tell you that you can't come back here. You or Seth. They'll kill you if you do—that's what they want. It's why they came after you in the first place: They keep talking about wanting to make an example of you and

Seth, like a symbolic slaying of the old president's show of weakness or something. It's sick."

I lean closer to the screen, wishing I could simply destroy it. That it would somehow destroy the distance between us at the same time. "I don't care," I say. "I'm not afraid of them."

"Well, I am. Listen: They aren't going to kill me. Not right away. They want to use me, and Jaxon and the president and now, I guess, Angie, too, to try to get you and Seth here. Don't let them use us like that. We'll figure out what to do in here, but for now, you have to stay away."

A more intense buzzing of metal being cut. Sparks fly from her left. I hear footsteps, voices, someone whooping in success as a piece of the steel door falls in, flashes across the screen for just a moment before slamming against the floor with a metallic clunk.

Catelyn clutches the gun to her chest. With her other hand, she reaches and ends the video call.

"No!" My hand flies at the computer screen, hits it so hard, I am surprised it doesn't crack it. I want to grab her and pull her back. I want to be where she is. I want to fight whoever was on the other side of that door.

But instead, I am here and useless and shaking, cut off from her yet again.

"She's joking, right?" Seth says. He's come up so quietly behind me that I didn't even notice him. "About the stay away part, I mean. She can't seriously expect us to." Somehow the words manage to break through to me, even as my mind blurs with desperate plans and an intense hatred for whoever was on the other side of that door.

I don't answer him, though. I don't want to talk. I don't even want to move my fingers from where they are still splayed against the black video box on the computer screen, as if I could keep our connection going, so long as I refuse to let go.

Then, to my surprise, a connection attempt message actually appears beneath my fingers. But when I manage to click accept, it's not Catelyn who greets me.

It's Josh.

And several feet behind him, instead of his usual gang, there are two older CCA members. Between them is Catelyn, with her arms and legs tied and a strip of tape across her mouth. She looks dazed. A nasty burn covers a large strip of the right side of her face, blistering red welts visible even at the distance she is from the camera.

"Hello again," Josh says. "Your sister tried to cut us off, like she didn't want you to see this happen or something"—he gestures behind him—"but it feels like it's been forever since we talked, doesn't it? And I don't think she relayed the message I needed you to get quite as clearly as I would have liked. I thought this might help clarify things."

Seth puts a hand on my arm and gently pulls my fingers away from the screen. He lets his hand linger there, and for once I am glad for his touch, for the weight of it, because the urge to hit the screen is even stronger than before.

"Is that Seth behind you?" Josh asks. "Tell him I'm sorry Jaxon isn't here too. He and his mom are tied up elsewhere at the moment—which is a shame, right? It could have been this whole weird little family get-together thing."

Seth's grip on me tightens.

"Let them go," I say.

Unsurprisingly, Josh laughs. "We will," he says, "when we're ready to. When we've made our point, and nobody else around here thinks it's a good idea to associate with the very things we're supposed to be fighting against. When nobody else wants to keep dangerous clones like you two as little pets, the way the so-called president of this organization was doing."

My eyes are still watching Catelyn, so I see her blink into an almost awareness—aware enough that she is able to look straight at the computer screen and start to struggle, screaming words that are only muffled by the tape.

Josh holds up a small tool that blocks my view of her; I would guess it is the same one that burned through the door and left that mark on Catelyn's face, because he walks over and presses the tapered nozzle of it against her other, unburned cheek. Her eyes widen at the sight of it, and then close tightly, bracingly.

"This is a useful thing," Josh says, digging the nozzle around in her skin. "As good at shutting mouths as it is at opening doors."

"Don't." I mean to shout it, but it comes out as a horrified whisper instead.

"'Don't'?" He pulls the tip away from her cheek, lets it hover just a few inches from her face. "I wonder: How many people have said 'don't' to you in the past, and you didn't bother to listen to them? You weren't a very good listener before Cross brought you back here, you know."

"I'm different," I say quietly.

"You look the same to me."

"Don't," I say again, as close to begging as I think I've ever sounded, which he seems to find amusing.

"Okay," he says. "Okay. I won't. So long as you understand what is going to happen next."

I want to guess that what happens next is I come to the CCA headquarters and rip his disgusting throat out, but I don't want to make him angry, because I know he would only take it out on Catelyn. So instead all I say is, "I'm listening."

"Good. Here's what you're going to do," he says. "Both you and Seth—you're going to come and hand yourselves over to us within the next twenty-four hours. And then it's going to be the way it should be: The humans get to live, and the monsters get to die. Just like in every story that's ever ended with 'happily ever after.'" He walks back to the camera, and I allow myself the first decent breath I have taken since he moved closer to Catelyn. "I'll see you soon, then?" he asks, leaning in so that I can't focus on Catelyn, or on the room behind him, or on anything except for his eyes, which are shining as if he has already beaten me.

"Very soon," I promise him. "And you will regret every second of this call."

"Doubt it," he says with a smile. Then he cuts the connection, and this time the screen stays black.

CHAPTER TWENTY-FOUR

"You two are both insane," Tori says. Again.

"We know," Seth says, taking the steps in a few long leaps and bounds. He pauses at the top of them long enough to glance at his communicator, and then he is disappearing into the sanctuary above as he adds, "Somebody was just telling us that. It was you, I think?"

I follow him upstairs without a word, ignoring Tori as she sprints to catch up with us.

"It was bad enough that you were planning on going back there when things were just tense," she presses. "But now there's a full-scale uprising, and they're expecting you two, and—"

Seth stops so abruptly that she slams into the back of him. "You saw the video." He spins around, brings his face level with hers so quickly that I think she is going to trip trying to get out of his way. "It's not like we can wait this out and see if things somehow shift in our favor." He doesn't elaborate past that, but I know he is thinking the same thing I am: Josh said we had twenty-four hours, but there is no telling what they might do to their hostages during those twenty-four hours.

Thinking about it makes me want to hit something all

over again, so I am glad Seth dealt with Tori. Because I honestly don't want to hit her. I have actually been growing sort of fond of her.

"You two are going to get killed," she says, her voice a little quieter as she warily watches Seth turn his back on her and keep walking.

"Well," Seth says drily, "at least we're no strangers to death."

We move as quickly through the city as we can while still staying discreet. It's just Seth and me now. We decided it was too dangerous, with the way things have escalated in these past hours, to bring the others. Tori halfheartedly argued with us about that—and forced me to sit still long enough to at least figure out a way to block the signal from the tracker embedded in me—but she finally agreed to let us go alone, once Leah insisted there were other things they could do to help us from the outside. I don't know exactly what Leah had in mind, because there was no time for her to elaborate; when we left, she was back at her computer and working just as intently and furiously as she had been the night before.

Zach meets us several blocks away from headquarters, with a handful of CCA loyalists in tow. "There's another team of us inside," he tells us, "waiting to create a distraction so we can lead you guys to where we think they're keeping Catelyn. And then to the others."

"The others," meaning more loyalists who have managed to get themselves locked up. Zach claims he wanted to help us, but he can't exactly stop in the middle of this uprising and focus on freeing only the ones we've come for. So he agreed that he would help us out in return for our help breaking these others free—more quid pro quo, as Seth called it. Though I think Seth partly agreed because he feels more loyalty toward the president, and the ones still following her, than I do; my main concern is Catelyn, though, which is why I insisted we free her first. Once I get her out, then I'll focus on these other people—but not before. My single-track mind working once again.

I don't care, though, because that track is going to lead me back to her.

I trail a little ways behind the group as we approach headquarters, only partially listening to the hushed conversation Zach and Seth are having. I feel like Zach should be a little more focused on the task ahead, but he doesn't seem to be able to stop giving Seth strange looks.

"Still having a hard time believing you're . . . you know," he finally says as we make it to the edge of the parking garage. "You look the same."

I hear muffled laughter from Seth. "That's kind of the point," he says. "That I look the same as a human? It's like . . . Cloning 101."

"You know what I mean. I've known you for a long time, and you were a human as far as I knew or cared." He shrugs—the smallest of movements, but it causes a light fluttering in my chest. A flutter of hope, maybe? That when this is over with, the more moderate CCA will prevail. That they really will be able to help the rest of the city shrug off the old mind-set toward clones as easily as Zach has accepted the truth about Seth.

Maybe we weren't fast enough to prevent what is happening tonight, but things won't end here.

I keep telling myself that as we huddle around Zach's communicator, listening. It's linked to the communicator on the wrist of his distraction team's leader, so that even though we can't see everything going on in the base, we can still hear it.

Zach sends a text message—a silent *We're ready*.

For what feels like much too long after that, we hear only silence over the communicator's speaker.

Then the leader, in a whisper, tells us they're in position. That the bombs are set and ready to be tossed.

Flash bombs, Zach explains. Not anything that will do any major structural damage, of course, but the noise and smoke and vibrations they create—along with whatever other noise the team can make—should be enough to draw people toward it, away from the entrance we plan to use.

We slip into our own position, moving our huddle to that entrance, which is a high-security one normally reserved for the president and only a handful of others; Jaxon provided Zach with a key capable of opening it, and Zach presses that key to the panel beside the door. The light around the scanner blinks from red to green. We all ready our weapons, and Zach lifts the communicator to his lips.

"Okay," he says. "Go."

The door in front of us slides up at the same time a barrage of noise begins to drown out any hope of communicating with the other team. One thunderous rumble after another as at least ten bombs go off, followed by shouts mixed in with coughing and choking.

We can't see it, but we can tell when at least some of the smoke has settled, because that's when we start to hear gunfire in the distance. Seth and I both just move faster, but the rest of our group hesitates, looking in the direction of the distraction point.

I think of Catelyn's burned face, and it's all I can do to not start grabbing people and dragging them.

"We need to focus on our part," Seth says, more patiently than I ever could have. "Let them do theirs." It snaps two of our group out of it, sends them sprinting to catch up with us. But the third still lingers behind. She is still standing there, wearing a torn expression, when two CCA members barrel around the corner behind us.

I'm irritated at having been slowed down, and it shows in how fast I aim and pull the trigger—almost before I can take the time to be sure the ones I'm shooting are part of the splinter group, and not the CCA loyalists we're planning to help.

I still only shoot to disarm. Even with all the intelligence we gathered, Seth is still convinced that we might be wrong about who is good, or bad, or something in between, so we decided before coming in that we would kill as few as possible. I hit the hand of the closest CCA member, and Seth makes an almost identical shot at the second one a moment later. Both of their weapons go flying as they clutch their hands against themselves and stumble to their knees. The lingering girl finally wakes up and remembers how to move. She grabs their guns and then races after us so fast she almost stumbles herself.

We make it the rest of the way to the north wing with only a few more encounters like that one—just the occasional CCA member or two interrupting our path. Some throw up their hands in a gesture of peace as soon as they see Zach, but it isn't always that easy to quickly tell who is on our side and who isn't. So we round every corner with guns drawn and raised.

Which is good, because when Zach finally leads us to the hallway outside the room Catelyn is in, we find ourselves facing four armed guards.

And they don't shoot just to disarm.

The first bullet sears through my arm—but it would have hit me in the chest if I hadn't twisted as quickly as I did. Focusing on dodging that, though, makes my own shot completely miss its target and hit the wall behind him instead. He takes aim at me again, but before he can fire, someone grabs his arm and twists it so hard, I am surprised we don't hear the crack of breaking bone.

"Idiots," snaps a voice that makes my flesh crawl. I allow my focus to abandon my target, and instead find Josh's face as he throws off his grip on the gunman's arm. "What do you all think you're doing? We haven't been given the order to kill or even harm them—my dad wants them alive and intact." He tilts his head toward us, and his eyes find mine. "It makes for a more dramatic statement that way."

Seth and I both lift our guns, train them on Josh's forehead.

He lifts his gun too. But not at us. Instead, he points it back into the room he just came out of. "Who do you think I'll hit if I pull the trigger now?" he asks.

My arm shakes, and my aim dips, just slightly.

"I'll give you three guesses who it is," he says. "Or, you could just refuse to lower your weapons, and then you'll find out the hard way."

I hate playing his games, but I don't see any other choice at the moment. I jerk my arm down, knocking Seth's down with it, and then turn to make sure no one else in our group has any weapons raised that might provoke Josh any further.

"Come on, man," Seth says. "Why are you doing this?"

Josh looks almost thoughtful for a moment. And then, in a voice so chillingly detached it sends a shiver through me, he says: "We're only doing our part to right her wrongs. To prevent more wrongs." He still doesn't take his aim off Catelyn.

Seth's voice is oddly soft as he says: "This isn't going to change anything that happened."

"No," Josh snaps. "But this is going to change everything that happens next."

"And what exactly do you think is going to happen next?" I ask, trying to keep my voice as quiet and calm as Seth's.

"The president was weak," Josh says, his gaze sliding to mine. "And the CCA has been growing weaker underneath her. But now? Now my dad will be the one to bring this organization back to what it was intended to be, only even more powerful than before—all of you clones and your disgusting creators will actually have a reason to fear us again. And with my dad in charge—"

"You get to be his idiot lackey who doesn't have to actually think for himself?" Seth interrupts.

Josh's eyes narrow dangerously.

"Or who could think for himself," Seth goes on without missing a beat, "but will still be too much of a coward to actually do it."

I want to hit him. Because Josh's finger is shaking, itching toward the trigger, and I swear, if Seth makes him pull it—

"At least we know you're smart enough to follow orders though, right? So not completely brain dead. Your daddy really must be very proud." I'm still considering hitting him, but then I see the way Josh's whole hand is moving now, tipping the gun back toward us, bit by tiny shivering bit, and suddenly I realize what Seth is doing.

Of course.

If there is one thing Seth is good at, it is making people want to shoot him. And that gun might be able to kill Catelyn, but it isn't going to kill either of us. Josh knows that, of course.

All it takes to make him forget it, though, are a few more taunts.

He swings the gun toward us. We move so quickly that by the time he fires, we're both already in his face.

Seth knocks the gun from his hand, and I do what I've been fantasizing about for months now, and throw all my strength into a punch, slamming my fist into Josh's face and sending him spiraling into the wall. Shots fill the air around us. The rest of Josh's group forget about any orders and simply shoot to stop us, and our backup answers with fire of their own.

I don't care about what happens in this hallway now, though. Josh is still lying on the ground. He and his threats are out of my way. I sprint for the room holding Catelyn, colliding with one last guard on my way through the door. I manage to wrench his weapon from his hand and shove him out of the room and out of my way easily enough. The chaos of the battle in the hallway falls behind me as I turn back, expecting to see my sister, to be able to finally make her safe again.

But she is not there.

CHAPTER TWENTY-FIVE

The fighting outside comes to an abrupt halt as I grab Josh, jerk him back to his feet, and throw him against the wall.

"Where is she?"

His head is lolling a bit from side to side, and his eyes are unfocused, still dazed from my punch. But he manages to laugh.

Seth has a gun in his face a moment later. "Answer the lady's question," he says.

"Did you think we wouldn't know you would come straight to where you thought your sister was being held? New life, but you still end up with the same old weaknesses. Fascinating stuff, right?" Josh finally manages to hold his head straight and look me somewhat in the eyes. "We made sure our false trail was well laid, of course."

His gaze flashes toward Zach. Zach, whose gun is raised and who, to his credit, looks mortified to have led us to the wrong place.

"Don't blame him," Josh says. "He tried, right? Shame none of you realized we had you heading as far from any exits as possible, just in case you thought about attempting any quick escapes once we had you cornered."

Now it's my turn to laugh. "Do you honestly think you have us cornered?" I glance to my left, at the four of his group still standing. "You realize one of me is worth ten of you, don't you?"

Josh nods. Or it's something like a nod, anyway; I have him pinned so tightly against the wall that he can't move much, his head included. "Yes," he says. "Which is why we planned for a lot more to meet you here. The little bomb show on the other side of the building, which I'm assuming you're responsible for, distracted a few, but they should be here"—he tries to glance down at his communicator, but I press him even straighter up against the wall and tighten the grip I have around his throat—"soon." He finishes in a cough.

"Guess I should hurry and kill you now, then." The threat has only just left my mouth when the hallway on either side of us starts to flood with people. So many people. Ones that we already knew about, of course—but there are some unexpected faces too. Some that we missed. Too many that we missed, too many people period, and all of them together are blocking any chance of our escape. Any chance of me getting to Catelyn.

I hear Seth curse, and then he tells the rest of our group to lower their weapons. I glance back to see them doing it. It surprises me. Even this outnumbered, they were still planning to fight?

Should I keep fighting?

I could still kill Josh, at least. And likely I could take out a lot more before they decided how to stop me. Especially if they truly do want to keep me alive on the orders of Josh's father.

"Go ahead and do it," Josh says. His voice is still strained from my fingers pressing in. "Finish what you started," he coughs. "You have a bigger audience now and everything."

I want to. More than I ever did in the training room, on the roof, in that parking garage. And whatever uncertainty I had felt toward him the night we watched him at Huxley is gone. I know exactly what I want now.

Destruction. I thought it on the day I was born, and I am thinking it now. And I still think it is the easiest thing in the world, maybe. To destroy.

"I know you want to," Josh says.

"Oh, I do," I assure him. "But I am not a monster."

So I let him go, and I step back and let the crowd surge over me and drag me away.

I've never experienced dreaming before.

There were things that woke me up at the safe house, of course—but they were never clear like this. I never saw them, or remembered them, and Seth had called them nightmares. This doesn't seem like a nightmare. Not at first.

But I know I'm dreaming, because I can see myself. A much younger self that I never actually knew, but that I've seen before, in pictures and through stories Catelyn has tried to paint for me. And she is there too. Catelyn. Even younger than I am, with her hair in pigtails and dirt smudged on one of her cheeks. We're both laughing at something like I've never laughed before, and the grass we're lying on is brilliant and green and the sun overhead is blinding.

Then the scene reels and goes dark. My stomach seizes, and it isn't a dreamlike gut wrenching, but a solid, wide-awake fear at the black loneliness around me.

"Come back," I hear a voice say. My voice, I realize. Only the younger version of it again. "Come back, come back, come back—"

Then she does. We both do. A little older looking, but still Catelyn and me and that same soft grass. That same warm sun. We're singing something. It starts out as a silly, high-pitched melody that we're both giggling too much to remember the proper words to, but soon she starts to hit actual notes, and I go silent and just listen while she finishes. Her voice fades off toward the end, and the blinding light of the sun fades with it, and soon I'm back in that blackness again.

"Come back, come back. . . . I don't want to be alone here."

Something hits me in the side. Hard.

My hand strikes toward it, grabs on to what feels like a foot. My eyes blink open, and after a moment of sleepy confusion, I realize that foot belongs to Seth.

"You were mumbling a lot," he says. "I thought you might have been having another nightmare."

Was it a nightmare?

"It wasn't all a nightmare, was it?"

I was wondering the same thing, but it wasn't me

who asked the question. It was Catelyn. I turn and find her staring at me, and I know it isn't a dream anymore, because her face is still burned—covered partway with a ragged strip of cloth—and, other than that, she looks just like she always has to this version of me. Like brightness and warmth and green eyes glistening with tears that she could shed at any given moment.

"It wasn't all a nightmare," she repeats, "because some of the words you were saying . . . some of them sounded familiar. In a good way."

"Words like song lyrics?" I wonder aloud.

She nods, eyes widening a little more. "From a song our grandma used to sing. I used to sing it while I sat with you after . . . when they were working on you a few months ago, I mean. You were still in that coma. I didn't think you could hear me."

I don't remember hearing her. But there is no other explanation for why I would have been dreaming about those words, so I don't tell her that.

"How beautiful," Seth says. "Sorry I interrupted your singing, Violet. But you should know that you're tone deaf."

"Shut up, Seth," Catelyn says. "Didn't you say you were going to try to figure out that security panel over there?"

"I told you, it's different from the system that used to be in here. It's been a long time since me and Jaxon played the lock-each-other-up-in-these-cells game—we're much more mature than that now."

"One of you is at least."

He ignores the stab. "And he was always better at actually escaping than I was, anyway."

"Well, Jaxon's not here, is he?" Catelyn says, her gaze dropping to the floor and her fists clenching. "So we'll have to settle for you. The least you could do is give it a few minutes' worth of effort, considering how long I spent trying to work on the stupid thing."

"If *you* can't break it, what makes you think I can?" Seth asks, not moving from his spot on the floor.

While they continue to bicker, I finally manage to take my eyes off Catelyn's burned face. The three of us are the only ones in here, but it's still cramped. A literal cell—no more than ten feet long, maybe three feet wide, with no windows and only one dim yellow light above. Just a vent of some sort on one wall, and the steel door with an operations panel on the other. Like most of the newer security measures in headquarters though, that panel is usable only if you can first put in one of the correct biometric codes— likely those of the programmer, the president, maybe higher-up heads of security. People who the CCA couldn't afford to have locked up in the event of an attack on base.

Not us, in other words.

And no matter how many times Seth and Catelyn try to override the program, the status display still remains a stubbornly bright red declaration of SECURE.

"What happened to the others?" I ask, maybe out of some faint hope that they could have gotten away somehow.

"Other cells, I guess," Seth says. "They blindfolded her," he adds with a nod at Catelyn, "and I was knocked out as cold as you were before they brought us in here, so neither of us saw. I'm betting nothing good happened, though. They tried to help us, so likely the fanatics are going to call them just as guilty as us. That way they can burn them at the altar with us—because, you know, the more people the revolutionaries have, the bigger their flame will be."

"Thanks for those cheerful thoughts," Catelyn says.

"Just being realistic," Seth replies.

This can't be how it ends, I think.

I won't let it end this way.

I jump to my feet and go to the vent on the wall, rip the cover off with an ease that surprises even me.

"We've already tried that," Seth says. "But it's the oldest escape trick in the book, so of course they've built against it. There's no way we can fit through."

I hoist myself up to peer inside anyway, but he's right—the vent opening itself is large enough to climb into, but the channels that stretch out from either side of it are much narrower. I don't bother reattaching the vent cover. I throw it as hard as I can at the corner of the cell, and it chips into the solid concrete wall with a metallic crash that reverberates through our tiny cell.

Over and over the sound vibrates through me.

Then it begins to change, into more of a tapping at first, and then a slamming that shakes the floor, travels up through my legs and all the way to the tip of my head, shaking in my teeth and sending shivers over my scalp.

My eyes shift from the dented vent cover to the door. There is a second slam against it. Catelyn jumps to her feet beside me, and Seth backs away from the panel he had been vainly messing with again. As we watch, that panel begins flashing, and we hear the taps and beeps of its counterpart on the other side of the door.

"Looks like they might be ready to start the bonfire," Seth says.

I grab Catelyn and push her behind me, make her promise to stay close. Then I take a deep breath, brace myself, and face the door.

"You think you're going to fight your way through them?" Seth asks.

"If we're going to burn, we might as well go down in a blaze of glory, right?"

He shakes his head, but he's smiling a little too. "You're insane," he says.

"I know."

"I like that about you though."

The panel on the wall flashes one last time. Then it glows bright green, and there's a sound like air hissing out of a tire as the door in front of us slides open, blinding us with the fluorescent white lights on the other side.

CHAPTER TWENTY-SIX

I'm not sure which one of us manages to adjust our eyes to the awful brightness first, but Catelyn is the first to move. She races past me, straight into the crowd of people blocking our exit. I'm a fraction of a second too slow when I try to grab her.

That same gut-wrenching fear from my dream tears through me again.

Come back.

I'm about to shout it out loud when I recognize a face a few feet back in the crowd.

"Jaxon?" Seth pushes past me and joins Catelyn, who now has her face buried in his brother's chest. I feel like Seth's voice is probably the only thing that could have torn Jaxon's eyes away from the bandage on Catelyn's face—and it does, though not exactly quickly. He is slow to focus on Seth, too. Slow and careful, like he is afraid of making the wrong move. The rest of the group Jaxon brought with him, who have to number at least as many as the ones who ambushed us in the north wing, all take a few steps back to give them some breathing room.

It's Seth who finally breaks the silence that is bordering on awkward. "It's about time you showed up," he says with his trademark grin, offering Jaxon his hand.

"I am so incredibly pissed at you," Jaxon says. But then he sighs, and he shakes Seth's hand anyway. "You weren't supposed to come, you idiot. And as soon as we finish dealing with everything here, I'm going to kick your ass for it." The threat makes Seth laugh. He pulls Jaxon into a one-armed hug, which lasts until I clear my throat impatiently.

"Speaking of dealing with everything that's going on," I say.

"Right," Jaxon says, "here's the plan." He glances over the crowd of us with a renewed, sharp focus as he talks, and it reminds me of the way his mother used to look. The way I thought she always looked, until that first night I saw her alone. And just like his mother, he delivers orders easily, sharp and quick and not leaving any room for pro-test—at least until he turns to me. "I want you to take your sister out of here," he says. "Most of the rebels have been backed up toward the training rooms now, and we've secured everything in the north and east wings, so you should be able to sneak out that way." Catelyn is in the middle of looking over a gun someone just handed her, but she is close enough to hear him, and she turns and answers him before I can.

"I'm not leaving," she says, and holds up the gun. "I want to fight."

"We have enough people ready to fight," he says as the group around us disperses, heading off to secure the next areas they've been assigned to. "We don't need you here, and I don't want you here. It's too dangerous." Catelyn gives him a stubborn frown, but she doesn't seem able to come up with a convincing excuse to stay.

"I was already planning on getting her out of here first," I say, and I can feel Catelyn glaring at me, but I don't take my eyes off Jaxon. "But then I'm coming back."

"I'd rather you didn't."

"I have things to settle here."

"I've seen the way you settle things." He steps closer to me, and for once the look he watches me with isn't wary or guarded in any way; it's just as it was a moment ago: focused, determined. He's changed. Hardened, some-how, since the last time I saw him. I wonder what these past months have been like for him, while he watched his mother lose her grasp on the power they were both so used to. Is it why he feels as if he needs to confront me like this?

I feel something like sympathy for him, maybe. For the way he has had to inherit this war from his mother.

But I am not sympathetic enough to let it control me.

"If you've seen it," I say, "then you should know better than to stand in my way." I step back and go to move around him, but he stops me with a hand on my shoulder, shoving me back.

"You're going to take her to her father's," he says. "And then you're not coming back. I'm not letting you turn this into the same mess you made back at Huxley's labora-tory." I resist the urge to return his shove, mostly because those last words catch my attention.

"What mess?"

"She didn't make it," Catelyn says quietly.

"Close enough," Jaxon says, and suddenly all the CCA members who are still nearby seem to be paying attention to our conversation, and they are all either nodding in agreement or else watching me as if they only wished they had the courage to really tell me what they thought about me.

As if they needed to tell me.

Here I am, standing in the middle of who I thought were the tolerant ones, the ones I planned to help, and nothing has changed. I am somehow still on the outside of anything they could ever accept or understand. One of the few people I thought did understand—Seth—suddenly seems much farther away than the few feet he is actually standing. He looks much more torn about the issue than the others, but he also isn't saying anything, so what does it matter? It feels enough like betrayal. From someone I never even wanted to care about being betrayed by. Which somehow makes it even worse.

"Fine," I say. "I'm not coming back. Have fun trying to fight this battle without me." Why should I help them, anyway? If this is the way it's always going to be in the end, then why bother trying? I shouldn't even have hesitated to just take Catelyn and leave and never look back; she is the only one who seems capable of remembering that at least some part of me is human, after all.

And when I grab the gun Seth offers me and turn to leave, she forgets her argument with Jaxon and follows me soundlessly. Of course, I feel like she is only going along with me now because she's worried. Because maybe I can only take so many hurtful words and glares, and it was inevitable that one of them would eventually cause a break. And Catelyn is good at spotting broken things.

"They just don't know how to deal with you," she says as we turn down an empty hallway, our guns drawn as a precaution. "You're just a . . . what's the word? An enigma. Yeah. That."

"Let's stop talking and start paying attention to getting out of here alive, shall we?"

"I am paying attention."

It's hard not to let my own attention slip and my guard fall in these quiet halls, though. The few people we've passed so far seem like stragglers, more interested in trying to pretend they aren't here than in trying to stop us; a few of them look like they might be thinking of following us, but probably only to escape themselves. Jaxon was right about this much: The fighting has been contained somewhere behind us. I still feel strange walking away from it, surrounded by this peace. Uneasy.

Because it may be surrounding me now, but something tells me it won't last. *Could it ever last?* I wonder. The fight can be contained, maybe. But the anger and hate that is fueling it will still leak out, just as it always does, and make a mess of things all over again.

A mess of things.

Like Jaxon accused me of making at Huxley.

"What was Jaxon talking about before, exactly?" I ask Catelyn. "About what happened at the laboratory."

"It doesn't matter," she says stiffly.

"It matters to me."

"Well, it wasn't actually you that did it."

"It was the old Violet?"

"Yes."

"The same Violet with the father and the memories of us you wanted me to call mine?"

It takes her a moment, but then she gets my point. "God, you're annoying," she says. Because she can't argue what we both understand now: that I can't pick and choose which parts of my past to keep and which parts to get rid of—even if it would be easier to get rid of some of them, like Seth said. Real people can't do that. So it doesn't seem like I should be able to either. Not if I want to pass as one of those real people.

"Okay, you really want to know the truth?" Catelyn asks after a moment.

"I've never wanted anything but."

"Most of the CCA thinks you had something to do with the fire that burned down Huxley's laboratory. And a lot of them, even the ones that trust and are still following President Cross, were afraid you might end up doing the same thing here. It's part of why the decision to bring you back was so unpopular."

And this is one of those moments when my brain is a curse, because everything connects in it almost instantly, and suddenly I understand. Suddenly I hear so many things from these past months so much more clearly.

I see Josh, walking toward me on the rooftop.

They didn't have to pay me for this. I've been planning this ever since you woke up.

I see his father, dragging him away from the gates at Huxley.

His mom was there. Her name was Michelle, I think.

I don't realize I have stopped walking until Catelyn reaches the end of the hallway without me. Even then, the distance between us isn't obvious right away.

Not until I see people I recognize—people who were there when Jaxon set us free. People who I thought were following his orders and had set off to secure other parts of the building.

Which is why the guns they have pointed at Catelyn don't make sense.

CHAPTER TWENTY-SEVEN

The distance between us is obvious now, because I am too far away to get to her in time.

It doesn't matter, though, because I have problems of my own a second later: double as many people behind me. And while my attention is still on Catelyn, one of them manages to slip one ring of a set of electronic handcuffs around my left wrist.

I could likely still jerk my way free at this point, maybe even fight my way through them all. Six of them. One of me. Not impossible odds.

But I am having a hard time getting any part of myself to move. All I can think about is the time I spent kneeling in the ashes of that laboratory. How I tried to brush them off, the way you brush off minor annoyances. Some part of me knew I had something to do with it all, I think. Jaxon's comment wasn't the first of its kind. And Seth was so strange toward me while we were in that hollowed shell, surrounded by the aftermath of all that destruction. The same sort of destruction that has been screaming through my thoughts since I woke up in this body.

Reborn.

But how much the same?

Do I deserve everything that is happening now? What else did the old Violet do that I might need to pay for?

They twist my hands behind my back. The other ring closes over my right wrist. It pinches a bit of skin, and a few drops of blood trickle down into my palms. All the while, Catelyn is shouting at them, telling them they're making a mistake. That they were supposed to be on our side.

But I wonder how many of the others following Jaxon were only hiding in that crowd as well, waiting for an opportunity like this. For us to separate the way we did, or to give away some other weakness. Maybe I would have seen it coming where Jaxon didn't—but I can't blame him for missing it, can I? A war wages long enough and all the sides begin to blur.

And how do you fight an enemy that looks the same as your ally?

The war in my own mind continues to wage, all the different versions of me colliding and blurring as they fight for control. Catelyn and I are marched through headquarters. Soon enough we fall into a route I recognize, one that I have walked a million times before. I know where they're taking us.

The noise as we approach the main training room is deafening compared to the peaceful halls. The scene that greets us inside reminds me of historical paintings I've seen, ones depicting vicious, bloody gladiator battles. A public spectacle of violence, and at the center, President Cross and Silas Iverson stand facing each other, both of them pointing a gun at the other.

I focus my gaze on Iverson. And I'm struck, again,

by how much his son looks like him. The same crooked nose and sharp chin, the same confident way of standing with shoulders just relaxed enough to suggest indifference toward the gun the president holds. Maybe he is right to be confident too. Because not only does he have his own gun, but he is also far from alone; there are dozens of his fellow rebels behind him, most of them armed, with their weapons trained on their former president as well. And there are people standing behind the president, of course—but not enough.

Not nearly enough.

Our captors shove us farther into the room, and the sound of Catelyn tripping a bit makes both Silas and the president dart a glance our direction.

"The others are coming," one of the men holding me says to Silas.

Silas nods, and I would swear he almost smiles, too. He turns back to President Cross to say something, but I don't hear it over Catelyn's renewed attempts at shouting protests that, unsurprisingly, set neither of us free. We're only pulled faster, more roughly, toward the observation room in the corner. The windows have been shattered, and pressed up against its outer wall, sitting in a pool of glass shards and surrounded by several more of those armed rebels, is the one person I was still hoping might have escaped all this somehow.

Angie.

They drag us over to her, push us up against the wall beside her.

Like little lambs being lined up for slaughter, I can't help but think. And then I hear Seth's voice in my head.

The more people the revolutionaries have, the bigger their flame will be.

He was right, wasn't he? Do they plan to make examples of all of us in the end? I was prepared to face my own death, maybe, but if they all die, then what happens next? If this fanatical, bloodthirsty group takes over the CCA, then what becomes of the work we did trying to free the clones from Huxley's control?

"Cross should just surrender already," says a voice to my left. "I'm tired of this standoff." I glance over and see Emily, mixed in with the armed group gathered around us to prevent our escape. On the other side of her is Josh, who looks like he is ignoring her. His gaze is laser-focused on that standoff between his father and the president.

Emily starts to say something else.

And then our eyes meet, just briefly, and her attention falls to studying her hands instead.

I want to know if she still thinks I saved her that night, and if that was the reason she wasn't in her usual place at Josh's side when I was attacked on the roof. And I want to ask her what she's doing here, and if she is certain—really, truly certain—that she is on the right side.

Because the way she can't seem to look at me makes me wonder about that.

But Josh, who apparently was listening to her, speaks before I can ask her anything. "She'll surrender," he says smugly. "Just watch."

And, as if on cue, the heavy metal door of the training room slides open again. President Cross's aim and focus never falter, but several of the crowd around her and Silas turn their heads almost at once toward it. I follow the crowd.

My stomach sinks at the sight of Jaxon and Seth, guns to their heads and hands bound, being led toward the center of the room. Seth must have put up more of a fight than I did, because from the way he is stumbling and fighting to keep his eyes open and focused, it's obvious he has been hit with some sort of tranquilizer. Still conscious, though. I imagine because there would be no statement of power to be made by killing an already unconscious victim.

They're brought to a stop just a few feet from the president. Close enough that she can't avoid seeing them, but too far for her to reach out and touch. She inhales a little more sharply than normal. But other than that she makes no movement, no cry for their release. No sound at all.

Then the man holding the weapon against Jaxon's head clicks the safety off. The pulsating sound of its energy charging fills the room. Jaxon closes his eyes and takes a deep breath.

The president's gun drops to the ground.

She still doesn't move at first, except to draw her gun hand very slowly back against her chest, closing it into a fist over her heart. Silas exchanges a look with Jaxon's would-be executioner, and the weapon is lowered, and Jaxon and Seth are marched the rest of the way over to us. And with all the calm and poise of someone out for a casual stroll in the park, the president walks herself over and takes her place beside her sons.

One little lamb, two little lambs . . . Six little lambs lined up for slaughter. . . .

Catelyn leans against my arm, silent.

The group of loyalists the president left behind shuffle uncertainly, leaderless now. Some move as if to attack, but then seem to remember they are outnumbered and draw their weapons back instead.

Silas kicks the president's fallen gun toward the crowd behind him, and then starts toward us. A group of his rebels converge in his wake, moving backward with weapons raised to protect him. "Now that we're all here," he says, "let's get started, shall we?" His eyes sweep over all six of us, without lingering long enough to meet any of our gazes.

Seth is the only one who answers. But the tranquilizer must be fogging up his brain, because instead of one of his usual quips, he manages only to call Silas a name, strung together with enough curse words to make Angie sigh.

"Always with that awful language," she says softly.

"You've just changed my mind about something, clone," Silas says. He steps in front of Seth, grabs him by the jaw and forces their eyes to meet with a jerk.

I try yanking my hands apart, testing the handcuffs one more time.

Still just as strong as before. My eyes don't want to leave Seth, but I force them to, searching for something I could possibly break the restraints against.

"See, my original plan was to take care of the former president first," Silas is saying, "just to settle any lingering hopes for her possible resurgence. But . . ."

The broken-out window frame of the observation room, maybe.

". . . now I have a better idea."

If I hit the middle of these cuffs against the edge of that frame, I may be able to weaken them enough that I can break free.

"You can go first," Silas tells Seth. I jerk my attention back to them just as Seth is pulled from our lineup and forced to stumble his way out in front of us, to be centered in front of the crowd pressing in, where everybody can clearly see him. "This way," Silas says, gaze flickering back to the president, "she can watch. And maybe it will be a reminder to her, as well, of what this organization is supposed to be about."

"It was never supposed to be about this." The president stares straight at him as she speaks, her voice as stoic and unyielding as the rest of her.

He abandons Seth for a moment and moves back to her instead. "Did you honestly think it could be otherwise? Especially after you brought that other monster into our very ranks?" He brings his face closer to hers, lowers his voice. "You are a disgrace, to yourself and to everyone who helped start this organization."

The president's fists, hanging at her sides, clench tighter.

I inch toward the window's edge.

Silas backs away from the president. He orders the ones holding Seth to turn him around, so that he has a clean shot at the back of Seth's head.

One of the guards sees me trying to move, and steps between me and the window.

Silas raises his gun, and I realize how serious he is about this slaughter, and that, for all my speed, I am still going to be too slow again.

I kick the guard as hard as I can in the stomach anyway, and I dive toward the window.

I slam the handcuffs against the wall, and a crack appears in their center at the exact moment that gunshots ring out behind me.

CHAPTER TWENTY-EIGHT

I spin around. Silas is lying on his back with his gun on the ground beside him, and President Cross is pushing herself off him, heaving for breath.

She stopped him.

But something is wrong.

She doesn't seem able to get off her hands and knees. She reaches for her chest, and that's when I see it: a burnt and ragged-edged hole, with more blood oozing from it with every movement she makes. Her eyes scrunch in pain and try to flutter shut, but she forces them open with a wild, defiant determination. Her hand swats for the gun Silas dropped, but he plants his foot in her side and sends her toppling the rest of the way over.

As Silas climbs to his feet, the president tries to do the same, pushing herself up with the arm on her unwounded side. But just seconds into the shaky attempt, she collapses under her own weight.

The moment her head hits the ground, the rest of the shocked room springs back to life.

A scuffle breaks out in the watching crowd. Someone breaks free of it and rushes to the president's side. Silas is closing the distance between himself and Seth with rage in his eyes, recharging the gun as he walks. I remember the crack in my handcuffs, and I finish the job in one quick motion, turning and smashing them against the window and then ripping them apart. I shake my wrists to regain the feeling in them, sending bits of metal raining down to the floor.

Several of our guards rush toward me. I knock one to the ground as I start to run, and as he falls I grab his gun and wrench it out of his hand. I toss it to Angie. Seth has told me she's a good shot—a result of all the years she spent hiding and had to be prepared to defend herself, I guess. Still, she looks hesitant for a moment after catching it, frowning down at it as if she'd taken a vow of pacifism at some point in her recent past. At least until a stray shot hits the wall behind her.

She fires a shot of her own then, hits the guard closest to Jaxon, and then races to his side and tries to help him and Catelyn break free from their handcuffs. I leave them and turn just in time to dodge a streak of gunfire. After that I don't look back. My sight is set on Silas now. And this time I won't be too slow.

I hit him just as he tries to raise the loaded gun toward Seth. I aim for his head, and I don't hold anything back. I don't want him getting back up anytime soon—I still have too many other people to deal with.

The ones holding Seth are next. I grab the gun from one of them, send him to the ground with a stabbing kick and keep him there by pointing his own gun at him. Seth has regained enough consciousness that with the first man on the ground, he is able to fight his way free from the second one, even with his hands still behind his back. He gives the man a vicious knee to the gut that makes him double over and fall face-first to the ground.

After kicking the man's gun out of his hand and sending it flying, Seth turns and races to President Cross. He stumbles only a few times from the tranquilizer poison pumping through him. But when he tries to kneel next to her, between the poison and the handcuffs still hampering his balance, he almost ends up collapsing beside her instead.

What good does he think he is going to do, handcuffed and half oblivious as he is?

I run to them, grab Seth by the arm, and yank him back to his feet. "Observation room. Now." He tries unsuccessfully to shrug out of my grip. "Get out of the middle of all this until the tranquilizer wears off," I say. "I'll take care of the president." He glances toward the room, eyes still unfocused, unsure, but then he finally listens and takes off.

There are two CCA members also kneeling beside the president, one trying to stifle the bleeding from her wound while the other swings his weapon toward anyone who gets too close. They both move aside when I bend to pick her up. I cross her arms over her chest, placing the gun in one of her hands so I have both of my hands free to cradle her against me and prevent jostling her as much as possible. She is still conscious, but her eyes have taken on a strange, glassy look.

She needs medical attention.

And I have no idea how we are going to get it for her in time.

Right now, all I can do is get her out of the center of the fray. I bolt across the room, dodging bodies and stray fire and plenty of fire that was actually intended for us, and reach the observation room. Angie and the others have barricaded themselves in the far corner with some of the loyal CCA members standing as protectors in front of them. Catelyn and Jaxon—and now Seth as he joins them—are still fighting with their handcuffs.

I've made it a few steps into the room when a shot hits me between the shoulder blades. The pain is blindingly, teeth-grittingly intense for a few steps. It passes almost as quickly though, my lightning-fast brain releasing the synthetic chemicals to block it and sending signals to the cells around the new wound to start healing it.

But then two more shots hit. One right after the other. The second is dangerously close to the nerve center of my brain. My head buzzes. My face flushes with heat.

I stumble and fall, and it takes all my focus to keep myself from crashing hard on top of the president's wounded chest. I have to drop her to catch myself on my shaking hands, and she hits the ground with a sickening thump that shocks life back into her glassy eyes for a split second. I close my own eyes for a moment, trying to bring myself back. The world has fallen away to only a few basic sensations—that heat on my face, spreading over my scalp. Footsteps pounding, vibrating the floor beneath my hands. Catelyn's voice screaming my name.

I roll off President Cross. Blink my eyes open just in time to see a figure step into the doorway, a silhouette against the bright lights shining over the battle outside.

Josh.

He fires another shot without even thinking about it, without even really aiming. It glances off my shoulder. The weak shot normally wouldn't faze me, but my brain is already struggling to keep up, to heal as fast as it normally does, and so the burn of it is enough to nearly well my eyes shut. I do close them—for what can't be more than a few seconds—and when I reopen them, Josh is somehow already directly in front of me. President Cross shifts beside me. The gun still in her hand glints in the corner of my vision.

Josh grabs it first.

He points both of the guns at my chest. I vaguely wonder how many shots my body could actually take, if my brain can continuously keep up with this brutal healing, pain-dulling cycle.

"One more move and you're dead!" shouts one of the CCA members behind me.

Death by firing squad, I think. Exactly what he deserves.

He still doesn't seem to notice the firing squad facing him, though. And the guns are shaking in his hands. My mind has controlled enough of my pain that I can focus on the tiny movements. Movements that seem strange, being made by this boy who has never shown me anything except a foolish, death-wish sort of confidence.

At least not when he thought I was looking.

It's like watching him outside Huxley's gates all over again.

His mom was there. Her name was Michelle, I think.

"My dad is dead," he says suddenly, talking more to his shaking hands than me.

I am not sure what he expects me to say.

"Not you, this time. I don't even know who it was, but does it matter now?"

I know enough about human nature now that the normal reaction to something like this statement would be to say "I'm sorry." Even to someone like Josh. So I try saying that.

But it only makes him laugh. "No, you aren't."

The strange thing, though, is that I am.

I am sorry enough that I don't want him to be gunned down in front of me, at least. Maybe it isn't true, what they say I did at Huxley's lab. I don't know. But I know what it is like to have things taken away, to wake up empty, and to not know how to fill those empty spaces inside you. So I make myself sit up, and then stand, so that I am blocking any clear shots at Josh. My body protests the entire time. The tingling around my healing wounds turns into more of a needle-pricking sensation, and my vision shifts in and out of focus as my ears fill with an odd whirring noise.

"Sit back down," Josh says, pressing one of the guns into my chest.

"If I sit down, they'll shoot you."

"I don't care." I don't think he really does, either. And I don't know why I do, but I stay on my feet. "Get back on the ground where you belong," Josh warns, "or I will pull this trigger again."

I take a step, shrinking back as if I am actually thinking about it.

Then I punch him instead.

It was for his own good, really. Because now he is the one lying on the floor, after tripping over the president's outstretched body, and he is too dazed to put up much of a fight when I disarm him. I peer over my shoulder to see the line of CCA loyalists lowering their weapons. Catelyn and Jaxon push through them and hurry over to me and President Cross, and I see that they've managed to get their handcuffs off too—with Seth's help, maybe. He follows the two of them a moment later, leaning a bit on Angie for support.

"I so wanted to be the one to do that," Seth says, looking down at Josh's still, curled-up body. "Except I probably wouldn't have been able to stop at just a punch." He says that, but I don't think it's sincere. As his voice trails off toward the end, he doesn't seem to be able to keep his eyes on Josh.

Maybe it's because of the way Josh is holding his head and curling into himself. As if he wishes, just for the moment, that he could make himself disappear. That he could get away from this place, and everything that happened here and everything that led up to it. No more of that confidence now. Just a small and broken boy as in over his head as I am beginning to think we all are.

I don't want to look at it any more than I wanted to watch his father pull him away from the lab.

"I'm fine. Just a bit light-headed is all." I am grateful for President Cross's voice, because it wakes me up, pulls my attention away from Josh. She is sitting partway up. Her arm is resting against Jaxon, while Angie tries to clean away some of the blood and other seepage around the wound. I reach absently up between my shoulder blades, checking my own wounds, and my fingers find the bits of my shirt torn and singed by gunfire. The cloth around them is damp with blood.

Human blood, I remember Angie calling it the night we met.

And it does look like the president's, maybe. But for me, unlike for her, that bleeding has stopped. My body has put itself nearly back together again, while hers is still too weak to stand.

Members of the CCA stand like sentinels around us, and even though I know they are mostly here for the president—that they are on the loyal, moderate side—it still feels strange to be protected by them like this.

"Mostly shock, I think," the president insists, trying to push Angie's hand away.

"That shot nearly hit your heart," Angie says sternly.

"Well then, it's a good thing I have a heart made of . . .

what was it you said that time? 'Painfully solid stone'?"

Angie looks sheepish. "This is hardly the time to bring up the past," she says, continuing to clean. "This looks bad," she says after a minute. "The bleeding doesn't seem to be stopping. And I'm not exactly this sort of doctor, but I would guess it's only going to get worse unless we get her stitched up. Soon."

"There are more pressing things to deal with at the moment," the president says. She attempts to stand, but both Jaxon and Seth are there to hold her down. She struggles. But only for a few seconds.

Then an alarm shrieks through the intercom system around the room, and she freezes.

"See? More pressing things such as that," she says in between the pulsing shrieks. She places a hand on Jaxon's and Seth's arms and pushes herself up, ignoring their objections and Angie's disapproving frown, and staggers to the broken window. We all follow.

The scene outside has gone eerily quiet. People are standing, staring up at the intercom speakers and at one another, looking as though they have no idea how they arrived here. It makes all the signs of destruction and death—the still bodies on the ground, the scent of blood and charred flesh and hot metal—even harder to stomach, without the cushion of chaos around to distract from them.

A woman breaks free from the crowd, walks over to the door, and presses the button to open it.

A wall of black smoke rages in from the hallway.

"Shut the door!" the president shouts, and even in her weakened state her voice carries through the room.

The woman frantically tries to obey, but the door isn't made to shut quickly; it creeps along its track, sliding shut only after it's already let enough smoke in to start a coughing fit rippling through the crowd. This room is huge, though, and with plenty of space to disperse, the smoke rapidly stretches into little more than a thin haze. People start to panic anyway. Some are tripping over themselves to get away from the door, others arguing over whether or not to reopen that door and try to make a run for it. All other fighting has been forgotten for the moment, it seems, but this isn't much better.

The president takes one of my guns, stumbles out of the observation room and fires a shot into the air. It gets the attention of the panickers closest to us, and then one by one more of the crowd behind them looks in our direction. A hush falls over them.

"That door is built to withstand all the extreme conditions this room can be programmed to simulate." President Cross still has to shout to make herself heard over the sounding alarm. "It's virtually indestructible, and certainly fireproof. Do not open it."

Her words cause a wave of almost-calm to wash over the room. But I noticed the way her voice faltered a bit at "indestructible," as if she didn't quite believe that was the right word.

"'Virtually indestructible'?" I repeat, dropping down

beside her as she kneels down to catch her breath. "Does that mean it's actually perfectly destructible?"

I would swear she almost smiles. "Always so full of questions, aren't you?" Her eyes close for a moment, and she takes several more deep, steadying breaths as the rest of our group gathers around her. "That was too much smoke," she finally says, and then she opens her eyes and looks to Jaxon, to the communicator around his wrist. "Contact the main operations control room, please," she says in her calm, understated way. "And let's hope there is still someone at the monitors."

Jaxon does as he is told. After he messes with it for a moment, a woman appears on the tiny screen, and he hands the communicator over to his mother.

"Hello, Rachel," the president says. "Status report? What exactly is going on?"

The woman on the other end wastes no time. "Fire observed in the main hall, in north wing corridor A, south wing corridor D, and the corridor of training room three. All doors have been sealed where possible to contain it until we are able to extinguish it."

"But why is it not already extinguished?"

"The automatic sprinkler system has disengaged some-how." The woman's words tumble out in a rush. "There are no cameras in the room that contains the system's control panel, and we tried to send someone to check, but—"

"They couldn't get through the D corridor of the south wing."

"Correct."

The president massages her temple. The hand she uses has blood from her wound on it, and some of it ends up smudged across her forehead. "All of those fire locations are blocking exits," she says. "I don't think the sprinklers being disengaged was an accident."

Angie says what we all must be thinking: "Someone was trying to trap us. All of us."

"Orders, ma'am?" says the woman on the screen.

But the president appears out of orders to give.

"It's contained, right?" Catelyn asks. "It will eventually burn itself out without getting any fresh oxygen, won't it?"

"It would likely take hours for that to happen," Angie says. "And by then the structural damage may be substantial, and it won't be contained just to those rooms. It will be a domino effect. When the supports of the hall outside this room go, for example, chances are . . ."

"We'll be crushed in this room as well," the president finishes for her. Her eyes have taken on that same glassy look they held earlier. "While we were busy destroying ourselves, we forgot there were still others outside, waiting to do the same. We knew this is what they wanted. We should have seen something like this coming."

"We just have to find a way to fix the extinguisher system before the damage gets too bad," Seth says. "We have to get to that room somehow."

"It is likely already up in flames," the president says quietly.

I stand up. Visions of the last time I was in this room flash through my mind. I think of blacking out, of that numbing, violent ringing in my mind and of a life that is a million miles away from where I find myself now.

And once that ringing stops, there are only two words left to find there, within all of my brain's artificial grooves and circuits.

"I'll go."

CHAPTER TWENTY-NINE

I step into blindingly bright flames and suffocating heat.

It looks as though those flames have already smol-
dered out some, as Catelyn guessed they would, because
the black melting streaks they've scorched along the walls
were made by flames much higher than the tongues of fire
that lash around my feet now. But it's still hot enough that
I already feel blisters bubbling across the unprotected skin
of my face and hands.

I cover my mouth with my arm, and run.

Almost immediately I slip, and catch myself in a pile
of flames that singe the tips of my hair. My nose fills with
the scent of the burning strands. I shove myself back up
as fast as I can, before any other part of me has a chance
to catch fire. There is something glistening along the floor
beneath my feet, beneath the flames. A fuel of some sort.
More proof that this fire was deliberate. As stray embers
land across the scattered drops of slick fuel, they explode
in brilliant little bursts around me.

I continue to run, picking my way around the slippery
spots as best I can with eyes watery from smoke.

Soon I turn a corner and leave the flames behind,

though the smoke remains, hanging heavy enough over me that I can see only inches ahead. I drop to the floor, where that smoke is at least somewhat thinner, and feel my way along the warm walls until I come to a more open room. The air in here is clearer, but it's still hard to catch my breath without choking on it.

But I have to stop for a minute. I have to give my body a chance to heal. I can still feel those blisters on my hands and face, along with more burning and an itching, pulling pain traveling up legs. It feels like my skin is shrinking, like it's too tight for my body. I lean my shoulder against the wall and close my eyes, and almost immediately I hear Seth's voice in my head.

Don't be stupid. You're tough, but you're not invincible. You can't walk through fire.

"Watch me," I say to the smoke. Because I guess I already miss having someone to argue with.

But of course, since he isn't here to answer, it's a short-lived argument.

I don't want him here, I remind myself. It would make no sense for us to both be in danger like this, and he has more life to lose than my short eight months. He has to realize that, doesn't he? How many times did I explain to him that we weren't the same?

Still, he is going to be so mad at me when I come back.

Catelyn, too.

Don't you dare, she warned me. *Don't you dare.*

I did it anyway, though. I pushed her away, like I've done so many times before. Too many times? Enough times that I know I will never hear the end of this when I come back.

"When I come back . . ." I repeat aloud. "When, not if." Speaking to smoke again. It is unsurprisingly silent as I shove off the wall and continue to part my way through it. I can't waste any more time. My feet and legs still itch and burn and ache, but I do my best to ignore it.

Your system is already overloaded from trying to heal so much.

Angie's voice, now. It sounds like I imagine a mother's is supposed to sound, and I wish I'd had a chance to hear more of it. That we could have talked about simpler things, things other than this war, or the monstrous things they created and the monsters who rose up to fight those things. The memory of her voice is a comfort, cool water against the soot collecting on my parched skin.

I reach the narrow hall in the south wing—which I recognize from the directions and descriptions President Cross gave me—and can only guess that my destination is at the end of it. I don't know this part of headquarters well, and I can't actually see the door to the control room, thanks to smoke and bands of writhing flame swallowing up the space between here and there. The bands seem to be stretching, reaching to consume me next. A little closer with every passing second. My hands and feet are numb. My mouth barren. Lips cracked. Eyes nearly swollen shut.

I don't know how much longer my body is going to hold up.

It's now, or it's never.

I sprint forward, pumping my legs as hard as I can,

desperately hoping I can move fast enough to keep the flames from latching on. Five feet, ten feet, fifteen feet—and suddenly the door materializes in front of me. I don't want to figure out any security codes, or think about finding another way inside. I only want out of this fire. Even if it means breaking my way out. So without much thought, I lower my shoulder and slam full speed into the door.

It stands firm, shaking only a little at my jarring impact. The tremor reverberates up into the ceiling. Glowing bits of molten metal and ash shake free from some support beams, and they float down over me as I back up toward the door, stripping off my jacket and attempting to beat the encroaching flames away. My hand claws for the panel beside the door, even though I know it will likely be melted, twisted into a nonfunctioning blob of buttons and screen.

It is.

I lean back more fully against the door, not caring anymore that it is searing hot, and that the heat hisses right through the thin cotton shirt I am wearing beneath my jacket. The support beams above me shift and groan, more radiant pieces of them drifting away, bit by bit. I shut my eyes, not wanting to see the moment the ceiling completely gives way.

The door behind me pulls open, and I crash backward onto the floor.

Someone grabs me by the collar of my shirt, drags me farther in, and quickly slams the door shut again. I hear the ferocious whoosh of the flames on the other side, as the fresh oxygen from this room is funneled out into them. More creaks and groans from the ceiling follow soon after.

"I expected Seth, maybe. Not you."

I rub the soot and tears from my eyes, and look up to find Leah watching me. She is leaning beside a computer that is built into the wall, her arms folded across her chest. The room is a relief from outside, but still sweltering, and now cloudy with the smoke we let in. It all makes it hard to collect my scattered senses. To find words.

"You did this?" I finally manage to cough.

"I had help." Her gaze drifts to the computer screen. "But, yes, I overrode the auto-program and activated the stop valves. There were others who sneaked in with me, during all that chaos and distraction the rest of you caused. Old friends of mine, if you could call them that. They started the blaze."

"Why?"

"Fire for fire, right?" she says, and suddenly I realize: I am brushing the ash from my clothes the same way I did in Huxley's old lab. "Or at least, that's what Huxley wanted. This wasn't my idea—I only carried it out for them."

"You were supposed to be an ex–Huxley employee," I say, staggering to my feet. "Why are you doing anything they want?"

"Because I made a deal." Her voice starts out sharp and sure, but it cracks and goes quiet toward the end.

My voice is equally quiet, an overwhelmed sort of calm, when I ask, "What could they have possibly offered to convince you to do this?"

"They have something of mine," she says. "And they promised to give it back."

A memory flashes to the front of my mind; but even though it came as quickly as my brain normally opens things, it seems oddly blurry. Surreal, almost. As if it came from a different life, even though I am sure that it was me—that it was this Violet Benson—who listened to Seth's explanation as we rode on that shuttle.

"You mean your daughter, don't you?" I ask.

Leah's eyes are haunted as they meet mine. They remind me of Angie's that night we sat at the kitchen table. Of all the questions I had, and how desperate for answers I was. How desperate I still am. Because even now, nothing I know seems right. There is no clear answer, no clear purpose for anything. No good and no evil like my rational mind has always longed for. No black or white, only shades of both and hordes of people caught in between, trying to fight their way out.

"You helped me, though," I say, "the very first day you met me."

She turns back to the computer and absently starts pressing buttons. "I wish Seth had never told us about you," she says. "I wish I'd never known you were coming. That you'd never shown up at all. You made it so easy to get the information about the CCA headquarters that I needed to plan this—so easy for me to get into your brain, and access a few key memory files while I was in there."

All I can do is stare.

I trusted her.

I thought that was what I had to do, that it was the right thing to do if I was going to evolve into something more human, something more right for this world. It was supposed to put us on the same side.

I thought we were on the same side.

"I fixed your blackouts because I really did want to," she says quietly, as if that makes up for anything at all. "I did want to help you. But you have to understand: I had to help myself, too."

"And everything else?" I demand. "The program you supposedly created? Was any of that even real?"

"Of course it was," she says. "It had to be. I was working on it with Angie—and she didn't know about any of these plans. So the program is more or less functioning, and I really was excited about that. But I altered a few things in the version I gave you, to prevent it from spreading the way it needed to. I couldn't risk jeopardizing the deal I'd made with Huxley; if that program did work, if it did spread and we'd managed to free all their clones, and they found out I had a hand in it . . . well, it wouldn't have mattered what I managed to accomplish here for them, would it?"

"I still don't understand: What good will it do if Huxley does free your daughter as promised, if you're just going to die in here?"

"Do you think I'm the one who set the fire outside this particular room?"

My sudden understanding must be obvious, because with a weary little smile she says, "I wasn't planning on dying here. I had this all mapped out so meticulously, you know—everything that would happen here, and what would come next. But I should have known there would be no next. That Huxley would avoid keeping its part of the bargain, somehow. I suppose that's what I get for making deals with devils, right? And this ending is probably the one I deserve, anyway, for what I did when I worked for them. Maybe we all deserve it for the things we've done— me, Angie, Cross. All of us."

There's a sudden crash from the other side of the door. It shakes the ground hard enough that I almost lose my balance. I fight to steady myself, and then somehow force my burned and broken body to move to the computer and shove Leah out of the way. "I am not dying here," I say. "Tell me how to put the system back online. Now."

Another quake from outside.

The roof. The support beams.

Leah looks from the computer to me, and holds my gaze for a long moment—too long. I can see the thoughts churning behind her eyes, restless and searching for answers we don't have time to find right now.

"You could have just left us all, you know," she finally says. "It would have been easy for you to save yourself."

"I know."

But I didn't. It never even occurred to me that I could have, until she said it.

And for whatever reason, that seems to cause a change of heart for Leah. She steps between me and the computer and silently begins to work. Minutes later we hear the shower of pings, the sound of water against metal, and the hiss and sizzle of fire being extinguished. Then more of those scrapes and creaks of support beams.

"The roof may not hold," I say. "We need to get out of here."

Smoke-tinted steam floods into the room as we open the door—so much of it that my clothes are already soaked and clinging to me before we even step out underneath the sprinklers. So thick that it's almost worse than trying to find our way through the smoke.

I almost don't see the falling beam until it's too late.

But I manage to push Leah out of the way. She hits the ground in front of me just as the piece of the crumbling ceiling lands on my shoulder, crushing me to the floor and pinning me underneath it.

The air feels even damper, heavier here on the floor. I can barely breathe. I glance at my pinned legs and try to convince myself that I am strong enough to move.

Leah's hand clasps around mine. She jerks and tugs uselessly, while above us, more of the beams are slipping, caving together into a long V shape that looks as if it will collapse in on itself at any moment.

"Go!" I shout at Leah.

"I can't just—"

"I'm faster than you." My words stutter out in between harsh breaths. Talking is taking too much of my precious energy, but she still hasn't let go of my hand. Her stubbornness reminds me of the last person I want to think about right now: Catelyn. "I'm faster than you," I repeat in a whisper. Quiet is easier, somehow. "I'll catch up."

And for a moment I would swear it actually is Catelyn staring at me. That it is her, finally letting her hand slip from mine, finally backing away as I tell her, one last time: *Don't worry. I'm coming back too.*

No matter how many times I run away, I always come back.

Everything feels cold all of a sudden. It must be because of the cool water raining down on me. There are still patches of defiant flames flickering among the debris, refusing to be extinguished by that water; I stare at the one closest to me and try to somehow will its warmth into my bones.

Get up, I remind myself. That is what I am supposed to be doing. Get up and go back to Catelyn. She was always warmth. From the first day I woke up, she was a steady flame to that inferno raging inside me.

That violent inferno has been all but snuffed out now.

The water is starting to bring peace as it slides over my skin, washing away the ash. I am getting used to its coldness. Fond of it.

Somewhere up above, things are shifting. Moving. Falling.

I close my eyes, and I drift into a deep sleep.

I took some of the flowers from my sister's funeral, because I thought I might need something else to remember her by.

There are no more replacements now. No more silly games to play, no more secrets to share, no more of her perfect face and perfect smile to be jealous of. No more us. Violet is gone, and she is not coming back, and all I have left of her is this vase full of flowers that have already started to die. That, and the tiny round tin that contains a sprinkling of her ashes.

Three times now I've watched my sister die.

It hasn't gotten any easier each time.

There's a soft knocking at my door, and I turn to see Jaxon standing with my coat draped over his arm. "Ready to go?" he asks.

I nod. Because this house has captured ghosts of my sister in everything I see, from the sandals I borrowed from her and never gave back to the red streak of marker she scribbled on the wall and then blamed me for. Ghosts I'm finally ready to leave behind.

I only wish we'd left sooner. Years and years ago, before anything that's happened could have touched us, back when we were still a whole family with all its pieces.

But that's a selfish thought, I guess.

Violet's sacrifice silenced some of the uprising—funny how quickly some of them changed their views on clones once one saved their life. Not all of them, of course; though even the ones she didn't completely silence have, in a lot of cases, still quieted down enough now to listen. And while they had their attention, President Cross, alongside Angie and Leah, shared the plan that Violet first told us in the park that night, what feels long ago and forever away now. I wasn't sure, back then, if the president was actually taking that plan seriously. But now she talks about it with a passion that makes me believe she's committed to seeing it through. All the way through. Which is good, because the virus is the easy part—but after that's done, there will still be a long way to go toward repairing this city and the ones in it.

I'm not as naïve as I used to be. There's no telling how Huxley will retaliate, once we deal this blow to them. And even if we do manage to unravel them completely, I know that the city will likely always remain unsettled, unsure in places, full of still-smoldering hot spots that could erupt at any point. Full of a fear of clones that runs too deep for it to simply be erased, even once Huxley's control over those clones is erased.

But at least now my sister will be remembered as someone who tried to fix it, at least in some ways.

"We'll be waiting in the car," Jaxon says. "Anything else you need me to carry?" I shake my head. There's only one other thing I have left to carry, and I'm the only one who can do it. Jaxon leaves, and I walk over and carefully pluck a few of the more vibrant petals left on the flowers. I open the tin and drop them in with her ashes.

The three of us decided a quick road trip was in order, while the dust of everything that's happened takes its time to settle here, and Angie and President Cross work out the plans for moving forward. So it'll just be me, Jaxon, Seth, and a couple of cars full of our closest bodyguard friends. We're going to the beach, to find the highest waves and roughest waters we can. It seems like a fitting place to scatter these few last pieces of Violet Benson that I hold in my hand. Because every version of her has been a little too wild for this life.

A little too wild to hang on to.

And because she'd be glad for the freedom of the open ocean, I think.

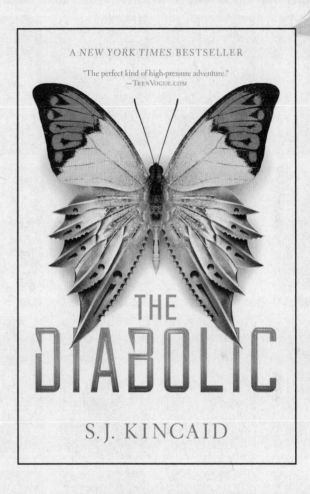